Tear Down the Mountain
An Appalachian Love Story

by Roger Alan Skipper

Soft Skull Press
Brooklyn, NY
2006

Tear Down the Mountain
© 2006 Roger Alan Skipper

ISBN: 1-933368-34-9
ISBN-13: 978-1-933368-34-4

Published by Soft Skull Press
55 Washington St., Suite 804
Brooklyn, NY 11201
www.softskull.com

Distributed by Publishers Group West
www.pgw.com 1-800-788-3123

Printed in Canada

Book design by Anne Horowitz
Cover design by Kari Rittenbach

Library of Congress Cataloging-in-Publication Data

Skipper, Roger Alan.
    Tear down the mountain : an Appalachian love story : a novel / by Roger
Alan Skipper.
        p. cm.
    ISBN-13: 978-1-933368-34-4 (alk. paper)
    ISBN-10: 1-933368-34-9 (alk. paper)
    1. Marriage--Fiction. 2. Appalachian Region--Fiction. I. Title.

PS3619.K568T43 2006
813'.6--dc22

2006019068

For Connie

I

All You Get

Blessed are they which do hunger and thirst after righteousness:

for they shall be filled.

Matthew 5:6

1

THE UNFINISHED CHURCH REEKED OF PINEWOOD and new-poured concrete and of asphalt from the shingles the men had hammered fast earlier in the week. And of cigarette smoke that slunk in through the open gable just above the altar. That stinking tentacle of sin snaked around Janet and strangled any other thought. Right where the Spirit of the Lord moved, someone smoked.

For all her sixteen years, the Spirit had left her alone, but no longer. He had grasp of her, had rattled her loose from her bones and crawled through her muscles till they thrashed under her skin like a cat lost in a feed sack. "Praise Him," whooped some man she'd known all her life but could attach no name to just then, huffing milk and onions through the beard that worried at her ear. "Praise His holy name." At that moment, Janet couldn't recollect her own name.

Her mouth stayed frozen shut till the thing growing inside her chest tried to bust her. A man's hard horny hand jiggled her neck every time he bellered, like he could dislodge the devil, or sift the Lord in. An old woman stinking of lard clawed at Janet's arm, helped her shake it, chanted just let it go honey just let it go honey just let it go honey and behind her a sharp little voice snapped like a pair of scissors hang on to God, put your hand in His and hang on to God don't never turn loose of God. All around people spouted out tongues lallalallomakallorabonni and screamed and pranced so that the concrete floor shivered through the rug under her knees. An accordion wheezed in a black-lung way, and the guitar player's old tube amp crackled and whined. Fingers walked on her back and head, some like soldiers marching, some like a blind man in a junkyard.

And somebody smoked.

That smoke, maybe, kept her from running over, stoppered up her tongues. Janet couldn't stand it any longer. Like a gyp dog shedding nursing pups, she wrenched free of the hands and staggered from the tangle of people around the altar to the back of the church where she sat on an upside-down sheetrock dope bucket and yanked her dress over her skinny knees and tried to finish shaking out. Her arms quavered on, but they weren't her arms anymore and she couldn't be liable for them.

Up among rafters spiderwebbed with temporary wiring, a bird-sized green moth merged with a thousand little ones battering against bare light bulbs. It banged the hot glass hard enough to start it rocking, its shadow on the bare stud walls that of an angel, or a vampire. As if summonsed by her thoughts, a bat darted through the open end and out again.

Even having church there before the building was finished—barely started—was crazy. But that same little bunch, the ones that couldn't hardly wait for Armageddon when everybody but them would get what they had coming, had overrode the ones with sense again.

Suddenly she needed to get *clear* away from it: the smells of new construction and hair oil and perfume and sweat; the hollering and tongue-talking and singing and out-of-tune instruments; the mismatched benches and folding chairs and upside-down buckets; the lump inside—a knot of guilt and revulsion and yearning to apprehend what these other folks were feeling, not just a bloating, clotting tumor.

She'd quit West Virginia if she could, or the world. But she'd commence by getting out of that place, right there.

For a moment Janet stood in the door hole under the yellow bug bulb, feeling as though she were launching out into a void. She stepped forth and felt her way along the outside of the church. The wall's coarseness against her sweaty palm and the arguments of clay and rock under her feet were both fresh and familiar, far removed from the wildness inside. She slipped off her shoes and set them on the concrete-block ledge that would someday support fieldstone veneer. If Jesus tarried, it would. Would her shoes drop down the holes in the block, she wondered, and would she care? Would her soul drop into hell? Her bare feet greeted the soil, warmed by the day's sun.

The tobacco smoke fattened as she approached the corner, a stench sinful enough to stop her there, brash enough that she had to know its source. Voices welled like a thunderhead and slopped out the open gable end, then receded and surged again. Some woman was cutting a shine inside, too full of the Spirit to comprehend what she was doing.

Janet slipped around the corner and leaned against the wall like she was just hanging out. Like she and the other girls used to at the fire hall when they lied and said the youth meeting was over at 9:30 so they'd have a half-hour to yak. Back when they had youth meetings.

A thin dark form stood propped like a crooked stick against the wall not three feet from her. A cigarette tip swooped up and flared and illuminated a bony face no older than her own.

Janet knew every face around, but not that one. "God'll strike you down dead, smoking on His property."

He hardened into focus one part at a time as the inside light faded from her eyes. A beak nose sheltering a slash of teeth. Rolled-up sleeves of a white shirt. Blaze of sun-bleached hair. Dark knots of arm muscle. Coal-shine from polished shoes. He dragged on his smoke, squinted eyes picking at her. "You're all aquiver." His voice was slow, soft, southern.

Janet clasped arms that still juddered like she was riding fast on a potholed road, like she was shivering, and her so hotted up. "Can't help it. The Spirit's lit on me." She was defending what she'd come outside to get shed of, but she couldn't help that either.

After a while he said, "You talk in tongues?"

The lump inside bulged again, and she shook her head, unable to talk in any tongue.

The cigarette spiraled away and expired in a shower of sparks. The dark seemed diluted by its death; the boy's face became clearer in the gentle light from a jagger of moon. "Can't you get over the hump?" he said, and she clasped his understanding against her cold knot and felt her hurt diminish.

"The words won't come out," she said when she could. "The Spirit's on me and in me till I can't stay in my shoes, but the tongues won't come."

Teeth flashed in a grin. "I wondered why you was barefoot."

"Aw." Blood rose in her cheeks. "I shucked them cause I was sweated up from . . ." Janet gestured toward where the blaze of voices had burned to a bed of hot coals.

"Why don't you fake it? Its not hard, if you practice up." His tongue flickered across his lips and he said, "Eye sheikomo hundi, elly matea hey mako eye hundi, kay elly mo hundiiii." His shoulders spasmed and his head jerked on the hard peaks of sound, and his voice tailed off tuneful at the end as though in a love song.

A chill wrapped in hot shame struck Janet for even hearing such blasphemy. "God's gonna strike you dead for that," she whispered.

His laugh was tender and fluid. "I thought He'd a done that already, for smoking. Like you said." Concern twisted his features. "I don't know that I could withstand being struck down twicet."

"It ain't nothing to fool with. That's a sin against the Spirit. The Unpardonable Sin."

A square jaw worked while he pondered that, and he spat. "Be a waste of time to beg repentance for it, then."

Janet wheeled and gazed into the night, shoulder to the wall and back to him, panting as though she'd been hauled back to the altar.

"Not that I'm sorrowful about it. Maybe for the smoking. But not the other. There wasn't nothing mocking about it." His voice was close for a moment, then away. "It's not sinful to want bad something good."

Janet found no response. Inside, the evangelist salted the pot for the next night's service. "Bring your friends-a," he said, snatching air between phrases, "bring your loved ones-a, bring the stranger you meet on the highways and byways-a." His eyes, she knew, coursed faces, warning them he'd take note if they let the Lord down. "God'll do the rest-a."

"Didn't you ever want to know what it feels like so bad that you had to give it a try on your own?" He was close again, his voice a whisper since the rumpus inside had died. Too intimate for comfort, but chaste as a bedboard after the wallering she'd taken inside.

"I wouldn't let on I could talk tongues if I couldn't."

"Don't you want to be took into the church? Talk tongues one little shot, and you'll be part of their doin's. Then you won't have to stand outside and smoke while they have a big fling in the Lord."

She turned into his hair oil and tobacco. "Life ain't about worldly selfish desires, and I ain't the one smoking. You need Jesus in your heart 'stead of that nastiness you got, and I ain't talking to you anymore."

"I got Jesus, but He don't cut much mustard with this bunch." The back of his hand found one of her arms, then the other, then his fingertips inquired of her cheek and she could no more recoil from his touch than she could stop quivering.

"You're an awful sinner," she blurted.

The boy fell away and spoke in a voice that ached like the lump in her chest. "I'm not one a-tall. I just wasn't chose to be a saint."

Janet fled to join the people streaming into the night, before she had to hear any more.

§

She cried in bed, after her shaking stopped. After the headboard's creaking in her parents' room ceased. What they did after a fire-and-brimstone service both shamed and roused up some part of her that she couldn't get a handle on. While she wept she smelled that boy smoking, heard his falsified tongue-talking, felt his voice go forlorn into the night.

His words slashed her again, eye sheikomo hundi, and she crushed lips against teeth before they could take root in her own mouth.

§

The next evening, Janet walked to the church early. To pray without distraction, she told her mom. The carpenters had been productive: gable ends closed in, windows installed. Though the parking lot was vacant, the boy sat alone inside on a low backless bench cobbled from framing lumber scraps. It was darker with glass in the window holes, but he perched in a beam of sunlight like God almighty on the throne.

Sunburned scalp smoldered under fine sun-blanched hair. A nose longer than she'd remembered, skin coarse and red, chin not so square where daylight could worry off the corners. Bright stiff jeans and a rolled-sleeve white shirt, engineer's boots run down at the heels but toes buffed bright as a leaf lizard. Plaited ropes of muscle, not sleek bulges, and a moustache that hadn't made a profile in the dark. Eyes not the blue of sky but of creek, and teeth so unspoiled they had to be artificial. All that gathered in a glance that never lingered.

The church was like an attic, akilter and unfinished. But fresh, not dilapidated like the old church back in the woods—unsafe to go in, some said, the people that couldn't wait to pile into the new one. The bunch that always started the troubles.

Like the new church *was* safe. She still felt bruised from the previous night's mauling at the altar.

New, raw-new. The concrete floor green-cast, lumber sawmill pale. Here and there nails from outside missed the wood and stuck in like a cat's claws.

She skinned forward along the wall and sat on a wood chair with loose slats that pinched your fanny if you squirmed, put her head in her hands and confided her want to the Lord, though she didn't know what it was. "Please dear God," she whispered down into the concrete. "Please." The trembling in her arms commenced again like she'd slipped a thumb into a light socket.

"Howdy," he said, but she didn't look up. "The holy fire's lit on you already. Just from venturing in the door."

Janet shot him the look her mom gave her dad when he farted. "This ain't the place to yak."

His teeth flashed, but he didn't reply. Like he'd took heed of her warning.

She jammed her head back into her hands. "Where you from?" If God wouldn't listen, maybe he would.

A callused thumb flashed through the sunlight like a grouse taking wing. "Top of the hill. Not but two hundred yards."

"You little liar." She knew everyone around, all ten of them. The words were out before she realized he lived in the new house they'd hauled in on two diesel-smoking trucks a few weeks back, four axles under each half. "A man lives there."

He popped his muscle and puffed his chest and grinned so big his jaw might splinter off and leave nothing for his top teeth to chomp against. "I reckon."

If she'd wiped her face, her hand would have come away red. "Not you."

A maple-syrup laugh. "I'm joshing. I won't be a man till next year. It's my brother Roddy's house."

She nudged an ant into a new course that it pursued with undiminished zeal. "You must be rich. That fine house, and a brand new pickup."

The bench creaked when the boy locked his fingers behind his head and leaned back to expound. He forgot the bench had no back and his feet tipped up and he grabbed at the bench but didn't go over, just made the bench clatter and himself look dumb. The way he sniggered at himself made Janet partial to him though she didn't want to be. But she didn't have to look at him. Not much.

"A piece of junk, that house is, made in a factory like tater chips. It's two trailers scabbed together, but if you weary of where you're at, you can't even move it again like you could a real trailer." He still smiled, but rocks dragged under his voice's smooth surface. "And Roddy bought a daggone Dodge. I'd ruther walk. A '79 wheelbarry would be a improvement on a Dodge. The worst F-150 there ever was would make two of it."

"We got a Ford," she said, not so much to concur as to demonstrate she knew what an F-150 was.

"You most likely voted for Ford."

Janet put a sting in her tone. "I ain't old enough to vote. And why would you talk mean, even if I could?" Though Jimmy Carter should have stayed home and farmed peanuts, where he belonged. And them that elected him.

"Cause holyrollers is all black-legged Republicans. Declare they're for good, then vote in the biggest crooks there is. Probably to get their sinning in without having to touch it theirselves. Or so they got something worrisome to pray about."

"You shut that talk in God's house."

"Or He'll strike me dead again. 'Fore long there won't be enough left of me for a tree to fall on."

"Why'd you come here, anyhow?" she said. No way to pray with him beating his gums.

"Roddy landed a job at the papermill, and I come too. He's all the folks I got."

"I don't mean Union County. Why'd you show up here? At this particular church."

"To hear you get filled up with the Spirit. I want to see your tongue flap when you do."

"Don't poke fun at what you don't understand."

He laughed sad. "It's not meant to be understood. Not by me, anyhow."

"You talk southern." Through her fingers she admired the multiple shadows the row of windows caused her to cast on the concrete. Like the light had come from inside her, and was split through her fingers.

"That's cause I am. From Logan County. God's country."

"Way down there." She glanced to see if that information had changed his appearance. He'd been examining her, she could tell. She tugged her dress down and the chair slats pinched her. "Ow." She hugged her trembling arms.

He winced like chair slats had nipped him precisely like that. "What's your name? Wigglewart?"

"You think you're funning me, but you ain't. It's God you're pestering."

He considered his feet, and his Adam's apple bobbed. "I don't mean to torment you. Maybe I'm covetous of what you got."

"Of what, Mister Flatlander?" She tested the word he'd said inside her mouth, wasn't confident, but she knew another near alike. "What we got to look jealous at?" She waved at the walls. "This half-finished church? We ain't even got a toilet yet."

"Sid. That's my name. Sid Lore."

"Well, Sid Lore from Logan County. You're poorer than a possum if you're covetousous of this place." Janet coughed to blame the extra syllable on a tickle in her throat. She oughtn't have tried it unpracticed. "I'm Janet Hollar."

"It's not this place. It's you." His watery eyes captured and held hers, but before she could get her words rowed up gravel rattled in the parking lot and doors slammed bang bang bang and feet crunched their way. "I watched you through the door hole last night," he said. "I know what you're going through, cause I been through it too. Only I didn't make it all the way."

Then churchgoers were coming in and he was gone and she was left there in the endless hollering and singing and the testimonies and the preaching and the shouting and the shaking, oh Lord through the shaking she couldn't turn into something more, but amidst it all she sensed him. Watching. Listening. With the gable end closed in, she couldn't smell his smoke, but she felt it. She knew Sid Lore leaned against the church, smoking and waiting for Janet to receive the gift of tongues he never could.

"Say a word or two to get it started," that hard old voice scissored from the tongues-talkers who were working her over. "You can't speak tongues with your mouth shut."

Janet yearned to babble those words that would make her fit in again, make it so she could teach Sunday school and take in money at the bake sales. Suddenly she wasn't a kid anymore, and without notice, the Jesus that had got her started wasn't sufficient anymore and she was expected to be a Holy Ghost growed-up. Six words, and she'd be one for good.

Janet turned up her face and wet her lips, and all around the voices jumped a notch and patting hands went to grabbing and mauling to work the words out. Sid's fakey tongue was laid right on top of hers like two frogs making babies, eye sheikomo hundi, she knew what to say, and she sucked a breath past the malignant knot and said the only words she could, her words and not His. "I can't. It can't be me that does it."

She fought free and waded away and fled outside, and Sid Lore was waiting, like she knew he would be, smoking and squinting off into the dark at things he couldn't make out.

Neither of them talked. Sid was calm and Janet all aquiver. She looked out there with him. Out beyond the rocks and fox grapes, through the snow-twisted maples, over the dented trailers and muddy barnyards lay the mystery and simplicity of that other world she'd seen in the TV, out where folks thought church stuff was funny. Out there was only one reality you had to fool with, just the one you could get ahold of and smell and see, touch to your tongue if you took the notion.

But standing with their feet in the clay and smoke in their nose and their backs to a thin, unfinished wall that could no way contain the Spirit that had broke plumb loose inside, they could no more glimpse it than they could poke a hole in the sky and gaze up into heaven. So when his face nudged in from the dark and his little mustache tickled her nose, she kissed him back and swallowed his smoke and gave him her hurt. It wasn't everything she wanted, but it was likely all she was going to get.

2

Sɪᴅ's ʙʀᴀɪɴs ᴍɪɢʜᴛ ɢᴇᴛ sǫᴜɪʀᴛᴇᴅ out his eyeholes like a runned-over rat, but he'd not flinch or holler quit like he knew all three men figured him to. It'd be a shame to die over a damned old rock before he was old enough to smoke legal, but he wasn't a kid anymore, and he wouldn't behave like one. Even if one of these old farts hammered him in the head.

The steel shivered, shimmied up his armbones into his skull. The three sledges crashed a foot from his face, ninety licks a minute, and Sid had to twist the bit a quarter-turn each time, torque it without budging the top from where the next hammer, already coming, would strike.

"Move the dad-blamed church to where there's not a rock in the way," he wanted to holler, but he squinted and turned the bit.

Bud's sledgehammer was the worst. Rock dust blew from the hole when Bud's hammer struck, and Sid had to hoist the steel from the groove it had just cut. Bud swung a ten-pound hammer, not an eight like Chester's and Sam's.

It was Chester's tentative tap that puckered Sid's bunghole, though. If the man wasn't no more secure in his aim than that, he didn't have no business driving steel. His hammer never struck square or timely, or if it did the face was off kilter and the bit skipped sidewards.

Sam was steady as the rock they bored. One eye roved like a hounddog marking territory, but the good one locked where the sledge would ring. "You always hit where you're lookin'?" Sid said when that off eye meandered his way.

"Ever time," Sam said, and the bit shuddered.

"Then I'm not turning this thing no more." Sid grinned to let them know he'd turn it till they collapsed.

Bud grunted and said "break" and they all took one more ram and stood back to appreciate Sid's words. "You always hit where you're lookin'?" Chester aped with crossed eyes and they laughed except for Sid, who spit and grinned sly like they would if they'd said it. A half-gallon jar of spring water kept cool in a falling-apart wet paper sack made the rounds, Sid last. Bud was damp around the armpits, Sam's sweat a vee over his shoulders and down the front like a horsecollar, Chester dark around the belly. All wore olive green or dark blue or tan work pants and shirts that seemed the same color. Sid, in jeans, felt too dressed up for proper work.

"Deep enough, ain't it?" Chester said.

Sid purely despised the way these hillbillies said ain't, even the ones that knowed better.

"Nope." Bud examined glasses scarred from welding and cutting, then scoured them with a blue paisley hanky the size of a bedsheet.

"We should have mudpacked it." Chester understood as much about drilling and shooting as Sid, but Sid at least knew that he didn't know nothing. "Lay the dynamite on the rock, shovel mud on it. I heard that works."

Sam streamed tobacco juice not far from Chester's boot. "Mudpack hell. Waste of dynamite"—he pronounced it dan-o-mite.

"If we break through, we'll have to drill another hole. I'm just saying." Chester mopped his forehead with an arm just as wet.

Bud nodded toward another boulder on the edge of the parking lot. "This rock's bigger'n that one, or the dozer would have fetched it out. You think we'd be through that one, yet?"

"Lay Chester atop the mudpack. Maybe then it'd bust," Sid said, and Bud and Sam chuckled.

"Where'd you learn to be such a smartmouth?" Nothing was amusing when it came at Chester's expense. He was younger than the others, had his hackles up like him and Sid were dogs squabbling for a place in the pack. "They teach you that down in Logan County?"

"Learned it off you."

Sam grinned, but not at Sid. "Brother Hamil tried to pray this rock out. Got the deacons here, done a Jericho march round the bulldozer. But she wouldn't budge."

"Who tole you that?" Bud could let loose a damn or a sumbitch, but he didn't care for mocking against the church.

"Hubert. Hubert Smouse." Like there were dozens of Huberts around. He fixed his good eye on Sid. "Not Jim Smouse—Brother Smouse—but his brother Hube that don't go to church. You probly don't know him."

Sid nodded, grateful for being included in the talk.

"It was Hube's dozer. Said every time he went to back up, one a them deacons had laid hands on his machine. Finally he backed off and said, 'Hammy, you go ahead and pray out however much you can, and I'll labor on what's left when you're done. But there ain't room for both of us to torment it simultaneous.'"

"That's Hube." Bud's grin exposed black stubs and snuff juice. "Him and Jim's from the same litter, but you'd never figger it."

"Maybe the Good Lord doesn't want the church built out here," Chester said. "In town, folks could get to it easier. Maybe that's why this rock is in the way. Hube or Hammy neither one got it out, I notice."

"Folks in town got more churches than is good for them," Sam said. "And God don't bother with stuff we can handle on our own. Catch hold of that steel, Sid. That hole won't get no deeper from talking."

Beat on it they did, till Sid's spine felt wormed into the rock. As the steel worried into the sandstone, its mushroomed head sunk closer to Sid's until he was keen to holler out for a fresh position.

"Break," Bud said before Sid could, and the hammers clanged three times and it was still.

§

Sid, Chester, and Sam hunkered with their heads peeking over the boulder in the parking lot—the one Hube's dozer had rooted out—but Bud leaned against a tree, exposed to the upcoming blast. "Get behind something," Chester said for the fifth time. "You loaded it heavy. A stick-and-a-half, that's a wad of dynamite."

Sid's eyes resembled gnats' asses stretched over rain barrels, though he willed them not to, and in them he saw again Bud crimp the silver blasting cap onto a coil of orange fuse, then slice open the oily-looking dynamite sticks and crumble the pale contents down the hole and around the cap. Sid cringed when Bud tamped the dynamite, and the three men smirked. Then Bud packed the hole with muck and mashed it with his foot.

"Won't that wet make the fuse fizzle out?" Sid said.

"Looky here." Bud knifed diagonally across the fuse, a foot above the hole. "There's tar that melts around the fire. It'll even burn underwater. Slice it slantways so it'll light easy."

"Is there anything you don't know?" Sid said.

"He don't grasp how to keep buttwipe kids out of his way," Chester said.

But Chester was paying keen attention too when the wooden match blazed off Bud's boot, and when tar dribbled from the fuse, but when sparks sizzled from the tip, Chester was gone, Sid and Sam close behind. Bud stopped halfway back and packed his lip with Copenhagen, then parked himself against the apple tree as though for a snooze.

Sid was seeing all that again when the earth tremored like someone one room over had stomped on the floor. The rock shrugged and a butterbowl-sized piece humped three feet straight up, and lesser sprags leaped out like a hoptoad hatch, and then the noise—a grunty snort like you liberated on a deer stand when you just *had* to cough. In the following silence, smoke snakes writhed from the rock. They went to inspect, Sid and Chester spooky like it might rare up again.

"Undershot it," Chester said. He'd hardly quit harping that a stick-and-a-half was enough to bust it twice, and gone to saying it wasn't enough. "Poop fire. We'll have to bore it again."

"You drill her this time, Chester," Bud said. "I'm tired a fooling with it."

The rock was rubble. Sid kicked at it, flabbergasted at the way it crunched inside, and at the smell—a fired shotshell, smoky and sour—and at the stark white of shattered rock.

Logan County, where Sid had grown up, had been a world of rock, pulverized by bulldozers and paddle pans, by hydraulic oil and diesel smoke, by the very bellow of the machinery.

Not by hammer and perspiration and match. Sid savored the sharp-edged pieces, the sandy dust trickling through his manlike fingers.

§

Sam departed to requisition concrete while the others picked out the broken pieces and drove stakes level around the ditch. Chester peered through the transit because he was worthless at driving stakes or holding the rule plumb. He couldn't look right either, couldn't keep his fingers off while he sighted, so he always jiggled the crosshairs. "Down a quarter," he'd say and Sid would bump it another shot. "Down an eighth. Down a sixteenth." Sid would give the stake a tiny tap and Chester would alter his grip on the transit and say, "Up a quarter."

Bud would say, "Drive her the other way, Sid. Drive her up a tad." And they'd progress to the next stake.

After getting the wheelbarry too close and knocking dirt into the ditch, then dumping one wad shy of the target, Sid placed the concrete where Bud pointed, twisting the handles sideways as the tub emptied so that it was already half spread out when it hit the ground.

"He might make a Uke driver," Sam said. "You know what a Uke is?"

"Shoot yeah." Sid imagined himself in a massive Euclid construction truck like Roddy used to drive, tires twice as tall as Sid's head.

Chester sulked when they commended Sid, and wiped down an extra big load from the chute—about six hundred pounds worth—instead of damming it back with his round-pointed shovel. Sid almost tipped over when he made the turn to square up with the ditch, but he never let on. "Give me a whole load this time, Chester," he said when he sidled under the chute again. "Running back and forth half empty is wearing me out." Chester's neck sure could get red.

§

The concrete truck had gone, and Chester and Sam, too. Sid stayed behind to scrub the tools while Bud slicked the poured footer. Bud's wooden trowel—a float, he called it—made licking noises. "Why you working here for nothing?" Bud said. "This ain't even your church."

"I'm not. My brother Roddy pays me two bucks a hour to help yous. He can't volunteer hisself, or even come to church, with all them hours he works at the papermill." Sid spat all in one knot, a talent he'd acquired by studying Bud. "What I think is, he don't want me laying around with nothing to do."

Bud's grunt might have indicated that he agreed with Sid, or that he thought him as intelligent as the wheelbarry. "You got kin in Logan County?"

"Nobody close. Ma died two years ago. Roddy sold the home place and come here to the mill."

"If I moved for a job, I'd move where it was."

"Roddy says it's muggy down there and smells like shit." Sid felt obliged to cuss a little. "He'd ruther drive sixty miles and live here. He don't always make sense."

The silence ground on Sid. He considered the rock at the edge of the parking lot, half the size of a dump truck, fat on one end like a lopped-off nose. Clawed-looking where the dozer's teeth had raked its weathered crust. "Maybe I'll bust up that other rock," Sid said, mostly to make some noise.

Bud made a face and belched. "It ain't hurting nothing. Leave it for the old women to back into. Give the body shops some business."

Sid imagined the rock's pallid insides, saw it as a heap of smoking rubble. The expression on Bud's face if he really got it done. "I bet I could."

Sid felt dismissed, and wished he could recall his words. But after a while Bud said, "If you commence to bust on it, you'll have to finish."

Sid laughed. "I'd stop if I wanted to. Who'd make me keep on?"

"You will. You won't have the guts to quit."

Sid considered the flat faces where he'd strike, the corners he'd work off a slice at a time. He saw himself in the rubble, smoking, or chewing tobacco. "Hell I won't."

Bud guffawed and leaned back to stretch his spine. He lobbed the float into the wheelbarry for Sid to scour. "How old are you, punk?"

Sid hid his red face by bending and scrubbing at the hardening concrete. "Seventeen."

"You won't be a kid when you finish busting that rock." Bud laughed. "You'll be a full-growed man."

Sid nodded, surprised at how painless growing up was turning out to be.

§

Sid labored with the men during the day, then beat on the rock at night when nobody would notice him. Two weeks after he started, a half-dozen beagle-sized knots had peeled off, had been knapped up and sailed into the woods. Another week would do it, he figured; it was time for folks to appreciate who'd done it. When cars rolled in for the first night of the Holy Ghost Fire Revival Meeting, he kept swinging the hammer.

Sid watched Chester's wife Laurie from the corner of his eye. Her freckled face was devoid of makeup, and she carried a little pudge. But the excess was in the right places, right where Sid liked it, and he despised Chester for possessing her.

Before Chester could get around the vehicle to head her off, Laurie came Sid's way. "My lands, Sid," she said, her eyes measuring him in a way he was afraid to mimic. "Didn't you toil enough today, carrying shingles up the ladder?"

She'd brought hot sallycakes and sliced ham at lunch, lemonade in the afternoon, and stood right in and talked while they ate. "Now you're going to break up that boulder." Like it was a done deal.

Sid tore his eyes from the bosom that stretched her dress taut. "Waiting for them old dudes to nail down a shingle oncet in a while isn't all that magnacious." He grinned, and felt his muscles stiffen wherever her eyes rested, concrete firming in the sun.

Her laughter was husky, as though her fingers, not her eyes, had examined him.

Chester looked even more stupid in church clothes—the same green pants but a white shirt buttoned around the neck. Hatless, his freckled bald spot was a toadstool hooved up through pine needles. "Don't be fooling around while church is going on." He snagged Laurie by the arm.

Sid flexed his bicep and swabbed his forehead. "You couldn't notice dynamite"—he pronounced it the way Sam had because Chester didn't like that—"with that preacher hollering."

Chester had seen where Sid's eyes flickered, or maybe Laurie had pissed him off by chatting with Sid. He poked a finger at Sid as he hustled Laurie away. "Tell you what, don't fool with that rock anytime."

If he didn't care for his woman looking at men, he ought to lock her up in the henhouse. Sid rubbed his nose with a middle finger, but let the hammer handle fall against the rock. Chester could instigate trouble—a quantity of it, from what people said about why half the congregation had took out for the Church of God.

More cars arrived as he studied from the shade of the tree Bud had sat under while the dynamite went off. He imagined the girls as Laurie, the men as Chester.

It was brainless to have church there before the building was finished. It created more work, rearranging the benches and chairs out of the way every day.

"This structure will be sanctified from the get-go," Chester had said when Sid voiced his opinion.

"Having church in it. That makes it holy?" Sid had said, and Chester had kept his head turned so Sid couldn't see how red it was. The neck give him away, though, like it always did when Sid called him out for being as dumb as a sled track.

The women, as they arrived, nodded and said "good evening," but the men said "bite off more'n you can chew?" or "ain't you something." Spitting words like tobacco juice. "How you like that Mexican jackhammer?" one said.

One girl stood out because her dress had a wide white belt like Laurie's. She strode on the balls of her feet so that her bobbed brown hair hardly bounced, and her dress trailed like she was standing still and the earth and wind were sliding past her. She didn't fill her clothes like Laurie, and her eyes were on her low-heeled shoes, but she gave Sid half a boner, especially when she said hello in a little breathy voice. Her nose bobbed at the end, just where Sid desired to place his lips.

After dark, when Sid could stand out and look in through the doorless doorhole without being seen, he watched her. She sat alone near the back, and when he slipped up beside the door he could hear her singing voice. Strong, but feminy, and she knew how to sing alto.

Sid had a notion to slip inside and sit close to her, but his pants felt like they had a wet spot in the front. He couldn't tell for sure in the dark. Wouldn't the preacher like to light into *that*. Naw, he'd just stay there by the door with his back up against the wall and listen.

During the preaching she said "Amen" once in a while, but it sounded like she was using the word to poke herself with. Not like some of the older folks, Chester's voice head and shoulders above the rest, that said the word like, "Now by God, I told you so." Sid allowed the preacher's words to roll off him like the bat turds that freckled the floor inside. Had Roddy been there, Sid would have to skedaddle home or go inside, one. Roddy didn't allow laying back.

What Roddy's amen meant, Sid wasn't sure. It came at the damnedest times, like when he stobbed a toe on the davenport leg.

During the altar call, the girl went forward. A swarm of growed-ups buried her in a mess of sweat and noise. "Give her your Spirit, Lord," one cherry-faced old bag bellered, and Sid shivered.

He'd been through it, back in Logan County: voices like dogs', give it up, turn it loose, hang on, let it go; hands belaboring him, wrenching out the devil.

How he'd tried. How he'd sought for God to light fire in his muscles and shake him and slam him on the floor and waggle his tongue like the others. He'd wanted it so bad that he'd hung onto an electric fence till he'd bit his tongue and made a streak in his britches, but it wasn't the real thing, and it made him fanaticaled crazy to get filled up. Maybe it wasn't wholesome to go so hard after something: wanting it that bad was coveting, the nastiest sin there was. Probably why God hadn't wanted nothing to do with him. Sid give up trying after a while, and thought he'd got over being locked out of the fold.

He glimpsed the girl's upturned face in the jumble of arms and heads. Her want had run out of her eyes, and in the bare-bulb lighting the tears looked like slug tracks, like something evil was oozing out of her, and it all lit down on Sid again, and he hurt with her and felt the fence between her and the Lord she couldn't get over, and he couldn't look anymore.

He felt his way along the outside of the church toward the rear, away from the parking lot. Light and sound washed over the gable end that hadn't been closed in yet. Bats hacked their way though the flood of bugs in the wedge-shaped rays above his head, and there where he couldn't see the earnestness in those faces, the spell slithered away. He lit a cigarette and sucked it deep and held it without coughing like he'd done when he first started the week before.

He detected someone scrabbling his way just after he lit his second smoke. Chester, most likely, come to give him hell. But the girl slipped around the corner instead, and leaned against the wall panting for breath like dogs had pursued her there. She was atremble, and he told her so, and they talked of tongues. Her smells and sounds—sweat and perfume and hard little breaths that made him breathe harder too—built around Sid till he couldn't think right. She couldn't get the tongues any better than he could, she said, and in the company of some-one just like him, his mouth got out ahead of his brain and he was mouthing the words he'd practiced back when he'd decided to talk in tongues whether they was the Lord's or his own, but had been too trepidatious to use them. He should have been scared, but there was no mischief in his heart or his mouth either. Standing close to her had opened him up so he could let loose words he never suspected he possessed—words he'd never said or thought, like he was finally tongues-talking.

Sid's head was afire with tobacco and with her smell, like lilacs but steamy, and he heard the words from a mouth he no longer controlled, and he observed his hand go out to stroke her cheek.

She called him a sinner, a dreadful sinner, and he knowed he was one. Not for smoking or for saying words that meant no wrong, that meant nothing a-tall to anyone but him, but for touching her like that with lust in his flesh, her so full

21

of the Spirit that the muscles crawled like snakes under her skin. It was like feeling up God, and it mortified him so that his bowels rolled, and he denied his sin though that was a sin too and then she was gone.

Sid slid down against the wall and sat with his head buried between his knees until everyone had departed. Again and again he revisited touching her cheek, tried to recapture what had passed between them. He smelled for her on his fingers, but found only tobacco. Sin. One of God's good plants that man had dried and chopped and ruined and turned to evil.

He thought of Laurie, but her face had become the girl's. A great confusion drove Sid from the rear of the church, but what had happened there kept him from walking home, just up the road. He couldn't put it to rest, nor did he want to. He found his way to the rock and took up his hammer.

§

The dead black softened just after five o'clock. Ten minutes later, Sid weighed what he'd done all night. Damn near nothing. Dust from his sledging had turned the rock pale, and his white shirt brown, but the rock was unfazed.

Most of the night he'd swung the hammer with his eyes shut tight against the peppering of dust. The hammer's head never hit exactly when he expected nor where, judging from the width of the scar he'd inflicted.

While he'd swung, he'd prayed. Not for blessing, or for acceptance or forgiveness, or even for an answer. A clearing of a divine throat would do, or the shifting of colossal feet. A grunt, to indicate that he'd been heard.

Sid's arms quaked from fatigue and dehydration in the cold light of the morning. "Time to git home. Roddy'll want his breakfast," he undertook to say, but his tongue was stiff and gritty and the words foreign to his lips and to his ears.

The day lay ahead not as an adventure, but as a sodden plowed field through which he must walk. Already he felt its accumulation on his feet, weighting him down, gobbing him fast.

He allowed the hammer to slide from his clawed hands and trudged toward Roddy's factory-built home. At the edge of the parking lot he turned tired eyes back again.

Bit off more'n you can chew, didn't you.

The rock lay iridescent as a turkey's back, from one eye looking as it would one day be, rubbled inside a circle of big men and pretty girls, from the other a tombstone that would immortalize where he'd died trying.

He groaned, a voice deep and dark and not his own. "I'll break you, by God. I'll break you or me one." Then he whirled and ran as a boy runs, high-kneed and springy on his feet. The breeze was pregnant with dampness that had gathered and streamed down his face by the time his breath gave out. He stood hands-on-knees and herded up his air, then squared his shoulders and walked on, feeling his bicep, whistling a tune he couldn't name, or get shed of. A church tune, or a mixture of tunes, worn-out ditties with timeless lyrics, terrible words from which meaning had faded.

3

"Yeah, people's great here," Roddy Lore said.

Like George Hollar—Janet's dad—had asked that instead of did Roddy like Union County. Like hills and hollers and folks were exchangeable. The squat, pockmarked man was brother to the boy that had kissed her behind the church, but Janet couldn't see how.

A month ago, that kiss, but she could still taste him when she wanted. Like just then.

Janet fastened her sweater against the fog that ruined every Labor Day weekend picnic. Even if it hadn't rained since dog days came in, you could figure cold and soggy for Labor Day. Then when school started, hot would set in till flies couldn't land for fear of their feet. Even Roddy's coonhound was staying inside his barrel, but maybe hiding from people instead of the weather.

"Don't fret about tracking in; it'll clean up," Roddy hollered toward the house. Nobody appeared worried: folks moseyed through the open front door as though they were at the feed store. Open House. Dumbest thing Janet had ever heard of.

Like every get-together, it had mutated into a church event. Family reunion, fetch the hymnals. Ball game, commence with prayer.

Janet smelled her mom, Nettie—Evening in Paris perfume and Pine Sol, church pew and farmhouse—before she spoke. "Go socialize with the youth, Janet."

Youth. Like the church had wadded individual kids into one lump. Janet selected a carrot from the picnic table, really a piece of plywood on sawhorses. What she most wanted was some of that cherry-cheese stuff, but no way was she going to fat up like the other women. Mom had taught her that much. "You call that socializing?"

Paisey Everds and James Peters were throwing and catching a wiffle-ball in wire cups like the ones around the barn lights. Paisey couldn't see past her snoot, and James couldn't scratch his ear without getting a thumb in his eye. The Roomer kids—Hattie, Doogie, and Ralph—sat chin-on-knees, watching. A Frisbee lay beside them, but they lusted after those glamorous wire baskets.

"It beats standing here alone."

"I ain't hardly alone," Janet whispered, and Nettie grinned and Janet loved her though she wasn't in the mood.

Across the table, Knobby Jerden swilled food off a paper plate. Chicken crust littered his shirtfront, and a smear of ketchup made it look like he'd tore his mouth hole even bigger. Yellow eyes like carp rolling in the shallows. "This your bean salad, Nettie Hollar?" Knobby masticated the words.

A good word, Janet thought: mastication. Sounded like what it was.

"Your sister Dez made it."

"It ain't fit to eat. Too vinegary." He sailed his plate into the trash and sloped off to his truck, walking like a dancing bear with the piles. The truck belched like it had overeaten too.

"There you teed Knobby off, Nettie." Harland Roomer—Dez's husband and the father of the misfit kids watching the wiffleball—spat and talked with the other men. "He probly won't come to church no more." Knobby never attended church, just the eating affairs.

Even George laughed, something he never did at home. Janet grinned because you couldn't hear Harland's voice without grinning. His or Clarence Bowser's either one. They talked like brothers, dressed like twins in drab dark shirt and pants.

Clarence wiped his lips on his sleeve and said, "You hear about Fats and Hammie and Will arguing about hogs?"

Janet had, but listened for the new wrinkle he'd invent. Nettie clutched Janet's elbow as they crept into the pack of men. All eyes were on Roddy and Sid, who hadn't heard the story. Sid sat on a big rock at the yard's edge. He winked brash at Janet.

She looked away, uncertain whether he was winking about the story or at her. Though she'd seen him helping the old men at the church, they hadn't spoken since the kiss.

"Them three got in a word brawl down at the Agway," Clarence said, "over what you got when you bred a Yorkshire to a Poland China hog. Fats said Beltsville #2s, but Willie was clarified firm the shoats would come out Palouse."

Roddy laughed out of time, and Clarence gave him a hard look before he continued with a smidgen of outrage in his voice. "Hammie said you got a mongrel hog with decent bacon but wouldn't win a ribbon at the fair cause you never knowed what color it would be. He'd seen them clear white, or plumb black. One marked off like a checkerboard, and a polka-dotted one oncet."

They hadn't heard that before, and everyone laughed but Roddy.

"Then Harland showed up, and Willie said, 'He'll know. Hey, Harland,' he said, 'what do you get when you cross a Yorkshire and a Poland China?'

"'I reckon you'd get a Jerden,' Harland said, and went on inside."

Roddy opened his mouth and closed it again like a toad with a nasty-tasting bug.

Everyone postponed laughing until Harland said, "I ought to know. I been hitched to a Jerden nineteen year."

When the laughter subsided, Nettie picked up the ritual: "Harland, you ought to be ashamed. Dez is the sweetest woman there is."

When Roddy didn't do everything wrong, he did it right at the wrong time. He wore that look a man gets when the situation is out of his control: like he probly messed his shorts, but didn't have nerve to check.

"But she's a Jerden," Harland said. "Decent bacon, no ribbon at the fair."

Nettie stamped her foot and that tickled everybody. They all knew Harland and Dez were bad in love as moonstruck teenagers.

"Heh, heh." Roddy, louder than the rest. "Come look at the house."

"We can't tramp through your stuff," Clarence said.

"I could investigate your bathroom." Harland hitched his pants. "Right soon I could stand that."

"Come," Nettie said. "All of you." She dragged George until he acquiesced, and the other men eased along with them. Sid and Janet lingered behind.

Acquiesced: another word that sounded like what it meant: started hard but gave way as it went. Janet's eyes caught Sid's, and she colored and looked down and then over at the kids. James was lecturing the others, warming up to the preacher everyone knew he'd be.

"Where you been?" Janet put barbs in it.

"Nowhere. There's nowhere to be around here. But that's where I'd be if there was."

"It wouldn't kill you to come to church."

"I been there every day, working with Bud and them, and I been breaking a rock there every night. That's about all the church I can abide." He looked at the ground, offered Janet God's perspective of his schnozz. A real eagle beak.

"I saw you doing that. What's the rock need broke for, anyhow? There's ten million more just like it laid around wherever you look."

The way he licked his lips made Janet taste him again. "Someone might need to park there."

"Shoot. Since Brother Martin left, there's hardly anybody to park. Since Dunn came. I liked it when we didn't have a preacher, when Clarence or Chester just stood up and talked."

"Chester. I can't picture that roundhead delivering much of a talk."

Paisey glared their way, tossed back her hair and made a snoot. Janet felt Sid's eyes all over her when she wasn't looking. She took a deep breath and said, "Scoot over." The rock Sid sat on was big, but that part fit for sitting wasn't. She sat sygogling for a moment, her butt out of level, then glanced at the house and slid to where it was comfortable, where their elbows brushed. "Chester ain't bad, but he bloviates a lot. So does Clarence. They're both real smart."

Sid snickered. "The way you people talk beats all."

"Me? You sound like you come from Alabam."

"I mean the words you use. Ain't and blomiate all in one mouthful."

"I guess you don't say ain't, mister perfect."

"No, I *don't* say ain't. And that other word I don't even know."

"Bloviate. Like it sounds. Means he's a blowhard."

"Then just say that."

"Words spice things up. I bet you like spice on food."

Sid snapped a twig in a most annoying way, again and again. "I take grub straight. If it's not fit to eat without gunk on it, I don't care for none."

She examined him and saw it was true. And sad.

"Salt and pepper, but no spice," he said. What dandy teeth. "Where you learn words like that?"

"From books. Don't you read?"

"No more than I got to. Just in school."

Though she'd judged him her age, school surprised her. "What grade you in?"

"Twelfth. Eleven too many."

"Same as me. But I like school. I enjoy learning."

"If you been there eleven year and still say ain't, it must not be a very joysome place for you. I at least know that much."

"It's the way we talk. Not cause we don't know better. Were I to be in court, or on the radio perhaps, I could speak the King's English with perfect syntax, and with impeccable enunciation." She said it hoity-toity, but teasing. Whether it was right she wasn't sure, but he wouldn't know. "Miss Riggs teaches English, but she talks just like us away from school. A French teacher don't use French less she's in France, does she?"

He squinted through the smoke from yet another cigarette. "Hell fire."

She hit him in the leg and his thigh was the same consistency as the rock. "Watch your dirty mouth."

"Why do something less good than you could? If you can talk right, let her rip."

"Do you go whole-hog at everything? Always do your absolute best?"

"Why wouldn't I?" That maple-syrup voice, irritating as cockleburs.

"You wouldn't go to France and talk Chinese."

"I wouldn't go to France to start with, and if I did, I'd speak American. What I knowed."

"They wouldn't understand you."

"Then they'd have to go without learning what I had to tell them."

"You could pick up enough sign language to share all you know. Might take three-four minutes to get all the words you'd need, but it would be worth it."

Sid shifted away from her sharp tongue and she made it softer. "You're different from your brother."

"Everybody's different from Roddy. Since Nam, anyhow."

Pike Baggart had been to Vietnam. Runny eyes that never lit anywhere. "Does he have dreams?"

"It's like the gooks reamed out his insides and sent the skin back. Different people show up in his hide now and again." He muttered something Janet didn't hear, shook his head. "Or maybe he got his rudder shot off. Just bores along wherever he got pointed last." The pile of broken twigs around his feet was enough to kindle a fire. "I shouldn't say nothing. He's been good to me."

"He see a lot of fighting?"

"He don't say."

But for the whine of locusts and an occasional laugh from inside, it was quiet. Before she could figure how to restart the conversation, a white Cadillac with rusty rocker panels wallowed into the driveway. "Oh, poop. Put that cigarette out."

"What for?" Sid stuck it square in his mouth like he was freeing both hands to fight.

"It's Preacher Dunn."

Before she could move away from Sid, the old geezer popped out and had Janet's hand in his. "Miss Hollar." His other skinny hand worried at a button on his old brown sports jacket. "Thank the Lord, the dry spell has broken." Like they'd had a drought, instead of two weeks without rain. She imagined him preaching about it, his voice going quiet and loud like a guitar amp with a loose connection: "Because of your WICKED WAYS, the LORD hath CONSUMED the LAND."

"Brother Dunn," she said, but he'd turned to Sid.

"Arden Dunn's my name, young man."

Before he shook, Sid squinted a while. "Warden?"

Dunn smiled, but sparks were flying. "Arden. I don't run a prison. I set folks free."

"Aw. Sid Lore."

"Hope to see you in church." Dunn whopped him on the shoulder, harder than necessary. Sid looked like he might give him a pop back.

Maybe Dunn noticed that too, because he pranced off toward the house.

"Why didn't you put that thing out?" Janet hissed.

"If I was ashamed of it, I wouldn't do it. He didn't say nothing."

"He saw it. He'll not let it slide."

"What will he do, call forth she-bears to gnaw me up? Here was his chance, if he wanted to rip." Sid drew the smoke short and flipped it toward the preacher's car.

"You sure don't know much about people."

"I know how they ought to be."

From the open front door voices swelled like baying hounds. "Let's walk," Janet said. "Before they break out in a prayer meeting."

Sid frowned as though she'd suggested he take up ballet. "Where to?"

"Come on," Janet said, and caught him by the arm.

Behind them her mother's voice thin and cutting. "Janet." She ignored it.

The fog had clotted thick; disembodied sassafras limbs—beggars' hands—intruded from the untrimmed edges of the tar-and-chip road that wound down the hill toward the church. Chicory and bee balm lit sparks of blue and red in a monochromatic landscape. "Slow down." Janet clutched the sleeve of his thin jacket. Fog discombobulated her till she didn't even think in the same words. She was in another world full of hair tonic and cigarette smoke, and she wanted to taste him, to nuzzle that downy moustache. She turned him to her and rose on her toes and he tensed, then her lips touched the tepid damp of his face. "There." She wheeled away, mortified. Hoped he couldn't see the glow from her face, the way you could distinguish your own taillights in the fog.

"What was that about?" He'd stopped.

"That's so I won't be obliged to you for nothing." As he fell behind she slowed, hips rolling like a Jezebel's. But she couldn't walk any other way, not slow.

"That little peck didn't even make a interest payment on the one I give you."

She stood with crossed arms and sassed, wanting to slide under his jacket and feel his hard thin frame. "You got a lofty opinion of your smooches."

"No other girls found fault with them."

"You probly never kissed anybody but your mom." Out and gone, the words were beyond grabbing.

"My mother's dead."

"I didn't aim to say that."

He came her way, tall and thin becoming lean and muscled as he sharpened from the mist. "Then you ought not to have done it." If he was offended or angry, his voice didn't show it. Just aggravating sensibility.

"I said I was sorry." Janet stepped back in beside him, nudging hips till they got in step. "Everybody says stuff they don't intend."

"I don't."

"What about those made-up talking-in-tongues words you used?"

Sid zipped his jacket tighter, as though to exclude Janet. "I never said them. I just demonstrated what they'd sound like if I was to, but then I didn't."

Janet laughed, felt dim-witted for it.

"How'd you know about Mom?" he said.

"People was just talking."

"Gossiping."

"No, it wasn't. There's so little to know in a place like this, if you don't know it all you're clear ignorant."

He grinned, and she felt forgiven.

"I despise that about these hicky little places," he said. "I hear stuff I don't want to know. Gives me the hives."

"The way I hear, you don't hail from a metropolis yourself."

"Maybe not, but if you peeked out our front window, you could see a house. Out the back, there was another one, and growing up here you might not believe it, but there was even one out the sides. You not only had the option of whether to look at a house or not, but you had some to pick from. Here, you got to settle on red oak or hickory."

Janet plucked a black gum leaf that glowed scarlet beside a golden sassafras, thrust it forward like evidence. "But it's glorious. And it's always changing." She swept her hand at the other coloring leaves hidden in the fog.

"That's the difference. I'll allow you that. Back home, you swibbeled your head for a switch of scenery. Here, you hunker down and set three months and everything will be a different color. But the same. If it's not too foggy to tell."

"On the farm I live on right down the road, you can look any way you want, see something fresh every place. Not just ugly old houses, neither."

"I know all about you. Where you live, what your daddy does. What color your cows are, and your tractor, and how many bottom plow it will pull."

Frustration edged into her voice, and she didn't care. "For someone hard set against gossip, you must have done right smart of it."

"I never done any a-tall. It's like I said, what disgusts me worst about this place. I don't *want* to know anything about you, but what am I going to do when people yak? Put my fingers in my ears and holler?" He demonstrated: "Wawawawawalalalala-wookywookywooky."

"You talk like a flatlander. You are one."

Sid stopped and lit another smoke in a manner that said she was just dumber than dirt.

She was a milksnake, raring her head up from the grass. "You go through them things like a dumb kid eatin' jelly beans. After your mom died of lung cancer."

"Yous most likely dug up her x-rays, passed them around after Bible study."

"It wasn't a secret that I knowed of."

"You want to know about Mom?" He jabbed at her with his cigarette. "She never smoked in her life. Never ate red meat, or drank. It's just the way stuff comes to pass. Dad done all them things, and he was hale as a horse."

"He died in a car wreck, I heard."

"He died of too much hurry by a teenage punk." Any sign of mirth had evaporated from his voice. "Dad worked in the mines. Dodged roof falls, smoked cigarettes by the wheelbarry load. Felled timber when the mines was on strike, or when some nasty half-rotten cowshade of a yard tree threatening someone's house had to come down. Weekends he'd do roof jobs that others was juberous of—the high steep ones all swarmed up with bees. If a troublesome bull got loose, they called Mack Lore. All that so he could get caught on an inside turn by a nineteen-year-old bread truck driver in a sweat to get his route done so he could go to the movies."

It was his longest speech, and it left Janet as breathless as if she'd given it.

He wasn't finished. "What we do don't matter. Handy Mullins drunk a jar of liquor every day. Ate nothing but slab-back bacon and longhorn cheese, sopped bread in the bacon grease. Smoked and chewed and rubbed and lied and took off a-whoring when he wasn't laying drunk. If he ever worked, nobody caught him at it. Got too drunk to tend the fire and froze off his outside toes. He thieved everything that wasn't nailed down, and would piss on a tomb-stone. Lived to be a hundred and two, and then died of walking pneumonia, not of nothing he inflicted on himself."

A long tirade around a smidgen of truth. "I've knowed some like that," she said. The church loomed ahead, the roof's peak stretching forever into the mist. Like if you could distinguish the top, you'd see God peering over the edge. To the side lay the rock, and it drew them like a refrigerator discarded in a creek would attract sucker minnows. "But those are just freak happenings."

Sid sat back on the rock like he was easing into a familiar recliner. "Maybe freaky from our side of the mirror, but there's another side. Maybe life's pure blind chance. But whether God lays it all out, or whether we're blundering through the fog waiting for a tree to fall on us or a meteorite to lam us in the head or for a bread truck to run over us, we don't have no input."

"Aw, Sid, you can't believe that. That's defeatist. That mind-set robs off your mettle. You got to twist life's tail, force it to go your way."

Sid snorted. "I twisted a heifer's tail oncet to make her hop up in a truck so we could take her to the sale."

"Then you see what I mean."

"She didn't care to hop. She pooped down my arm and tromped a hole in my boot and jumped the fence and run off. Time we found her, a month later, she was so poor, her hamburger would a been tough. Pap took mercy, never butchered her till she got fatted up again, but before that she got loose and eat half the garden and then got bogged down in the sawmill swamp and croaked without getting her throat cut and spoiled. We never got one sliver of meat." He talked like he was explaining Tinker Toys to a toddler. "That's what comes about when you twist life's tail."

She wasn't required to believe that way, just because he did. "You sift out one single time and pretend like that's the way things always is."

"Pap got run over just oncet. But that's the way she was."

"It ain't that way. Life's how we manage it to be."

"You believe what you want." He unzipped his coat like the debate had warmed him. "I'll take it clean, without spice. That's the way I am."

"You got the right to be wrong."

"I'll show you how right I am. I never had one notion of kissing you today. Don't even care to, actually. But here it goes anyhow. So it must have been laid out somewhere to happen."

He snugged her into him, and she leaned harder than he pulled. Their noses nestled like sow and piglet, and their breath mingled as though made for the purpose. His body was hard, so solid that she couldn't tell where Sid left off and the rock took over. With their mouths stoppered against talking, they got along real good.

4

RODDY WORKED SECOND SHIFT, sucking up double-time holiday pay, and left Sid to tidy up the mud tracked into his open house. Roddy showed off, Sid cleaned up. He'd be wormy in the head to expect anything different.

Grass was thriving better inside than out. If he'd scatter some chickenshit on the carpet and let in some sun, maybe they'd have nice grass somewhere. He could vacuum the hardpan yard, mow the living room. Not that there was any dearth of chickenshit already. Sid slammed the sweeper into the baseboards, intentionally leaving dings.

His bile festered overnight. After the breakfast dishes were washed, Sid joined Roddy in the driveway. Eleven hundred miles on the pickup, and Roddy was already changing the oil. Sid bounced pebbles off Roddy's shoe. "Funny how you find time to fool with your stuff, but not housework." He lammed a rock hard at Roddy's shoe, but hit his ankle.

Roddy slid from underneath the pickup and aimed the wrench at Sid. "You hit me again, I'm going to thrash your butt."

"Pack a lunch if you decide to. I'm not a kid no more."

"No, you're seventeen. Clear grown up. Old enough to smoke and cuss, and threaten your elders. Probably breaking laws right and left that I don't know about."

"I would be, if I could figure out how to do it where there isn't nobody to break one on. If I thought I could get a commandment broke, or even bent, I'd take a run at it."

Roddy brushed at the khaki trousers he'd started wearing. "Who've you've been hanging out with to catch an attitude like that?"

Sid failed to keep his voice level, like Bud could. "With those old farts you been *paying* me two bucks an hour to hang out with."

Roddy polished grease from his wrench. Just once Sid would like to see that much effort applied to a greasy skillet, or a load of laundry.

"I supposed those Christian men would curb you from taking up with the wrong crowd. Guess I figured amiss."

"I been trying to tell you, there isn't no wrong crowd around here." Sid kicked a tire, scuffed the white lettering. "There isn't even a right one." Roddy was quick for being squat, and strong, but Sid kicked it again before he got hauled away. When he levered Roddy's fingers loose, Sid's jacket tore. It looked like he'd have to take up sewing, too. "Keep your nosepickers off me."

The person who'd showed up in Roddy's hide that particular day didn't get mad. "There's no call to quarrel."

"You think a new truck and house makes you something, but it don't."

"It's more than you'll own, the rate you're going."

"Look what it's cost you. You work all the time. Smell like crap when you come home."

"That's the smell of work. Of money."

"You think you're the cheese, set and operate a machine and never soil your hands. But you're just a paper roller at a humangous mill. If that mill was a fish pond, you'd have to hide under a rock to keep from getting ate." Roddy's dog Stride bawled from inside his barrel in answer to Sid's raised voice. "You got a high-dollar dog, but you don't have time for him. Or me either."

Sid shied from Roddy's hand, but it was palm up. "Give me a cigarette."

"Why, so you can have a sin to dump at Jesus' feet like when you got drunk that last time? And then you preached at me like I done it."

Roddy drew back his hand and brushed his coal-black hair. "All right. I'm not partial to cheap smokes anyway." He leaned inside his truck and came out with a pack of Marlboros. His lighter was a worn silver thing that he flicked open and shut like he'd done it a billion times.

"Now you took up smoking again." Watching Roddy, Sid didn't feel like smoking anymore. But cigarettes had become necessary to speech. Like kicking tires, your feet delivering what your tongue couldn't tote.

"Old habits." Roddy sat on the front door stoop, too old for his years.

"Is that Dad's lighter?"

Roddy handed it over.

A hinge had been crudely mended, and the plating was so used up that it was neither chrome nor brass. It was heavy, and warm. A whiff of lighter fluid brought back the sound of flicking open, snapping shut. Late at night, early in the morning, revealing the black spiderwebs around Dad's eyes.

"I doubt you recollect much of Dad," Roddy said.

Did he think an eight-year-old had no memory? Sid tested the sparker, and it birthed flame despite his fumbling. "Why are you smoking again?" His memories were his own, not something everyone could dip into like they were standing around a water jug.

"He had a manner of talking that made people partial to him," Roddy said. He motioned for the lighter, and Sid dropped it into his outstretched palm.

"You mislay your religion?"

Roddy drew on his cigarette, then spit between his feet and worked his slaver into the gravel with his shoe. "When you get away for a while, church loses its grip."

"I wouldn't have no way of knowing."

"You don't go to church. That much I'm certain of."

"I spend my whole time at that church." Sid toed the reddog gravel, spritzed some against the house's aluminum siding.

"You don't attend services. Church isn't a place. It's about people."

"How's that work? They divvy God up and take Him home? So the only time He's there is when they come and put Him together?" The notion tickled Sid. "What if you get the bunghole? Can you swap it off next time, or are you stuck with it? Or if you go to a big church, maybe your allotment would just be a corn off'n His toe. There'd be a blessing."

Sid had finally pierced the skin; Roddy nibbled at his lip. "Shut that talk."

"Would some churches get better cuts? Backstrap for the Baptists, lips and earlobes for the Piscopalians."

"That's enough."

"You never could chew a conversation with meat in it."

"That's not meat. It's blasphemy." Roddy had his lip half gnawed off by then.

"Mom talked about anything, and Dad didn't shy from it. He wasn't skeered of nothing."

Roddy lips had paled like he'd sprung a leak down low. He started to talk, then shook his head and stared at his feet for a spell before he tried again. "Mack passed away before you got to know him."

"Don't call him Mack, like he was a cousin or something. Call him Dad." Sid paused to get his own voice reined in. "I probably knew him better than you did."

Roddy stood and walked a few paces into the yard. Yellow clay, churned up during the open house, squished under his loafers. "Boys always imagine their father is special. Before they find out the whole man." His shoulders hitched like he was chilly.

"I'm no hero worshipper. I know he was drinking when he died, and the day before and the one before that." The more Sid tried to sound reasonable, the more his words came like potatoes poured from a sack. "He didn't hide his smokes in the glove box like you do."

"You think he was brave and exciting, but he was just foolish. 'Get a drink into Mack, he'll climb your barn roof.' That's what others thought."

"I don't reckon it's ever *smart* to be brave. Hell no. Someone might get injured. We couldn't allow that."

"He was reckless with his life, too. He didn't have to go underground. He liked the mines because of the strikes and shutdowns. Gave him opportunity to drink and be irresponsible."

"I can see why that would stick in your gizzard. That he could enjoy life, and work too."

Roddy prodded one of the sawhorses that had carried food the day before with his mud-smeared burgundy shoe.

Everything felt like an accusation. "I'll put them sawhorses away when I get a chance," Sid said.

"Mack's amusement made it hard on the family. Someone's got to foot the bill for good times, and it usually isn't the one that had it."

Sid took out his smokes, but put them back his pocket without taking one. "Life here ought to be a free ride, then. Godamighty, Roddy, you act like Dad run over himself."

"If it hadn't been that day . . ." Roddy shrugged. "You been hanging with old men who got nothing left but to bitch and moan, and it's clabbered your out-look. Turned you sour. Now's the time to have your fun, not after you have a family. And don't let on there's none around."

"We're nine miles from town, if you can call it one. And could I get there, there wouldn't be nobody else there except more old men."

"What do other kids do?"

"The poor ones is milking goats, and the rich ones are packing to leave. If there is any rich ones." The dam had burst on Sid's frustration. "I can't do nothing without a car, but do I have a job so I can get one? No, because I don't have a car so I can get to a job."

"That's why I paid you to work at the church this summer."

"Two dollars a hour. That's just a bribe to keep me from getting a job, which you don't want me to have cause then you'd have to wash the skid marks out of your own undershorts."

Sid couldn't keep under the skin of the Roddy that had showed up. "You're right," he said, and sat again beside Sid. "I've done you wrong."

The confession let some of the gas out of Sid. "I just can't hardly tolerate it here. You've give me a passable home, but there's nobody in it but me."

"Maybe I shouldn't have moved here." Roddy was arguing, not doubting himself. "But I won't work underground, and construction jobs are worse. Look how many died when that scaffold fell over at Willow Island last year." He leaned to bump shoulders with Sid. "You got to have a decent job, and one that's safe. Without money, life's one wretched bitch."

"Then let's move where there are some jobs. You drive all that way every day, and I'm left here in the middle of gobbler's knob. We been here all summer, and I don't have friend one except for them old farts at the church." And Janet, but he didn't say that.

"Down at the mill is no place to live. Too much crime, and you can't even drink the water. I won't settle down there."

"Then let me quit school, go off on my own."

"No. You need a good education to get a job that pays."

"You hear these hillbillies talk? The schoolteachers won't be no different. You'd be lucky to get any education a-tall, much less a good one."

"I know it's troublesome to start a new school. But you'll make friends, and you'll have something to occupy your time."

"How would you know? You never done it."

"Adjustment, that's what I'm talking about. I know *all* about that. When I come back from Nam, Mom was dead, and I had you to take care of. You think that's not change?"

Sid had to move; talking wasn't working out his dander fast enough. He stacked one sawhorse on the other, then put it back and sat on it. "That's just coming home to something different. Like going to a house that's burned down, nothing left but the ashes. You plumb missed the change. You got to be there at the fire to grasp it."

Roddy looked at his watch, scratched under his arm and yawned. "I've got to get some shut-eye."

"You working tonight? Again?"

"Somebody's got to. That mill spits out paper whether it's a holiday or not."

"Not unless some other butthole crams trees into the far end, it don't. Tell them not to put none in. Daggone it, I was hoping we could run over to Morgantown. Get me some jeans, and a shirt or two. A better pair of shoes."

Both looked sharply toward a sudden clamor that became the individual voices of geese as it drew nearer. The fog-hidden flock skimmed so close overhead they could hear the whistle of wings. "It's clearing up above us, at least." Roddy said when they'd faded from hearing. "Geese won't fly blind."

"It's too bad we're not up there," Sid said. "We got to fly along where we're at, whether we can see where we're going or not."

Roddy's chuckle was as infectious as pimples. "You got a way with words, Sid. I'll give you that."

"Speaking of giving." Sid used the ceremony of lighting a cigarette to assemble the right words. "You hinted one time that there might be some money for me from when you sold the home place." He blew smoke from the corner of his mouth so Roddy would be able to see his face. "I'd like to have some of it."

"What little there is, I've set back for when you need it."

"Right now's the time. Just like today. I need clothes, but you can't take me."

Roddy stood and considered his watch again. "I'll buy you some new clothes before school starts. Don't fret about it."

"I got cash for clothes," Sid said. "I sure haven't been no place to squander any." He knew he'd already lost the case. The frustration hove up in his voice. "I need a car so I'm not beholden to you to haul me places. So I can get a job."

"A car would keep you flat broke, and hinder your schoolwork. I know, because I tried it at your age."

40

"Then I ought to get to try it too, show you how it's done. I want some of that money."

Roddy retreated up the stoop and attempted to go inside, but they hardly ever used the front door and it was locked. Like there was someone around to break in, or that they had something anyone would covet. Sid moved closer, where Roddy would have to crowd past him to come down the steps. "It's only right."

Roddy chewed on his lip, then jumped sideways off the stoop, landing stiff-legged like a brittle old man. "I won't let you fritter your money away on a car. It's not much anyway, and I have some extra expenses coming up."

Sid's cigarette ash was long and rigid and wouldn't flick off, and when he scraped it against a thumbnail, the fire fell away and left him with a dead smoke. He hurled it against the siding. "You spent my money. I reckon that's my Dodge truck there, then."

"The money will be there when the time comes." Roddy niggled at the seat of his pants like he'd soiled himself. "But I have some extra expenses right now, like I said."

"For what? I'm at least due to know where my money went to."

"I don't know how to explain."

Sid looked sharp at Roddy. "Just blabber it out."

"All right." But he didn't. He tongued his lips and adjusted his hair and fooled with his pants some more and looked everywhere but at Sid. "I've been seeing a girl. Not from work. But down there. I been taking her out to supper and stuff. I haven't been working as much as you charge me with."

The idea rattled in a hollow place Sid hadn't noted before.

"I thought you ought to know." Like Roddy had volunteered the information.

"I guess you mean a wedding, then." Sid tried to picture the girl that would be attracted to Roddy. "Is she pretty?"

"She's beautiful. Big deep eyes like Mom's. Short hair. Just a little bit of a thing." Roddy gnawed his lip like he was trying loose it from a steel trap. "You have a home here, irregardless of how it works out with me and Judi."

Somehow having a name firmed Sid's picture of the woman more than Roddy's description had. A quiet pretty woman to wash dishes and vacuum the carpet wasn't something Sid was prone to disallow out of hand. "You're a growed-up man; do whatever you've a mind to. It's your sneaking around, making everything a big secret, that grinds on me."

"I guess I was juberous about how you'd take to her. To her being Jewish."

The word exploded from Sid like it was a dead mouse he'd identified too late in his chili: "Jewish? Can't you find nobody your own race to marry?"

Roddy grinned like Sid was joshing. "That's no more a race than our being Scotch Irish is. Your lineage."

Lineage. Already talking Jew lingo. Sid wheeled and kicked over the saw-horse. "I'm a American, by hell, not a Scotchman or a Irishman. But a Jew . . ." Sid couldn't frame the words, so he kicked over the other sawhorse.

"There, that makes you look grown up." That Roddy could laugh just then was beyond Sid's grasp. "You've never even known a Jew."

Sid tried to restore reason into his tone: "I don't have anything pacific against Republicans or redheads, neither, but I'm not about to allow one into the house."

"Well, this isn't your best day, because she's a redhead for sure, and I got a strong suspicion she leans Republican too."

"Aw, Roddy." Words for his feelings had flown away to the moon. "You was raised better."

"You cool down a little, you'll see you're thinking crazy." If Roddy's tick-ledness was put on, Sid could have withstood it better.

Roddy hollered before Sid could get very far out the driveway: "Where you going?"

Sid stopped and looked back, wondering the same thing. "If I knowed that, then maybe I'd know at least one thing. But I don't."

§

Sid headed toward the church because that's the only place there was to go; every-where else was just woods. Sunday-morning services were underway, and the church parking lot was cluttered with the same family sedans that had mashed ruts into Roddy's yard the day before.

The sun had burned through the fog, and gave the mist collected on his arms the look of a bindweed's dew-frosted skin. Sid shivered and leaned against the back wall of the church, elbows on the unfinished stone veneer, an ear pressed against the coarse sheathing above. Close-by in the nursery a baby fretted, and from further away came the chicken-babble of kids. Dunn's words were clear but incomprehensible, familiar strings of sound that didn't need be picked apart and made to mean something.

He spat into the space between the stone veneer and the sheathing—a void half-filled with chunks of grimy concrete, a wadded Red Man tobacco pouch, and cigarette butts. Filth, skinned over with respectability. Little Jew babies traipsed through his mind in hordes, as faceless and unknowable as any creature from Venus.

Roddy vowed Sid could stay on, but when the babies started puking around the house, there'd be no place for Sid. Just like before, when Roddy had that Sharon woman. It hadn't took an Einstein to see they'd ruther he was elsewhere.

Republican redheaded Jew babies.

Somewhere along the line, life owed Sid something. Not as much as some, maybe, but something.

The sun raked along the wall and warmed Sid's right side at the expense of the left—a disagreeable sensation that mocked the way he felt inside. He leaned with eyes closed through the congregational song that followed the sermon. Through a lingering closing prayer. Through shouted goodbyes and slamming car doors and rattling engines. He picked Janet's voice from the rest, clung to it for a while.

He wondered if God was listening too. A blind man with hobnailed boots and a blunt stick, Sid had Him figured for, treading and whacking here and there as though trying to exterminate a rat.

"You going to stand and play with yourself all day?"

Sid jumped so violently at Bud's unmistakable voice that he lammed both elbows into the rock. "Ow," he said, and peered around the corner. "Startle a man to death."

Bud sat in his rusted Jeep, packing his lip with Copenhagen. Fernlike wands of brown stained the vehicle's faded canvas top.

"How'd you know I was here?"

"You're scrawny as a rubber stretched over a rail fence, but you still throw a shadow. Specially that nose."

Sid rubbed the appendage in question.

"Maybe you'll grow into it someday. I'm going sangin' this afternoon. Come along, if you've a mind to."

"I never could see it. And ginseng don't do you any good. That's just old wives' tales."

"I don't eat it, dumbhead. I sell it. One forty a pound right now."

"That's all?" Sid recollected the piepans of gnarled grubby roots his father had dried atop the refrigerator. A breadbag full to make a pound. "I remember when it fetched eight dollars. Down in Logan County," he added, lest Bud think him stretching the truth.

Bud ground the Jeep into life, then raked the gears into reverse. "I always considered a hunderd forty more than eight, but I ain't allus right." He started to back away, then stopped again. "You could find a wheelbarry load of sang today, I figger. The berries is brighter'n a baboon's ass right now, and it's still standing up straight. Not yellowed and laid over yet."

"A hundred and forty dollars?" Sid attempted to see that number, but a car kept getting in the way. Sid's car. "Maybe I will go along."

"You want to stop and tell your brother?"

"He don't care." He looked at the sun, straight overhead. "Let's go, before it gets dark."

5

"WE'LL GO TO PRESTON COUNTY TO HUNT SANG," Bud said. "The ginsengers up there are all dead or got crippled up."

Sid doubted the Jeep would hold together that long; it wheezed like a one-legged fat woman in an ass-kicking contest. Though August was hardly gone, the maples were speckled scarlet. Enough leaves had fallen to blur the joint between blacktop and berm, but Bud drove in the center of the road and eyed the woods, obliterous to the possibility that someone else might be using the road. Sid's bunghole constricted at every turn, and there were lots of turns. "Why don't we just hunt sang here?"

"I'm saving the close stuff for when I get too old and feeble to go far."

"They're probly coming from Preston County to dig our sang. Saving theirs."

"Nah, they come for women."

Sid snorted. "Surely to fire they got more women than we do."

"Yeah, but they're saving them for when they get old."

The day was passing, and they weren't even in the woods yet. "We could be digging sang right now."

"Amos Tucker was fixing to drive to North Carolina for a set of teeth oncet. I said, Amos, time you drive down, rent a room and buy grub, you won't save a nickel. Be cheaper to get teeth here. And Amos said, 'But then I wouldn't get to go to North Carolina.'"

North Carolina: flat ground and pines, though Sid couldn't say where that picture originated; he'd never been south or east of West Virginia, and only quick stabs north and west into Maryland and Ohio. He'd grown up almost on the Kentucky border, but had never crossed the line. "I wouldn't go to North Carolina for ten sets of teeth."

"Then I reckon you'd just have to stay in Union County and be dumb and toothless."

Sid felt his straight teeth with his tongue. "How long's this trip going to take, anyhow?"

"You punks tether your mind to the ass end of things. You're fretting cause you ain't making money when you should be taking pleasure in the experience."

"What experience? Riding in this old wreck?"

"Of being with me." They were descending Allegany Front toward the Cheat River, the road so curly Sid expected to see their own brake lights ahead. Bud hung over the wheel, tilting back and forth with the road gradient.

"I'd ruther have money than sang," Sid said.

"You got it backwards."

"Money you can spend. Buy a box of Slim Jims and new Redwing work boots and a .22 Colt Huntsman pistol and a Chevrolet Chevelle two-door sedan." Sid's ideals. "All you can do with sang is set it on the refrigerator to dry and accumalate dust."

Bud's grunting laugh could have been mistaken for a fart. "You got plans for your money, anyhow. But you're missing what sang's good for."

"You said you don't eat it."

"I reckon it'll make your sticker peck up, like the Chinamen says. I don't care whether mine does or not, and you most likely need something to lay yours down." Bud slowed, peered toward the river and up the hollows. "The good of sang is in the hunting." He pulled to the side and hauled the emergency brake and elevated a cheek and scratched his rear. "You bring dinner?" From the nest of papers and tools and snuff cans behind the seat he extracted a dented aluminum can.

"I wasn't expecting to go nowhere."

"I never knowed anyone ignorant enough to go sanging without dinner." Oily juice dripped into his lap when he ruptured the seal.

Sid's stomach was as empty as an Irishman's cupboard. "Eat it down, and let's get out there."

Bud pulled out a short wiener the hue of cold oatmeal. Congealed fat glistened on the ends. Its rich smell found Sid, and his belly groaned. "There's more Viennies back there somewhere. Get you a can."

Bullheadedness and aggravation heaved up at the expense of Sid's appetite.

"Let's go."

"If I knowed you was on the rag, I wouldn't have ast you along."

Until the words popped out, Sid had forgotten what was really chafing him. "I'm pissed at Roddy. He's got mixed up with a Jew woman." Bud would understand.

Bud scrutinized the second wiener as though it was a mutation of the first. "You probly ain't the only one pissed."

"I knew you wouldn't care for it," Sid said.

"It don't unsettle me, but that woman's family is likely got their dander up. They're as pissed as you, with their daughter messing with a hillbilly."

"It's nothing to poke fun at."

"I wish there was more Jewish women to compete with them Selders girls. There's nothing else to pick from around here. Would you be happy if Roddy took a Selders woman?"

"Don't joke about it."

"I ain't. We got Selders girls like bedbugs, and nothing else. Jews would be good. And Irish. Indian women. Colored mammys."

Sid's skin felt too small. Like flies had blowed him, pumped him full of maggots. "That's sick."

"Look at the kids' ears around here. Ever one has them shriveled up Selders' ears. If they kiss a stranger, they're still kissing their cousin. They probly all got the same fingerprints."

"That's trash talk, and I won't set here and listen to it."

"Don't ever think you're special, hillbilly, cause you ain't. Me either." Bud finally popped the sausage in his mouth and dabbed his fingers on his shirt. "Go on, if you're in such a heat. I'm going to taste the day, not swaller it down like cod liver oil. Go," he said when Sid made no move to leave. "You won't hurt my feelings."

Sid resurrected what his dad had taught him about ginseng: five leaves to a prong, spread finger-like, three big ones flanked by two smaller. Three prongs on most, with four on a big one. Once in a great while, five. A cluster of berries that sprang from the juncture of prongs and stalk. "All right," he said, and reached for the door handle.

"Slip a water bottle in your pocket." Bud offered a flat brown-glass syrup bottle.

"It's empty." Sid shook it and handed it back.

"It won't be once you cross the crick."

"We can't drink out of the crick. We'll get beaver fever."

"That'll clean you out like a dose of salts. Do you good."

Sid wished he'd stayed home. "I'll not drink out of a crick. That's all there is to it."

"Well, carry it for me, then. You'd do that for an old man."

"Right," Sid said as he slid down onto the ground, but he jammed the bottle into his hip pocket. Bud had parked so close to the brink of the fill that when Sid's feet found ground, his head reached only to the top of the seat. "You old farts are about to drive me nuts."

Sid slithered down the fill bank, directly through a patch of nettles. He heard Bud laugh at his curses. Welts sprouted on his arms and on the side of his neck till he found some touch-me-not to crush and rub where the stingers had brushed. At least he knew to do that. At least he knew something.

He set off down the hill, pausing every few steps to scan for ginseng. He'd not gone far till the Jeep's door slammed and Bud scrambled down the bank, arms and legs flapping, keeping his feet in front of him and arms above the nettles.

"Here's one already," Sid said, and knelt beside his find.

"No it ain't." Bud didn't even look. "A hickory, most likely. Has a woody stalk, and no berries."

Sid examined the plant. "How'd you know?"

But Bud had moved on in long easy strides that forced Sid into a lope to catch up. "First you set in the truck all day, then run through the woods without even looking for sang."

"We'll slow down when we get in a good place."

Sid couldn't see anything wrong with where they were: a north hillside, shaded and steep. No white oak or greenbriar to indicate sour soil. Sparse vegetation, the kind of uncluttered conditions sang craved. "You've been here before."

"Nope. But a blind man could judge sang won't grow here."

"How?"

"By how the ground feels. We ain't slipping and sliding, cause there ain't any little rocks. You could plant flowers in this. Good for hickories and striped maples, but not sang."

Sid remembered scrabbling a root from a hodgepodge of rocks. "Then how come you stopped here?"

"My gut told me to. That and the topo map I got at home. Up ahead the mountain twists east, then falls off hard southeast. We'll find sang there."

Sid was not going to ask what a topo map was. "I thought it did best on a north slope."

"That's what everyone thinks, and why there ain't much there. It's all been dug." The old man snapped off a dead standing sapling, tested it for cane duty. "There's two places to look: where sang grows good, and where everybody else don't go."

Sid nodded. "Let's get out there where it is."

Bud aimed his stick at a gnarled tree further up the hill. "What kind of a tree is that, just apast that tumbledown?"

Tree names swirled through Sid's head like trash floating on a creek eddy. "Locust?" he guessed.

"Looks like one, but it ain't. The leaves are different, and there's yeller in the chinks of the bark. That's a butternut. Look under a butternut good. Them and sang likes each other."

Sid spat into the forest litter, stirred it with his foot.

"Well. Git up there and look."

"You said sang won't grow here."

Bud shook his head and started walking again. "You still got it in your head that sanging's about digging roots. Making money."

"Hold on, I'll go up. I just didn't think it was a likely place, after what you said." He spoke to Bud's receding back.

"Things that are likely ain't much worth; everybody figures them out. It's stuff like knowing to look under a butternut that sets you apart. Gives you one of life's front tits."

"How can a sang and a butternut like each other?" Sid said when he caught up again. "They don't have feelings."

"Don't know, but they do. If it was a morel mushroom and an apple tree, them science people would call it a mycorrhizal relationship. The fungus on the tree's roots makes it better able to take up nutrients. Then the tree drops apples for just the right kind of mushroom fertilizer. If you go mollymooching, find an old apple orchard. You'll find morels." Bud inquired in his ear with a finger, then looked to see what he'd got. "I don't know how it works with sang and butternuts, but it does."

"How'd you learn that?"

"By noticing what's around me instead of pondering the money I'll make, or how fast I can get done."

"I mean that mikeyrizzle thing."

"From books." Bud stopped to fill his lip from a black-and-red snuff can. The raw smell of tobacco flung a craving on Sid, and he lit a cigarette while he caught his breath. "You read, don't you?" Bud said.

"I hate books."

"Get used to being dumb, then."

"If books are smart, why don't they talk about sang and butternuts?"

Bud scratched his back against a leg-sized poplar that had sprung up where a tumbledown allowed the sunlight in. "I guess I'm the only one that's took notice of that."

"You ought to let the people that writes books know."

"You must have had your brain out playing with it in the sand, and lost it. If I told all I know, there wouldn't be no sang left to dig."

"You just told me."

Bud grinned with dark-edged teeth. "You're too dumb to remember. Besides, I kind of like you."

The one small compliment cancelled the insults, made Sid feel important. "What else you know that I can forget and not tell?"

"Come on, let's look for sang. I'll teach you."

Sid scuffed his foot in the soil. "The ground's changed."

"Yep." They set off at a deliberate pace, angling down the mountain. Bud prodded a dark green clump of vegetation. "This is a companion plant that grows where sang does. You see one of these Christmas ferns, you're in the right soil. Proper light. Good drainage. Rattleweed's another one. Blue cohosh, some calls it."

"I know rattleweed. Gets blue berries. Down there's one."

Bud squinted through scarred glasses. "I don't see it."

Sid bounded down the mountain and lifted a long frond of leaves.

"I can't hardly even recognize you that far."

Sid plucked the plant and delivered it to Bud.

"You seen that way down there?" Bud said. "If I had eyes like that, there wouldn't be no sang left." He plucked a leaf from a low-lying plant, tasted it. "God done that so sang wouldn't go extinct—give me the brains, you the eyes."

"Maybe I ought to poke one out, just to make it fair. I wouldn't want to show an old man up."

"You'd be better liked. Folks'll think you're a asshole, when they're really just envious of your good eyesight. Poke one out, grind dirt into the other one, they'll plumb love you. It don't pay to stand out."

Had anyone else ragged on Sid that way, Sid's dander would be up, but Bud made him laugh. "Then what you trying to make me smart for, if dumb makes you better off?"

"You're the worst breed there is: flatlander and hillbilly both. If you get smart, folks here will charge you with putting on airs. But out in the world, they'll assume you're dumb because you talk different, and because you don't know how to work all the doodads they have to have to tolerate such a place." Bud punched Sid lightly on the shoulder. "The trick is to get smart enough to fool people into thinking you're dumb. Then you can be sharp and liked both. But I doubt you can pull that off."

"I got em fooled already."

They both laughed, then Bud gripped Sid by the bicep, hard. "You do your best. Don't worry whether you're liked. And whatever foolishness I come up with, don't drag your ass in it like a dog with a itchy butt, don't care whether he's picking up grit or scraping out worms."

"I don't pay attention to nothing you say," Sid said. Grinned.

"That's good. You just keep that up."

Bud started along the mountainside again, pointing and teaching until Sid's head was slopping over with more companion plants: white baneberry; the wild sarsaparilla Sid had always known as fools' sang. With places where sang would thrive: the downhill side of log road grades, where the soil was loose and shaded by a tangle of cleared brush; under trees brought down by grapevines— shelter for the birds that planted the berries with a squirt of fertilizer; near old homesteads, where some old-timer had planted a savings account for hard times. With places often overlooked: emerging clearcuts, just becoming pass- able; in nettle patches; in snaky-looking places ("a snake bites me, he better have a high tolerance for tobaccy juice"); on "islands" formed by runoff in the steep hollows.

And when the mountain curled toward the southeast, they found sang. Bud, with his bad eyes, spotted most of it. "You going to dig that one, or do you prefer to tramp it down?"

If there was a sang near Sid's feet, he couldn't see it. He fingered the leaves of a sun-starved blackberry plant.

"Watch the jaggers on that one."

"I know it's a bramble, but it's the only thing even close to a sang." Then he noticed a short plant with a trio of tiny leaves. "This?" Sid felt the serrated edges, no bigger than his thumbnail.

"That's a sang, all right."

Sid wormed his finger toward the root. "It's awful little."

"Anyone that would root out that little infant thing would poop on his grandma's grave." Bud spat close to Sid's hand. "Dig that big one between your legs."

"Aw," Sid said, sure that he was being made light of.

"Right here." Bud nudged with his stick the remnants of a deer-browsed plant.

Sid examined the stalk, the inch-long forks that remained. His mind provided the missing pieces to recreate a ginseng. "How did you ever see that?"

"Didn't. I seen that little one. After a while I made out its mammy."

"It's yours. You dig it."

"No, my back hurts. You root her out."

Sid's fingers traced the lumpy stem into the coarse soil, felt the long string of knots that signified years of growth. Many knots, many years. Fifteen or more. He reached the bulge of main root, and a smaller fork that wandered away through the rocks.

"You hunt squirrel?" Bud said while Sid labored at his excavation.

"I'm not good at it."

"Can't you hit them, or can't you see them?"

"I don't get enough shots to tell if I can hit them or not. They see me before I see them." Sid admired the root he'd dug, fat and as long as his middle finger.

"There ain't no way around them seeing you first." Bud brought forth two more dented cans of Vienna sausages from somewhere in his loose clothing. He tossed one to Sid and sat on a flat rock. Sid slavered on his shirtfront while he keyed the top from the can.

"You're looking for a squirrel," Bud said after he'd chewed his first one. "That's why you don't see none."

"What should I look for, then? Billy goats? Striped-assed apes?"

"You look for squirrel parts: a ear, or the end of a tail, or the corner of a eye where it sidles around a tree to see a little piece of you."

Sid nodded and chewed, soaking up words and grease.

"Sang's the same way. The whole ones have been found. Learn what a single leaf looks like, or the place where the prongs fork. I spotted one back there from a single red berry that had fell off."

They mashed their empty cans and wedged them under rocks. "Now you skin down to the crick and fill up our water bottles while I dig a sang or two I seen while we was gabbing."

The trip down and back took longer than Sid had anticipated. Four times he had to stop and dig sang, then plant the berries in hard-to-find places. Just like Bud had taught him.

§

"You getting that rock in the church lot broke?" Bud asked as they chugged toward home. The low-hanging sun cast his face as ancient as the mountains.

Sid fingered his pocketful of dirty roots, but felt the glow they'd given leaking away. "You seen it." All he'd accomplished in three months of beating was to make it round. The unwanted suggestions—*drill holes in it, and drive dry wood plugs in the hole. When they take up water, they'll bust her*—hadn't been worth a thimbleful of toadshit. Then people were saying *winter's coming. Pour water in the holes, leave it freeze. That'll split her.* Right. Just like *build a fire agin' it, then quinch it with spring water* had.

Nearly every evening he'd hammered away, pimpled it with plugged and watered holes, blackened it with fire. The corners fell away quick and easy. But once he'd made it round, he'd just as well try and spawl a piece off an anvil.

Bite off more than you can chew? Don't send a boy to do a man's job, they allus told me.

Bud's words about the job—you'll be a full-growed man when you finish—chafed at him, and he suddenly came to a decision. "I've give in beating it," he said. "I got better things to do." The evening air raised goosebumps on his sweaty arms, and bloody threads where briars had dug stood proud of his hide as if he'd eroded away around them. He drew his cigarette down to the filter and tossed it out the window.

Bud spit snuff juice out the opposite window, keeping them balanced. "You can't quit now." He wiped his mouth on the back of a hand dark and rough as his tobacco.

"I'd just as well beat on the road, try and bust the yearth in half."

"It'll bust one day," Bud said. "I never knowed anyone but you would worry at it this long." His laugh was dark and phlegmy. "Not near this long."

"Too long."

"You quit now, you'll evermore be seen as a quitter. It won't matter that you did more than anybody else would have."

"Like you said today, it don't matter what folks think."

"No, they don't matter." Bud rubbed at gray chinwhiskers, looked at the palm of his hand as though it had surprised him to find them there. "It's what you think of yourself."

"I've hammered it everywhere there is to. That's what I think."

"You got to keep on. You might not care right now, but you will. You got to bust it, however many lams it takes." His face twisted in concentration as he searched for a lower gear.

Neither spoke again until they chugged past the church. Cars parked for the evening service appeared nosed toward the rock, waiting for something to happen.

"Don't look at the far end of things. Don't look for a whole squirrel, or a full-growed sang. Don't look at how long it takes to break a rock, but what you'll learn a-doing it."

"All rocks learn you is that they can't be broke."

Bud downshifted into Roddy's driveway. "There ain't much to know about a rock. It's what the rock learns about you."

§

Sid listened to Bud's fading clatter, to the steady thump of Stride's tail against the dirt and his barrel: thump bong, a retard in an arm cast trying to hambone. Flies swarmed around the dog. "I'd ruther crawl into your house than that one." Stride danced on the end of his chain, hungry for attention.

"Daggone you, Roddy," Sid said. The water can was empty and dirt-frosted.

"You can't even keep your dog fed and watered." Sid filled the can from the outside faucet, then fetched food from inside while the big hound drank. Sid's fingers smelled gamy from scratching behind the tick-freckled ears, but he sat in the dirt and hugged the dog, hefted the chain and wide leather collar. "This here's one lonesome place." The dog licked Sid's mouth, his breath sour and wet as red oak sawdust.

"What if I turned you loose?" Sid fingered the snap and pictured Roddy's face when he discovered his three-hundred-dollar dog was gone. Without Sid's conscious effort, the snap dropped free of the collar.

Stride stepped forward and shook his head, then loped over and watered the corner of the house. Sid felt sick, but good sick. "My feelings exactly." The dog nosed the air, then returned to stand in front of Sid. "Git on out of here, if you want."

But the dog snooted under Sid's arm and leaned hard against him. After a while Sid said, "Dogs is so dumb," and rehooked the snap. The dog went in his barrel, Sid in his.

§

Sid showered and dressed and was restless in the gloomy, sullen house. Roddy's room was as destitute as Sid's, but the picture on the dresser attracted Sid. He touched his mom's face, then wiped the glass with a hanky from Roddy's top dresser drawer.

The .22 pistol was there, too, where Roddy imagined it was hid good. Like Sid could put away undershorts and not find it. The clip was full, the chamber empty, like Sid left it when he was through aiming at people on the TV. Sid stepped back two paces and aimed at Roddy, careful not to let the sights wiggle over onto Mom. "Pow, you Jew-kissing asshole." The weapon made him dangerous, and feeling dangerous made him reckless. He was not a shell around a void, but a hollow inside a husk. It was the place, the people. Nothing to do. Nowhere to go. People that didn't know him, and didn't care to.

Outside on the porch, Sid worked the slide to arm the pistol. Stride bawled and rared against the chain. Only once had Roddy hunted him, but the dog had acquired a taste for it.

"You had your chance, buttlicker, but you'd rather have your ears fooled with than run loose." Sid thumbed off the safety and fired in the general direction of a white oak, surprised at the pistol's buck. He squeezed the trigger twice more as fast as he could. Empty brass casings tinkled in the gravel, and the dog went completely wild. He hit the end of his chain and went over backwards and spilled his water can.

"This here"—Sid aimed at the dog—"is a Colt Huntsman .22 caliber semi-automatic pistol." The dog was carrying on so that Sid could hardly stand not to drill him, so Sid sloped off into the dark, aiming here and there at his adversaries: hillbillies; schoolteachers; deacons.

Church had wound up good, and poured out of the open high-placed windows. Sid stood on his rock where he could see inside. In the darkness, the pistol's front sight was invisible until it slid across the freckled dome of Chester's head, then back again. Sid rested his finger lightly against the trigger. "Pow," he whispered.

Janet's dad got one in the head, the out-of-tune guitar player another through his ink-stained shirt pocket, then again through a Coke-bottle eyeglass lens. Dunn was coaxing them to the altar, his voice nagging like the mosquitoes that whined in the dark. "God's speaking to souls."

"Then He don't need you to," Sid muttered, and rested the front sight on the preacher's nose. Dunn's eyes found Sid's and widened as though he could see him there, and his hand came up to shield his face. Sid eased further back, though he couldn't possibly be seen.

Dunn lowered his hand, his eyes riveted on Sid's. "There's a hindering spirit in our midst, folks. I discern him plain as day outside that window. But he can't come in God's house. Not unless we allow him."

Without warning, Sid's hand trembled so that he had to grasp it against his chest to maintain possession. "Aw, no," he said when he tried to release the thumb safety to unload the chamber, found it already clicked off. The enormity of his finger caressing the trigger while the sights wandered across faces and heads mashed him down, down, until he crouched on the rock, head between his knees.

§

In the night, each time he woke, Dunn's words echoed as though it had been that voice that woke him. *He can't come in, folks. Not unless we allow him.*

6

It took months for Sid to work up enough nerve to prove Dunn wrong. On a Wednesday night in November, Sid slipped into a Bible study and sat alone in back, as surly as if he'd elbowed his way into a shit-eating tournament and won.

He counted thirteen others.

Afterward, Sid escaped before Dunn could catch him in the hand shaking. He stood in the trees while old folks hobbled across the parking lot. "Don't tell me I can't come in," he said when the last was gone.

But on Saturday while Sid hammered the rock, Dunn watched from his car. Sid tried to stare him down, but the windshield's glare made it a one-sided contest. He smoked too many cigarettes in the hour Dunn watched, made his throat scratchy and his eyes tired.

Sunday was a wet-cold day that penetrated Sid's core and shriveled him up like two raisins in a prune. Every ten minutes he checked the thermostat, knowing Roddy stirred in his sleep each time the furnace kicked on. He knew he'd get the sermon about squandering fuel oil before Roddy lit out for the night shift.

He did TV with the sound off until his brain threatened to shut down, then went outside and fooled with the dog until he wearied and returned to his barrel. Sid put on his best jeans and an almost-white shirt and the too-big Carhartt coat Roddy had bought for Sid's birthday in May and walked to the church again.

He waited outside while they sang "Power in the Blood," then sneaked in during a prayer while everyone was standing. The kids were together near the front, and Sid slipped forward and stood beside Ralphie Roomer, one space over from Janet. When the prayer concluded, she leaned across and shook his hand and said, "Glad you could come." Ralph shied from her breasts like they were dan-o-mite.

Dunn sat on a bench behind the pulpit, reviewing his sermon notes while the song leader pumped up the congregation. When he noticed Sid, he smiled and folded the paper twice and tucked it inside his coat.

Come preaching time, Dunn leaned over the pulpit and stared at Sid for an hour or two, then commenced to crucify him. He read from Proverbs: *There is a way which seemeth right unto a man, but the end thereof are the ways of death.* The be-temperate-in-all-things part was drawn from another place. "Put behind you the obsessions of the world," Dunn said in the whisper that always followed a spell of hollering, "and fix your obsession on the Lord Jesus Christ." He was down at the pews by then, sharing deodorant and sweat.

Sid took it for twenty minutes, then hauled out for the door. Dunn had a verse ready for that as well, and stabbed it into his back. *The wicked flee when no man pursueth, but the righteous are bold as a lion.* Sid wanted to retaliate, but his tongue was tangled with his guts. His knees quivered and sweat trickled down his back where icicles had formed earlier. It was the same reaction he'd had in English class the week before, when the teacher called him forward to perform for the hillbillies; they'd snickered while Sid read.

Falling snow shrouded the scars on Sid's rock. He sat on the clammy surface, let his fire sink into it. Dunn's voice bored through the stone walls, indistinct but haranguing. Sid hung his coat over a limb and found his hammer, hidden behind the rock. As he swung, stubborn shame—*the wicked flee, the wicked flee*—became a rhythm of hard indignation—*unto a man, unto a man.* Nervous perspiration washed away in honest sweat.

Finally the doors opened and kids spilled out, then the grown men with nicotine fits. Two of them—Harland Roomer and Clarence Bowser—conferred under the porch light, then came and watched Sid. He nodded without breaking cadence. Twin stumpy silhouettes, the men said nothing. A foil pack rustled, followed by the tang of sweet harsh tobacco.

"It's not an obsession." Sid puffed words in lumps, between swings. "It's just a rock. And I'm going to bust it."

"That's what we come to say." Which man had spoken was impossible to judge.

"Go ahead and bust it," the other said. "There's no call to make a sin out of everthing."

"I wouldn't be too up in arms if my kids give you a hand." Harland.

Sid leaned on the hammer handle. "I'd as leave do it myself."

"I appreciate that, too," Harland said. The men turned to their vehicles, Sid to his beating.

Reverend Dunn didn't emerge until only his car remained in the parking lot. He buttoned his coat and inclined his wristwatch to the light and headed Sid's way. He nearly fell twice. He looked like a wind-twisted scrag pine, lopsided with hair frousled above his head.

Sid watched him approach. "You need better shoes," he said. "Leather soles don't cut it here."

"It's what I've got. They done all right in Tennessee."

Not knowing what else to do with his hands or his mouth, Sid lit a smoke.

"If my sermon caused hurt, I can't help it. But I'm not your adversary."

Sid grunted.

"I love you, son. Love you like you was my own."

"You concealed that pretty durn good tonight. If I was preaching and new folks come in, I'd make them at home. Not ram the Bible through them and hold them over hell like a hot dog."

"You're not doing the preaching, son. And comfort's not my gift. Just the contrary."

"Don't call me 'son.' My name's Sid."

Dunn peered up into the falling snow, breathed deep. "I'm sorry. Sid."

The apology dandered Sid more than the sermon had. "From what I see, there's others took affront, too. The church appears right underpopulated to me."

Dunn calculated. "If blunt talk suits you, I can handle it." He jammed his Bible under an armpit, brushed at his hair. "Coming here's the last thing I wanted to do. A busted church in the sticks. Everyone related, ready to take up arms if one gets their toes tramped on. Skinny paydays, if there is any. This isn't my first time."

"Then you ought to have stayed where you was." Sid's cigarette fried a snowflake.

"God called me here. That's the only reason I come. When my assignment's lifted, I'll be gone so quick it'll take a week for the dust to settle."

That manner of talk gave Sid the hives. "God ring you up on the phone? Or did He holler down from heaven?"

If Dunn took offense, he kept it out of his voice. "Just like this. I dialed my brother's number, but someone else answered. Wrong number. So I dialed it again, and the same man answered."

Sid snorted and hawked and spat into the trees. "That there's a sign to leave out for new ground, all right. That's exactly the way I'd took it."

Dunn wiped his lips on the back of a wet sleeve as if he'd spat instead of Sid. "It was past midnight, and I had the need to talk, so I called the nursing home. Like I do when sleeplessness lays heavy on me, to talk to the night nurse and check on the folks I know there."

"Aw. She told you where to go. Calling after midnight, I'd a done the same."

"That same man answered. Chester Preston."

Sid slid back into his jacket, zipped it tight against his Adams apple. "That was a pleasant conversation, I reckon." Chester always bragged about how early he went to bed.

"He was waiting by the phone. Said, 'You're a preacher, ain't you.'"

Sid shivered inside his clammy coat.

"After we talked a while, I spent the rest of the night packing. I left home that morning, got here before dark."

"Just because you got a wrong number three times in a row. You ever figure maybe you pushed the same wrong buttons?"

"I considered that real careful. Trouble was, I dialed a local call. Seven numbers. This here was long distance, eleven. And none of those three calls showed up on my next bill."

Sid recalled Dunn staring at him when he couldn't possibly be seen: *He can't come in.* Sid's cigarette was only half smoked, but he was jaded with it. "There you go. A phone company mixup."

"Believe what you want. I'm not trying to convince you. But you asked."

Sid didn't think he had asked, but he wasn't sure. Of anything. "God assigned that sermon tonight too, I reckon." Knowing the answer.

"Not at all." He riffled the pages on his Bible. "I found that in here. That's my job."

Sid couldn't get ahead of him. Like in school, where by the time he figured out what was going on, they'd advanced to something else. "You don't reckon you was a little rough on me tonight? I mean, I'm breaking a rock. It's not like I'm taking dope or something."

Dunn nudged Sid's cigarette butt with his toe. "What do you call that?"

"The Bible don't even mention smoking. Smoking's just one more thing you preachers have whipped up into a sin, so you can rare on everybody. Like

TV, and dancing. Going to the movies." Sid stood and discovered himself closer than he wanted to be. "I'm not a bad person."

"I don't figure you are. But you're a wedge that will split these youth off from the church. This here's a fragile congregation. It's seen one split already, and they're still skirmishing over what's right. Harmony is what they need. Reinforcement. Not a challenge to what little authority there is here. Flee the very appearance of evil. That's what my Bible says."

"Now I'm evil?" *I just saw him plain as day, right outside that window.*

Dunn said nothing.

"Hell fire. I'm not even *welcome* in your church?"

"I didn't say that. But when you set a bad example for others, it'll be you that's made example of."

Sid eased sideways to where there was more breathing space and turned and stared off into the woods. "What about the ninety and nine you preachers talk about? You're supposed to leave the flock and go after the one that's went astray."

Dunn moved with him, feet scrabbling through to the gravel. Sid imagined he could feel breath on his neck. "This ship was sinking," Dunn said, "and there was one three-man life raft left, but three sailors and the captain still aboard. He called them together and said, 'What you heard about the captain going down with his ship is baloney. I do things the democratic way. I'll ask you a question, and if you answer right you can get in the boat. That's the fair way to do things.' And he asked the first one, 'Which ship hit the iceberg?' And the sailor said, 'The *Titanic*, sir.' 'Get in the raft,' the captain said. He asked the second sailor, 'How many perished in that tragic event?' The sailor said, 'One thousand five hundred and seventeen, sir.' 'Get in the raft.' He asked the third one, 'What were their names?'"

Sid's skin felt like it was crafted for someone smaller. Someone that the raft would accommodate. "That's not funny a-tall."

"No, it's sad. Every soul is precious. But just like the captain going down with the ship is baloney, so is a lot that you believe about preachers." Dunn's hand lit on Sid's shoulder just for a second, then withdrew. "This one, at least."

Sid's knuckles brushed the hammer's handle; he gripped it hard.

Dunn's tone dropped low, not his preaching voice. "Preachers that hound off in pursuit of just one sheep come back to find their flocks drunk and knocked up and backslid. I wasn't called to account for the world, just this one little bunch. When the wolf comes around, I'll appreciate him, cause he'll herd my sheep tight together. And then I'll bust my staff across the top of his head."

"That's the most hellish talk I ever heard from a preacher. And I've heard some bad."

"You and me are outsiders. However long we're here, we'll always be apart. You're not losing a thing if I put a little distance between you and them. Get used to it."

Sid glanced to make sure Dunn was clear, then swung the hammer with everything that had to get out. He left it where it bounced to a stop, and turned to Dunn. "I'm going to bust this rock, and you'd best get accustomed to that."

"I recognized that yesterday, when I watched and fathomed your heart. You'll break it with your head if you have to. Sometimes stubborn pride will drag you along when times are tough, but I'll not let it drag you through my church."

"You can't keep me out if I decide to come."

"Come on. But your head's gonna feel my staff. Is that fair enough?"

"All right." Sid shook hands before he could decide not to. Dunn slipped his way toward his car. Just before the door closed, Sid said, "What size shoe you wear?"

"I can squeeze into a nine, but tens feel so good, I wear eleven. Why?" His voice as strong and clear as when he was close by.

"I hate to see even a preacher bust his ass for want of a decent shoe. There's some boots I growed out of that would fit you. If you want them. Though it might knock some sense into your head if you fell on it."

"I'm not too proud to take them."

"I'll leave them there beside the door."

"No," Dunn said. "Put them behind your rock. Everyone doesn't need to know our business." The smoke from his old junker lingered like the Old Testament, bleak and heavy and full of promise and threat.

§

The following Saturday, a balmy Indian summer day, Sid raked leaves to the edge of the yard for a while, then walked down the hill to the church and was greeted by the ringing of steel against sandrock. He stopped to rein in his anger. Doogie Roomer swung Sid's hammer while his brother and sister— harelipped Hattie looking like a dog that chased parked cars, Ralph with a green bubble percolating in his nose—sprawled in the shade, their bicycles a scrapyard of rusting chrome and tattered streamers. Long-muscled Doogie swung out-of-kilter, and Sid noticed they all had those scrunched-up Selders' ears.

Mostly though, his attention was for Janet, leaned against the wall, head back, breasts tracking the sun through a thin yellow blouse. Dark smooth legs between sneakers and pleated skirt. A lady slipper among ragweeds.

"What's going on here?" Sid said. "I told your pap I didn't want no help."

Hattie and Ralph managed to hunker down without moving, like rabbits in the headlights, but Doogie took issue. "It ain't your rock." His voice was changing, and made him sound as threatening as a house finch with a sore throat. Janet opened her eyes and smirked.

"I'll not have my handle split out by somebody who don't know how to use one."

"Daddy never said anything about not helping you. He don't even know we're here," Hattie said.

"You ain't very nice," Ralph said.

"This is no job for kids. A spawl might put out your eye, or the hammer-head might fly loose."

"We just want to help," Doogie said. "I can go home and get my own hammer."

"No. Kids shouldn't be fooling with it."

"I guess you're a man now after all," Janet said.

"What are *you* doing here, anyhow?"

"Hattie asked me to help them work around the church. I didn't realize there'd be a man around could do it all himself."

"I'll show you how much man I am." Sid took three quick steps and kissed Janet on the mouth. She didn't return it, but she didn't back off.

"Ewww," Ralphie said.

Doogie leaned Sid's hammer against the rock. "Let's go home."

"I came to work," Hattie insisted. "To pull weeds out of the flowers."

Sid considered the scraggly flowerbed along the front of the church, and how pleasant it would be to spend the afternoon with Janet, away from tattletale eyes. "Yank the flowers out of the weeds, you'll get done quicker."

"It ain't important to get done," Hattie said. "It's the pleasure of doing it."

Godamighty. People there not only had ears alike, they shared the same brain. Ralph stuck his tongue out at Sid before he pedaled off, and Doogie didn't even look back. Hattie busied herself at ridding the flowers of weeds, Sid at liberating smooches from Janet between licks on the rock.

But she had cooled. "Don't." She pushed him away, glanced at Hattie.

"Let her tattle. I don't care."

"It ain't her telling that troubles me." Janet's whisper was a burlap sack being torn. "She shouldn't have to watch what she can't have. Don't you understand nothing?"

"I reckon not," he said after a time. But he spoke to the girls' backs as they walked toward Janet's place, Hattie pushing her bike and yammering like it might be her last opportunity.

§

Sunday night, Sid went to church because he'd be a coward if he didn't. Dunn nodded when Sid came in, a little half-smile playing at his mouth. The sermon commenced with a hushed reading of the scriptures: *For the flesh lusteth against the Spirit, and the Spirit against the flesh: and these are contrary one to the other: so that ye cannot do the things that ye would.*

Sid saw in the hazy reflection from his shoes the Roomer kids' expressions when he'd kissed Janet. Or had Janet told? *Don't you understand nothing?*

As Dunn warmed into his reading, he wandered down to stand in front of the youth.

Now the works of the flesh are manifest, which are these: Adultery,
  fornication, uncleanness, lasciviousness,
Idolatry, witchcraft, hatred, variance, emulations, wrath, strife,
  seditions, heresies,
Envyings, murders, drunkenness, revellings, and such like: of the
  which I tell you before, as I have also told you in time past, that
  they which do such things Shall. Not. Inherit. The. Kingdom.
  Of. God.

His words thundered down like apples onto a car's hood.

Witchcraft and murder too?

Dunn's face drooped with remorse, his shoulders slumped as he reclaimed the pulpit. "It grieves me that the Board has been forced to institute new policies for the youth group." Each deacon nodded as Dunn's eyes queried them again.

"No longer will unchaperoned events be permitted. Formal or otherwise." He leaned toward them as though they were half deaf or daydreaming. Or stupid. "An adult has to attend your activities. All activities."

A rustle of closing Bibles scurried through the church. Dunn glanced at Sid, as though prompting his part in a skit they'd rehearsed. *When the wolf comes around, I'll appreciate him, cause he'll herd my sheep tight together.* The immense melancholy of responsibility struck Sid a glancing blow, left him too mature to suffer denigration with the kids, too unformed to strike out alone.

Dunn waited. Other eyes inspected other shoes.

"This is about me, I suppose." The words jumped out before Sid thought them. He stood, and all eyes came up with him. "Don't lay what I done onto these kids." He addressed the preacher. "And don't pretend you have a youth group. Youth groups got stuff to do. Picnics, and ballgames. Maybe a bus trip somewhere oncet in a while."

"Set down, Sid," said Harland Roomer. "Church ain't the place to argue."

Sid thrust his hands in his pockets, but they still jittered with adrenaline. "Is it better to argue about church at the dinner table? Bitch behind the preacher's back?"

"Oh," said one old woman, her hand over her mouth like she'd said it.

"That's the trouble with church. You can't say the way things is."

"There *ain't* nothing to do," Ralph said.

"You come here, boy, and set with me," Harland said.

"Pastor Dunn, you need to close this service." Chester spoke over a clamor of voices.

Sid raised his own. "The service is over when folks go home. That's how you tell."

"Reverend," Toots Friend, one of the deacons, hollered. "Reverend Dunn. You got to bring this service to order."

Harland stood, motioned for his family to leave with him.

"Wait, Brother Roomer." Dunn raised his hand. They all waited. And waited. Harland sat back down. "You're not just folks who come together at church. You"—Dunn pointed here and there—"and you, and you, young lady. Ralph. Hattie." He continued until he'd named everyone but Sid. "You're the Bride of Christ. You're the church. Do you really believe that God's institution can't withstand this little assault?" He looked prepared to make roll call again, to single out a vote, so they shook their heads and nodded, each one meaning the same thing.

"Go ahead, Sid. Get shed of what's eating you up."

"Touch not mine anointed." Toots, timid like, but determined.

"I don't want to hear no more," Clarence said.

"Just one thing, and then I'm leaving." Sid found little friendship in the faces. "You got to make something for these kids to do. They're good kids. Some of you are good folks, too, but you'd best wake up. These kids got nothing but church, and here you herd them into a bunch and ignore them. One of these days, when they get a little older, you're going to take notice and realize maybe they ought not be so close together, and all of a sudden the herd you put them into is going look sinful itself. And anything else they take a notion to do. I seen it happen down in Logan County.

"Then they'll have to choose to be like you—to hunker in a church where they can't ask a question or put forward a idea—or to go have a life that has something besides church in it. You don't offer them no other choice."

Toots licked his lips like he was going to pile back in, so Sid singled him out. "Where's your middle-age people, Toots? You old gospel-hardened pew-setters are here, and these kids. Where's the ones that has a choice?"

Sid hitched his pants and started to go, then turned back. "Treat these kids like heathens, that's what you'll get. The first chance they get, they'll haul out of here.

"If there's wrong been done, I done it. Not them." Sid eased to the aisle and walked out of the church. When he closed the door behind him, he felt righteous as hell.

He checked behind his rock; if the boots he'd left for the preacher were still there, he was going to reclaim them. Instead, he found a New Testament in a sandwich bag. Sid chucked it into the woods.

Too full of vinegar to go home, Sid wandered back a log road to an abandoned field behind the church. Not long after he'd settled on a decaying split-rail fence, two deer frolicked into the grass. One caught his scent and approached stomping her front feet, not so fearful as vigilant. Sid whistled, and she wheeled and bounded to the other end of the field. After a minute or two of watching and tail-switching, both deer began feeding. Neither paid further attention to Sid. Like they'd learned all there was to know about him. Sid smoked and watched until he tired of both activities.

When he got home, he pulled up short at the driveway's edge. The kitchen light was on, and Roddy's pickup still sat in the driveway.

"Hey," he said when he opened the door.

"Get out here." Roddy sat at the kitchen table. Only ten years Sid's elder, his eyes were pooched and bleary. He'd never gotten accustomed to swing shift, hadn't learned to sleep in the daytime. The stink of papermill never left him. Lean muscles had softened and sagged, and an eyeglass case jutted from his pocket.

"Why aren't you at work? You sick?"

Roddy drank from his coffee. "I hear you're stirring up trouble."

Sid slipped into the chair across from Roddy. "I reckon someone called."

"Chester came here."

That Chester would make Roddy late for work riled Sid more than his tale telling. "That asshole."

"You were brought up to respect the church, if nothing else. At least that much."

"Who are you to say that? You that's throwed over your faith for a Jew."

Roddie's empty-eyed expression said that life was fixing to tear off in a new direction, like it had every six months since he got back from Nam. "What you said struck a chord with me, Sid."

"What I said was ignorant. I don't got a thing against Jew women. Not knowing anything about one just made me juberous. One might be good."

"I'm through with her, Sid. I've repented for it."

"You got dumped again, didn't you. What'd you do, try to get her saved?"

Roddy dropped his eyes and muttered, "The bitch," then lit back into preaching. "We've been brought up to love Jesus. It's time we got back to doing it."

"I knew when you smoked that cigarette I'd be at fault, sooner or later. And since you raised the subject, I haven't noticed a lot of bringing up." Sid waved his hand at the unrinsed dishes on the counter, at the lunch bucket he'd packed before going to church. "Who takes care of who, anyhow?"

Roddy pushed his eyeballs in with the heels of his hands. "We got to straighten up and fly right."

"I haven't soared off crooked yet."

"This deal at the church. Leave it be. We can't be agitating these folks up all the time."

"Churches stir theirselves up. They got to, or folks loose interest, stay home and watch rassling."

Roddy stood and shook out his shoulders and checked that his hanky was in his hip pocket and looked in his lunch bucket. "When you get a little older, you'll understand. But till then, listen to me. You leave off causing trouble."

"I'm busting up a daggone rock. Is that a sin?" Sid followed Roddy to the door, hounding for an acknowledgement of a credible position.

Sid stood with his hand on the doorknob after it had closed, then leaned back against the hallway wall. A family picture hung there. His dad looked too young, too strong to die. Forage cap cocked on his head. Rolled-up sleeves biting into biceps. Mom gaunt as a rail, so pale and translucent they should have noticed the cancer forming inside. "I know what the hell you'd a done, Dad." He opened the door, but Roddy's taillights were winking out of sight.

§

On Thanksgiving Day, Sid and Roddy squabbled again. "A boy your age should be hunting deer. A normal boy."

"Is it normal to dog a double shift on Thanksgiving?" Picking holes in the last thing Roddy said was simpler than reasoning with him.

"I've downed lots of bucks. Now it's your turn. I've never seen the likes of this place for deer. There's hardly a sapling that's not horned up."

"I got work to do. Like you."

"The only reason you keep after that rock is that everybody's against your doing it."

"Think what you want."

After Roddy left for work, Sid beat for four hours on the rock. Without warning, a foot from where his hammer struck, a slab the size of Chester's belly peeled away and spiraled to a stop like a quarter spun on a tabletop. When his pulse settled, Sid examined the exposed face for clues as to why it had sheared just there. It looked no different from any other part of the boulder. After he'd knapped up the split-off piece, he lit into the whole with new energy. By dark, all he'd accomplished was to make the rock round again.

He commenced at daylight the following morning, worked into the rhythm, stretched out the kinks from the day before. Around ten o'clock, just after he'd waved at the mail carrier, the rock sighed. Before Sid could strike it again, a crack inched across the top. As he watched bug-eyed, the boulder eased apart until the earth below showed through the fault.

By late afternoon, no chunk was too big for Sid to carry into the woods. As he walked home in a twilight filling fast with cold, tears ran down his face so unexpectedly that he smelled his fingers after he'd wiped them away. "You let yourself get too wore-out," he said aloud.

Perhaps fatigue made him cry, or relief that his labor had ended and he could go hunting the next day. But a new thought skittered past, and returned: maybe he cried because the broken rubble couldn't be reassembled again. Without the rock, what would he do for an adversary? "That don't make no sense a-tall," he said, close enough to the house that Roddy's dog hollered back.

7

JANET STRAINED TO OVERHEAR what might be happening in the living room, but there was little to hear. Sid sat red-eared with his hands cupped tight in his lap, knuckles gleaming like bone. Stone-faced, Janet's dad rocked and contemplated the evening news and pretended Sid wasn't there.

Janet's mom pushed her a plate of cookies, steaming and soft. "Take these in before that boy has a stroke." A safety pin highlighted a broken bra strap when she extended her arms.

Sid looked up with hopeful eyes. His crooked rocker had inexorably rotated on the out-of-level floor till he faced Janet's dad. Sid's shirt was ironed, but he'd forgotten to take his cigarettes out of the pocket, and his fingers wandered there when they weren't busy elsewhere.

"Cookie?"

"Not for me," her dad said.

"George." Janet's mom stood in the kitchen doorway, "I left the nuts out." Nuts got under his dentures, which wouldn't be in if Sid weren't there. "You eat some."

"Nettie, I don't want one." But George motioned for the plate.

Sid dropped half on the floor before he got the cookie to his mouth, his face red enough to bleed.

"Give me that." Janet exchanged a glass of milk for the dirty cookie. Thank the Lord she hadn't invited him for a meal.

"These are good, Mrs. Hollar," Sid mumbled from a full mouth.

Before she sat, Nettie switched off the television. George stared on at the blank screen.

"How is school, Sid?" Nettie said.

Bad start. Janet knew Sid wasn't stupid, but his ignorant teachers had persuaded him that he was. After that, he didn't even try.

"I done all right in Building Trades." He wore a milk moustache that both magnified and trivialized the down on his lip. "That's what counts—learning a job. And construction's the only fit job around." He blushed again. "Unless you was to farm."

"Will you stay here after you graduate?"

"I don't know. I don't have family nowhere else, but jobs is scarce here." He rootched the chair around like they were still watching TV, then turned it right back.

George wore the expression he saved for barn rats and chicken hawks.

Janet tried to herd the conversation in another direction. "Did you get in the last of the corn, Daddy?"

"Yep." He deposited the word like a lump of mud.

"What the bears didn't thrash down," Nettie said, like Janet had hoped. "It's hard enough with the milk prices falling. If the government doesn't do something, there won't be any family farms left. Watch what happens then, when the big corporations get it all. And the deer—they wallow the hay and eat all the green beans."

"I got a dandy deer this season," Sid said, as though he'd killed a hundred before that particular monster.

"Yeah?" The first interest George had exhibited all night.

"Just a four-point, but they was big ones. Probably weighed one-ten, one-fifteen. They don't put em on the scales here."

George snorted. "That ain't big."

"Another one was running with him—maybe a six—but this one was limping, and I figured it was wounded and shot it instead. So it wouldn't suffer." Sid glanced around like they might not believe him. "Turned out it didn't have a mark on it, though."

"I'd a shot the big one," George said.

"I'd a shot both of them," Nettie said. "I'd shoot bears if they wouldn't put me in jail. And now we have coyotes, they say. And they eat housecats, they say. Just watch the rodents, when the cats are gone. And the coons! I got just two messes of sweet corn before they pulled it all down. They carry rabies, too. I wish they'd all get the rabies."

72

"I ought to bring over Roddy's coon dog."

"Keep your dog away from my milk cattle," George said. "My chickens, too."

"This dog wouldn't run anything but coon. He's a pureabread Treeing Walker."

"You hunted him before?"

"Roddy had him out, back in Logan County."

"I asked if *you* ever hunted him."

Sid's eyes tightened. "It's the dog does the hunting. Not me."

Visions of walking with Sid in the moonlight, bumping softly together with each step, filled Janet's head. "Let him hunt, Daddy. It can't hurt."

"You go learn to hunt on someone else's cows first." George adjusted his dentures with a work-roughened thumb. "Hunt your dog with Harlin Wall's. Then I'll let you hunt here."

"Stay away from that man," Nettie said.

"Don't worry," George said. "Sid ain't got the guts to hunt with Harlin."

"I don't know Harlin, but I'll hunt with him," Sid said. "I'm glad there's someone around that hunts. Or does anything, for that matter."

George removed his top plate and put it in his shirt pocket. His face collapsed into a pout, and all traces of civility left it. "You're right proud of sassing the preacher, I reckon. But that don't make you a man."

Sid wet his lips. "I'd hunt with Harlin, was I invited."

"George," Nettie said. "Don't . . ."

"I'll see Harlin at the Agway tomorrow. What night you want to hunt? Friday? Or do you have to go disrespect a preacher that night?"

"I was just trying not to get preached clear down to the bone. Friday's all right."

George laughed for the first time that evening. "I'll tell Harlin you're coming."

§

"What was I supposed to do? Let him call me a coward?"

Janet wished she'd not walked Sid to the mailbox. He'd tried to hold her hand, but she hugged herself. "I thought you'd be polite to my folks. Not bicker with them."

Sid kicked a rock that rattled ahead, then hopped into the frost-killed weeds.

"Don't go. Harlin Wall's crazy, and Daddy will put him up to something. He's killed people, they say."

Sid hawked and spat. "Everybody's heard them stories. Bud says Harlin Wall's just a thimbleful of stale piss."

"What could I do to stop you from going?" Janet slid her arms inside his coat.

"Shoot me. I don't know no other way."

§

When the sun faded, Stride metamorphosed from a lazy dog-box sleeper to a panting hellhound with eyes that glowed alternately red or foxfire green in Sid's weakening flashlight beam. The chain bit into Sid's hand, and slobber glistened on the dog's neck and forelegs.

"Hold back, dammit." Sid went to his knees when his boots slid out of the center of the grassy road and into one of the rutted mud tracks. He hauled the dog away from the black hollow that fell away to his right. "Surely nobody lives back here." The dog lunged forward again, dragging Sid across a creek in a clatter of slippery shelving rocks. There was light ahead—flickering, so faint that Sid looked away and back to verify its existence.

Then came the bellow of dogs, coarse-throated and demented, and the hollow-pumpkin thumping of chains tested against doghouse boards. Stride let the chain go slack for the first time since they'd left the hard road two miles back. "Hello," Sid yelled. A momentary silence, then the dogs erupted again: new meat. Stride tightened the chain in the other direction, hanging back.

When Sid first saw the house, he thought the swaybacked two-story structure was aflame. But the shadows behind the rippled-glass windows moved without firefighters' haste. A chill December night, the door stood open. As Sid edged forward, the flickering light source—a hanging kerosene lantern—appeared through the window.

"Hey," he called through the open door as he hooked the dog's chain to a post and eased under a porch roof that hung like a partially sprung boxtrap. The doorway was squat and the windows lowslung, as though the earth were tidal, rising around the house. Long indefinite shadows crept across the porch floor, but nobody answered. The thought of waving his hat inside the door as though to draw hostile fire, like Roddy always did for laughs, was tempting, but he suspected nobody would find it funny.

Sid stood dumb in the doorway for a long moment.

Before he could apprehend the kitchen before him, he had to address the bull that hung from a cable that mashed the broomed horns tight against the ceiling, then disappeared through a splintered hole. A tongue like a hot-water bottle stretched toward where the steel rope bit into a testosterone-swollen neck. The hide, dark and mottled, glittered wet around the gaping slash that divided the ribs. Hindquarters rested on a dirt floor, legs splayed as though the bull had been sitting examining his crotch. Iridescent coils of intestines spilled into his lap. Sid's first unspoken question was, who would eat a bull, rank and tough and gamy? The next was how they'd gotten the bull into the kitchen. Then he wondered whose bull hung there.

The lungs were flung off alone, pink and frothy, trifles the breeze should ruffle. Non-reflective pools of blood sulked here and there on the uneven dirt; more half-filled a galvanized tub. The liver huddled gray and malignant in a stained enameled basin. Beside it lay the bull's bag—a gaping purse, hairy and sad. Twin fist-sized testicles had the lightly blooded gleam of new-pulled teeth.

Too much to look at, yet every detail impossible not to see.

Lanterns flickered amid the smells of blood and hot meat and male animals and kerosene and soot and dirt and batshit and oil. A coal stove leaned into the wall, back legs eaten into the dirt, and meat hissed in a blackened pan. Fire raged in the stove's cracks and around the lids, a network of flame that made the stove seem nebulous, a colander of fire. At head height, the heat was oppressive, yet the gut pile steamed.

A short thin man with possum hair straddled the guts to work inside the cavity. A brown-bladed knife, slim-shanked from sharpening, made soft wet sounds as it severed scraps of diaphragm and the pale vacuum cleaner hose of windpipe. A nose prominent and hawkish, lips puckered with the set of toothless decades. Yellow and shit-green suet cuttings flittered over his shoulder onto the floor.

The remnants of a woman and a dress hovered in the shadows, and Sid had the unwarranted sense of others in the rooms beyond.

"Harlin?" Certain he'd made a horrible turn, had taken the fork to hell. "Is this the Wall place?"

"Depends." His voice, like the knife, one of soft wet slicing. "If you're the asshole punk that's been after George Hollar's girl it is." The seat of Harlin's pants touched the guts as he carved at the bull. He stood and tossed the knife into the liver basin.

"That's me. Sid Lore." Sid nearly extended a hand before he reclaimed his wits. "I didn't know you were butchering. I can come another night."

"Butchering ain't a special occurrence here." Harlin rinsed his hands in a bucket of water. "Finish this," he said to the woman, and crowded past Sid out into the dark. Sid followed as though snagged.

The dogs restarted their chorus when a match flared between Harlin's cupped hands. Sid saw his age: forty, maybe. Forty hard years. A .22 pump rifle had risen from nowhere like an erection beneath Harlin's arm. "Lemme fetch a dog."

"I hope our dogs will hunt together." What he really meant was, please don't let your dogs eat mine. Roddy's, rather.

After some cursing and yelps from the dog boxes, Harlin retrieved a lowsagged bitch that dragged tits in the frost and bared yellow teeth. The dog racket was undiminished by her absence. The two dogs snarled and hackled and sniffed hind-ends.

"What's her name?"

Harlin grunted. "I don't squander names on curs like that one."

"I thought you were going to learn us some stuff. Me and the dog."

Harlin's laugh was low and harsh. "If you don't learn nothing, it ain't my fault."

A chill unrelated to the night air wormed under Sid's collar as they set off along the suggestion of a path. The dogs towed them across a misshapen clearing, a bleak space unsullied by barn or manure or fence. Or bull: "Do you raise cows, Harlin?" Harlin said nothing, and Sid wished he hadn't spoken.

At the foot of a hollow they loosed the dogs, then worked their way up an old log road, and for a term the world juddered toward normal, at least coon-hunting normal. Sid began to wonder if he'd imagined the butchering scene. They stood wide-legged in the trail as the dogs opened across the way, moving fast. Too fast.

"They're running deer," Sid said, anxious to show that he wasn't perfectly ignorant. His eyes had adjusted enough to see the dark hole of Harlin's mouth flatten and spread into what Sid realized was a grin. "I got to head them off. I can't let Roddy's dog chase deer."

"Leave em run." Harlin's voice was brutal enough to stall the protests that lay rancid in Sid's belly. Sid stood speechless and impotent as the dogs faded away. Later, impossible to judge whether a half-hour or five had passed, a single dog's baying ruptured the malevolent spell. Harlin's head swiveled toward it like an owl's.

"That don't sound like either one of ours," Sid said.

"Shut up. And keep your light off." Soon a light flickered on the opposite slope, three hundred yards away. It probed along the ground. When it was directly across, as close as it would come, a gun cracked beside Sid. Whether Sid grunted or barked or let go a pent-up fart, he didn't know, but he had a visceral expulsion followed by another as Harlin deliberately worked the pump. After five or six shots, the light went off, and only then did Sid accept that Harlin was shooting at it. Eighteen times, or twenty one, how ever many shells the tubular magazine held, the gun cracked, the slide clacked, the spent brass tinkled into the still night.

Sid stood petrified, knowing he'd forever despise himself for doing so. Aggression so sudden and wanton and foreign to his experience or imagination had vapor locked him, left him with no response to offer. His mind trudged on separate of his soul, already manufacturing excuses: a .22 wouldn't kill a person at that range, even if Harlin could hit one; Harlin had a gun, and Sid was unarmed; it was just a dream; the whole circus was staged, arranged by George and Harlin in advance.

Hell yes. Why hadn't he suspected. The horror and adrenaline and self-disgust coursed out of Sid in a long sigh, and hatred for those who would do such a thing swept in. The night was still again but for the steady shoop shoop of fresh shells sliding down the tube as Harlin reloaded. Sid hauled a slow breath to make sure he could talk. "This your property way back here, Harlin?" He wished he'd brought Roddy's pistol, so he could fire some shots too.

"Keep your voice down. It's mine as much as it is that sunsabitch's."

Branches rattled above their heads, then the dry leaves beyond. A half-second later, a small-bore rifle cracked from further out the mountain than Sid antic-ipated. Harlin was gone as though he'd evaporated. "Get down, you idiot, he's shooting back." His voice was close by, but Sid stood alone in the night.

Sid wanted to laugh as much as he'd wanted to cry out earlier, but he bit it down. He played along instead. "Here I am, fellers," he called across the hollow. He turned his dim flashlight on himself, stared into its fading beam. "Make her clean. You don't want Sid Lore after you." Harlin's footsteps pounded away down the trail. No more shots came his way.

When his eyes again cleared, he wandered toward where Harlin had disappeared. The night closed in fierce and lonely, but he didn't call out. A rising moon highlighted frost-whitened leaves that crunched under his feet. Then a shadow shifted under a hemlock ahead. Sid stopped, waited.

"Are you *tryin'* to get shot?"

Sid moved closer, confident but cautious. "You about done with your little scare-the-poop-out-of-Sid show? Who's your buddy across the way?"

After a moment, Harlin laughed. "I got no idea who was over there. But he sure knows who you are, since you was ignorant enough to tell him."

"Don't tell me George Hollar didn't instigate this."

Harlin emerged from low-hanging branches. He'd struck Sid as being whip-like and vicious earlier, but by moonlight he looked ragged and skinny, like a sick rat. Shifty. "George Hollar don't issue my orders. Fact is, I told him I didn't care to hunt, but he must not of passed that on."

"You should have told me, instead of bringing your worthless mutt out to teach a good dog to run deer."

Harlin shrugged. "Was your dog any account, he wouldn't run deer. And you was there, wanting to hunt." Closer, he smelled of stale smoke and something sharp and medicinal. Whiskey, maybe, or snuff.

"You can fire at a man from the dark, but you can't say to my face that you don't care to hunt with me?"

"There's no call to make a enemy if you don't have to. And I wasn't aiming at that feller. He'd be dead, if I was."

The night was bleak and clammy, and Sid wanted to be home. "How we going to get the dogs back?"

Harlin had eased away. "They'll come back dreckly. Or leave your coat and come back in the morning. Your dog'll be laying on it, if someone ain't shot him." He was just a shadow again, sliding away up a side hollow.

"Where you going?"

"I'm going to the house. I got to work tomorrow. Go to the top of yonder hill, you'll see where you're at. It's closer that way than for you to come clear back to my place." Harlin's voice was fading fast.

"Harlin. How you break a dog from running deer?"

"How you break anything of anything? Kill it." Harlin was gone like Sid had just nightmared him up for company.

§

Just after 2 AM, Sid paused on the ridge to reclaim his bearings and his breath. He pieced together the roads and fields and forests from the touchstone of distant headlights where Union Highway topped Peck's Hill. Closest was George Hollar's farm. Janet curled there in a warm bed, belly filled with cookies. Longing gripped him before he could anger it away. A craving for Janet, but maybe more for his own bed. He stepped out along the hillside, walking in the pasture where weak moonlight lit the way.

A muted thump of running feet behind, and Stride was on him before he could brace himself. The big hound bowled him into the frost-slick grass, then licked at his face with a tongue that smelled of yesterday's breakfast. Sid lusted to strangle the dog, but instead hugged him close. "It's about time," he breathed into the dog's ear while one hand fumbled in his pocket for the chain.

The dog was docile, petered out from running deer, and barely pulled the slack out of the chain. While Sid stepped through George Hollar's barbed-wire fence the dog crawled under, then waited like they'd been practicing that maneuver. Halfway across the field, when Stride bawled and hit against his collar, Sid was off guard; the chain snatched from his fingers and was gone. Sid glimpsed a dark scuttling form that disappeared into a tepee of fenceposts curing above the barn. The dog raged at the pile, howling and slashing at the sharpened ends. In the house a light flared, then another, and shortly a flashlight bobbed down the porch steps.

Sid was still trying to subdue the dog when the gallump of unbuckled artics approached. No use to run, even if he had vinegar enough to haul the dog away.

George Hollar, in white pajamas and an old barn coat: "I told you not hunt here."

"I wasn't. We was on the way home when the dog ripped loose. I can't shut him up."

"What's he got cornered?"

"A coon, I reckon."

George grunted. "Probly a possum."

"No, it was dark-colored. I seen that much."

"Where's your gun? We just as well kill it."

"Harlin had a gun; I didn't take one."

"You went, huh?" George was shining the light into the pile when Janet touched Sid's shoulder. She was dressed like George, but for tennis shoes with dragging strings. George shined the light in her face. "Git back to the house, girl. It's late."

"I want to watch."

George started to argue, then shrugged. "All right, we'll give you something to watch." He turned to Sid. "You ever seen a dog and a coon in a evenhanded brawl? Where the coon don't have bullet holes in him already?"

Sid dodged the question. "Stride can handle a coon."

"We'll see about that." Grinning. "Help me peel these posts off. Janet, you hold the light."

As the posts fell away, the dog went so crazy that they couldn't keep him out of their way. "Haul him back, but be ready to slip him loose," George said. "I seen something move." His face a jack-o-lantern. "Ready?"

"Do it."

"Leave him loose," George yelled, and threw back the last couple of posts. Faster than Sid's mind could operate, the dog dove into the pile and extracted a small black-and-white form and was among them shaking, shaking and Sid's eyes were afire and his throat stoppered with stink, ears battered with the howls of five desperate animals and the two words Sid heard again and again: Skunk. Asshole.

§

Sid's knees wobbled with tired as he clipped Stride's chain to the doghouse. Sid dry-heaved a final time, scanned the forest with sandy eyes, then crawled inside the barrel. The dog retreated to the end of his chain before he settled into the dirt, like Sid was the source of the stink.

8

Sᴅ sᴍᴇʟʟᴇᴅ ʜɪs ʜᴀɴᴅ, something he'd done till he couldn't determine if his skin retained the stink or if it had got fast inside his head. "I won't apologize to nobody. And there's nothing you can do that's any worse than what I already done to myself."

Roddy hammered his fist on the end table, careful not to break anything or knock anything off. "We got to fit in with these folks." His whiskey stunk worse than Sid's skunk, but Sid didn't have the energy to challenge him on it.

"Maybe you do. I graduate in May, and then I'm out of here."

"Is a simple apology too much to ask?"

"You go repent to them people if you think it's in order. Take your damn dog with you, maybe he'll want to clear his conscience too."

"You never even asked to use him."

Sid stood from the couch and zipped his jacket. "I should have shot it. It's not worth tits on a boar hog."

Roddy had already lost the trail of their contention. "You ought to of asked."

"You'd a said no, and I'd a took it anyhow."

Roddy passed his hand across his face, top to bottom. "There's skunk everywhere."

"I wisht everybody in this whole county got a dose." Sid straightened the couch cover, just so he wouldn't be like Roddy, and headed out the door.

"Where you going?"

"I'm going to hell. If you get there first, save me a place by the fire." Actually, Sid didn't know where he was going. If it was to be someplace skunk-free, he'd have to leave his skin behind. Union County, too. He walked down the hill past the church. Just after Dunn had issued a new commandment about unchaperoned kids, a pole light had been installed in the parking lot. It buzzed like a baby rattlesnake, and Sid bounced a gravel off the reflector, hoping to bust it out but too depressed to try again.

Well past the church, he stopped at the end of the long lane that led to Janet's house. He ran his fingers over the mailbox's reflective stick-on letters: HOLLAR.

Janet Hollar. That deal was done with, he reckoned. When he called her house, Nettie had answered, then eased the phone into its cradle when she heard Sid's voice.

Ignorant whistledick, George had tacked onto the tail of his tirade.

Maybe if the hives had kept George out of the fourth grade like they had Sid, he wouldn't be smart either. When they'd tutored Sid during recess, it was more punishment for falling behind than an attempt to catch up. The teacher looked out the window more than Sid did. So Sid didn't read good, though he could do his numbers okay.

But he knew not to fetch a skunk out of a post pile, and not to pay $300 for a skunk-killing dog. Five dollars for the dog, $295 for the fancy papers. Knew better than to papermill himself to death just so he'd have $300 for a dog but no time to hunt.

What he couldn't grasp was how to get shed of people who called him stupid but couldn't work in a pie factory. Getting away wasn't the rub; he'd thumb a ride, or walk. But he'd need a place to stay, and a car. Food, and clothes. Money for the laundromat. Any way he ciphered, the money wouldn't reach.

And maybe he was a little bit trepidatious.

A stone clinked further up the driveway. "Git," Sid said, in case it was another skunk seeking an ignorant whistledick.

"Sid?" A shadow beneath the overhanging trees. Janet. He recognized that smell.

"That there tomato juice does the trick, don't it." Half a dozen people had called to tell Sid to wash in tomato juice, so he guessed she'd heard it a hundred times. He'd just as well of bathed in cow piss.

"What are you doing?"

"Checking your mailbox, making sure there's no treacherous beasts treed in it."

Her giggle surprised him. "It stunk so bad in the bedroom, I had to get out." She was wrapped in an old bathrobe, like she'd been the night before. Or that morning, rather.

"It's worse at my place. I got Roddy and skunk both."

"He preach at you?"

"There's no call for the way he's went on."

She giggled again, like a skunked girl oughtn't. "He can't be as ridiculous as Daddy. He even took the Lord's name in vain."

"Mine got utilized a little reckless in there, too."

Her teeth flashed white. "He prayed forgiveness for it. Begged Mom to lay on hands and pray too, but she swore not if she had two pairs of rubber gloves. He's holed up in the barn, out of range of her tongue. It's been a circus."

"You're on her shitlist too, I reckon."

"She's never treated me better. The more Daddy rails on you, the harder she lays into him. He'll rare at the cows till they won't let down their milk, probly." Janet permitted Sid to pull her close to him, but kept her hands at her sides. "Don't. I'm stunk up bad." She buried her face in his chest.

He kissed her hair. "You ever watch a hound roll in a dead groundhog?"

She nodded.

"That's what I'd do, if there wasn't no better way to get your smell on me," he said. "I'd roll in it."

Tears glistened when she turned up her face. They tasted salty, not like skunk a-tall.

§

The windshield wipers on Roddy's pickup hacked the rain, and Roddy sawed at the wheel the same way. He sped up when he could see, then rode the brake when another sheet of rain washed over them. "Just three more months, and then you'll have your diploma."

Sid slipped his cigarette butt out over the side window; Roddy didn't allow him to use the ashtray. The cab reeked of smoke and wet clothing and the blue-jeans and flannel shirts they'd bought in Morgantown. "That's when the class graduates. I'm flunking English for sure, likely history too."

"You're smarter than that."

Sid wiped at the window. "Maybe so. But I got the thimbleshits with boredom. This school thinks because I'm in the Building Trades, I'm too dumb to tie my shoes. You know what you do in Consumer Math?"

"Sleep, from the grade you brought home."

"You learn how to figure out if you got money enough at the grocery store."

"That's important to know. And you got to learn English. You can't get a good job if you can't talk right at the interview."

"I can talk right. But I'd be putting on airs to do it here."

"Trouble is, you'll get to where you can't do no different. Any different." Roddy shook his head like a bug had flew up his nose. "See what I mean." His hands shook from drinking, like they'd done before they had moved.

Had Roddy got fired? Was that why he was off work?

A log truck's horns blatted when Roddy strayed too far. "I wish they'd paint lines on these roads," he muttered. "You can take summer classes."

"They don't have none, and I wouldn't take them anyhow. I'll be eighteen by fall, and then you can't make me go back."

"Sid, I won't sign for you to drop out. Pap would roust up out of the grave."

"Let him come. Maybe he'll have some sense."

"You'll be poor the rest of your life."

Sid lit another cigarette, though his mouth was parched from the last. "Like I said, I got a job tomorrow. If you don't let me quit to take it, I'll leave out of here. One way or the other, I won't tolerate another minute behind a desk. If these sorry-assed teachers haven't taught me nothing in this time, they never will. Not if I stayed till my knees wouldn't fit under the desk."

As they climbed the mountain, patches of thin cold fog crowded out the rain. Roddy's driving improved to where Sid could turn loose of the armrest.

"A mason's helper. What kind of a job is that."

"A six-bucks-a-hour one."

"A orangutang could do it."

"It's outside. Healthy, not like that cesspool you work in. You look like bread dough."

"There's no future in it. Without that diploma, a laborer is all you'll ever be."

"Lestoil don't have a diploma, and three men work for him. If he don't feel like working, he goes fishing. Spends winters in Florida in a motorhome."

"Lester came up when hardly anybody had a diploma, when it didn't matter."

"He's offered me a job. I'll either take it, or I'll run off. It's your pick." Sid slid down in the seat and pulled his cap over his eyes.

§

"Mud," Greasy yelled. "Get me mud, boy. I can't lay block without mud."

Sid was too out of breath to answer. "Mud," Tom brayed, then Huck. The mortar buckets stretched his arms till he could have scratched the bottoms of his feet without bending over, if he had the energy to scratch. "Block," Lestoil growled. "And turn them the right way, the big end towards me. And stretch a line on that far wall, so we don't have to wait. Godamighty, boy, you're the dilitariest tender I ever seen."

And build the scaffold and haul water from the lake and knock dried mortar from the mixer and check the oil before the engine burns up and Lestoil takes a new one out of my pay and pick gravel out of the sand and strike the joints and fill up the anchor-bolt holes and tar the wall while you can reach over the top and burn the empty sacks before they blow away and piss off the neighbors and place the drain tile and haul gravel over it before the banks collapse and you have to shovel it back out, and godamighty, boy, get straw on that gravel 'fore it rains don't you know *nothing*, boy? The mud's too thin. You'll make somebody a good wife, good a soup as you make. What'd you do, shit-for-brains, run out of water? This is horse biscuits, put some juice in it boy. Block, we need block you worthless ass dragger, set up some blocks, and pick the leaves out of that sand, we ain't building no compost pile. Fetch my smokes off'n the dashboard, and set that water jug up where I can reach it. Boy, if you don't get them joints struck, you're gonna have to do it with a chisel. Lestoil, where'd you find this schoolgirl anyhow. Keep them blocks out of the dirt, boy, so I don't got to trowel em off before I lay em, I can't make no money troweling off every sorry-assed block twicet. How'd you ever find your way to work, you ain't got a gut in your head, ignorant as a bowl of toenails. Dumb as some of my wife's people.

By lunchtime, Sid's back ached so that he lay on the ground with a bag of mortar in the small of his back. He never knew he could swallow uphill before, but it wasn't any harder than sitting up. Though the masons took a full half-hour to work through their sandwiches and deviled eggs, Sid wolfed down his lunch and struggled to his feet. He greased and gassed the mixer and loaded another batch, ten and a half shovels of sand to a bag of mortar and not too much water to start with because it got thinner as the paddles belabored it, and then he caught up striking joints while the mortar mixed. At 12:30, when the men belched and loaded their lips with snuff or finished their smokes, the mudboards were filled and the scaffold lined end-to-end with blocks, every one turned the right way. Sid leaned against a cube of blocks and smoked a cigarette of his own.

"Godamighty," said Lestoil as he climbed up the steel bucks, "how we supposed to get back on the scaffold with all this stuff piled in the way."

"Just kick some down if you can't drag over it," Sid said. "I'd a thought the four of you would be able to keep up."

"The boy's getting cocky," Huck said. "I'll dump some mud down the wall if he gets ahead." The rest of the afternoon, though, instead of bellering "mud," one of them would say "Greasy's dumped his mud down his pants cuff again, better bring him a jag," or "Huck, you want me to come over and kick some of them blocks out of your way so's you can keep up with the big boys?"

When they'd finished that evening, after Sid had hosed out the mixer and while the men drank a beer from Lestoil's after-work cooler, Sid collected onto a mudboard what mud remained in the wheelbarrow and in the buckets. He chopped water into the drying mortar with the old trowel he used to scrape the mixer. He loaded the trowel, shook the extra back onto the board, and ran a bead of mortar down the top of the wall. It didn't string out perfect, a little too much where he started and not quite enough at the end, but it was acceptable.

"Better watch, Huck," Greasy said. "Learn how it's done."

Sid mudded the ends in two quick strokes and set the block on the wall, bumping it with the trowel's handle to tighten the head joints, then tapped it into alignment with the string.

Tom lifted his hat and scratched the top of his head. "You're fouling the end where the mud hangs over."

Sid cut off the mud that had oozed out and flicked it back onto the board, then repeated what he'd just done. That time he didn't distribute quite enough mortar on the wall, so he picked the block off and did it right.

"Looky there," Huck said. "A damn perfectionist."

"It don't have to be even near perfect," Sid said. "Just as good as yours."

They laughed. "You ought a heard Huck his first day," Tom said. "He asked what he was getting paid, and Lestoil said, 'How much you worth?' Huck looked around kind of desperate and said, 'Hell, I can't live on that.'"

They laughed loose and not too rambunctious, telling an old story for Sid.

Tom went on: "At dinnertime Lestoil asked Huck how many blocks he'd laid. Huck scratched numbers on his mudboard with his trowel for a while, and he said, 'This'n and one more will make two.'"

Sid's grin grew into a laugh. Not enough mud remained to lay another block, so he dumped it inside the wall, careful to find a hole where a bolt would need mudded in, cautious not to waste mortar.

"Looky there," Huck said. "He's a-laughing. Ain't many mud punks can laugh this time of the day."

Greasy raised a cheek and liberated a fart that burbled and blubbered and petered out with a squeal. "Any old horse can fart in the morning, but it takes a stud to fart come suppertime."

"Spud, you mean," Huck said.

"A spud would go good right now," Tom said. "I need to head home." But he tossed his can toward the woods and opened another beer.

"Git down off there, Sid," Lestoil said. "You're making me tired. Where'd you learn to lay block, anyhow? Not that it's good or nothing."

"I watched yous." Sid jumped down, landed on his toes. "It's not hard."

"Tell Huck that," Lestoil said. "Thirty years, he ain't yet got the hang of it."

Huck, Sid knew, could lay almost as many blocks in a corner, where each one had to be leveled and plumbed and squared, as the others could on a straight course.

Huck took a long pull from his can and belched. "I'll mix mud and watch Sid tomorrow, learn how. I sure ain't learned nothing from you roundheads."

Lestoil passed Sid a beer. "Don't blow beer breath on nobody, get me in trouble."

The beer was sharp and yeasty, not what Sid expected. After the first sip, he turned up the can and emptied it in one long swallow, then crumpled it and tossed it away. The brew was icy in his belly, but radiated warmth. A gas bubble budded in his stomach, and he held it until it bellowed out in one long bray.

"Damn," Tom said. They pitched the cans and loaded into their pickups.

Lestoil grabbed Sid's neck with a hand the consistency of the blocks Sid had toted all day. "You done good. Want a ride?"

"It's not far, and I need the exercise."

"We'll see how much exercise you need by week's end. Our next job's mostly twelve-inch, none of these little pissant eight-inch blocks."

"Bring em on," Sid said. "I can handle them."

"I believe you just might be able to."

§

"I'll be all right." Sid's breath caught as he bent for a sack of mortar. "Give me a minute."

Lestoil splashed water on his trowel and tossed it onto a cube of blocks. "There went another one," he said, and climbed down from the scaffold. Though the others had been yelling for mud and blocks a moment ago, they had gone silent, scraping at the wall with their trowels, not looking Sid's way.

"I'll catch up. I got to turn my back the right way, then it'll be all right." He groaned when he couldn't find a painless position.

"You just as well set in the truck," Lestoil said, and tossed a bag of mortar onto the mixer's grate as though it were Styrofoam. He split the bag with the spade, shook the mortar free.

"Don't be doing my job. I can do it."

"Jump in the truck and rest your back for a while. Maybe it'll come back." Lestoil shoveled sand into the mixer, slopped in half a bucket of water.

"Don't get it too soupy. It's easy to do."

With one hand Lestoil turned Sid toward the pickup. "I'll be careful."

From the truck it was hard to hear what the men were saying. Tom's high thin voice was the only one that carried. "Maybe we could get that Baker boy."

Twice Sid started to work, but couldn't operate the door handle without crying out in pain. Later, when the men cleaned the mixer and covered the sand and mortar—Sid's job for nearly six weeks—the pain moved behind his breast-bone.

"I'll give you a ride home," Lestoil said. "Don't argue." When they got to Roddy's driveway, he counted twenty-dollar bills into Sid's hand.

"I'll see if there's change inside."

"Don't bother," Lestoil said, and placed an additional twenty on the short pile.

"Just a little rest, that's all I need. I'll be back tomorrow."

"I hope you are," Lestoil said. "I sure hope you're right."

9

"I DON'T KNOW WHAT TO DO," Janet said. Sid's arms were barrel hoops around her, hard and too tight. He smelled of aftershave and of tobacco. "Daddy's decided to sell, and me and Mom can't shake him loose of it."

"Where you going to live?"

"He ain't said. Somewhere south. He hates winter. This last one worked on him fierce."

"You mean move clear away?" Sid held her at arms length and read her face like a newspaper. Their reflections danced in chrome he'd polished to a mirror shine. The old Chevelle was more rust than chrome, but Sid treated it like it was a new Cadillac. "Good geeminy, Janet. You can't leave."

"I don't have a say in it." Relocating was cold, gelled fear and hot excitement. What would it be like?

Sid studied her nose, her mouth, her hairline. "I got a idea what to do about it. You can marry me."

Janet stared at him for a while, then rested her head on his chest. His shirt was wet where her cheek touched. Sid. Oh, Sid. The fender popped as their weight shifted to Sid's car.

"You don't seem overly joyed."

"I don't know what I think anymore." She sniffled, liked the feel of it, did it again. Sid couldn't support them. Did she love him, even if he could? Maybe. Yeah.

"Just say yes, lay the thinking behind."

"It ain't that easy."

Sid lifted her chin. "Make your mouth like this. Eee esssss."

"I'm not of legal age. Daddy would have to sign."

"Is that yes-if-Daddy-goes-along-with-it then?"

"Sid." Plaintive.

"Well, excuse me. I figured you'd be tickled."

"I am." Was she? "But you just hatched this up when you found out I'm leaving. Tomorrow you'll get the fantods about it."

"I haven't thought of nothing else lately. I'll mean it tomorrow, and all the days there is."

Something rolled over inside that she didn't want to deal with. Not yet. Not so quick. So young. "Where would we live?"

Sid's eyes shifted to a point beyond her shoulder. "We could lay up at Roddy's. He's never there anyhow."

"I couldn't live with nobody."

"Then I'll buy a place. I'll build a basement house we can live in till we save up the money to finish it."

"Sid, how you going to build a basement house? With what you make pumping gas, you couldn't pay for a house in a hunerd years."

"Pumping gas is just the little end of my job. I ring up sales, and change tires and oil. Wednesday Shorty let me put on a muffler. I'm learning to weld. I got a future there, Janet. Someday I'll be a mechanic and someone else can pump gas and scour bugs off windshields."

His future she could not perceive, nor could she sell short his promises. "It takes a wad of money to build even a basement house. It'd be years before we could."

"It's all ciphered up. I can do the work in the evenings. I'll dig it out by hand, and lay the blocks. There's nothing to carpenter work that I can't figure out. I'll even do the wiring and plumbing; it can't be that hard." A prayer-like fervency drove Sid's voice.

"That's what ruined your back, that blocklaying." Enthusiasm percolated inside her, and she didn't care to be excited about living in a dingy basement.

"It's when I have to rip on it day after day that my back gives out." He pulled her close again. A steady heart. Powerful arms. "I broke up that rock in the church lot, didn't I? Building a basement isn't any harder."

Janet scratched "SID" on his bicep, the skin so tight and hard her nail rasped. She wrote "LOVE" and "HOW." "What land you going to build our little cinderblock mansion on?"

Sid didn't answer for a while. "That's the rub. A few year ago you could get land anywhere for $500. But since the lake people come, that won't pay the taxes." He took a deep breath. "I'll find someplace. Roddy might sell a corner, if we could tolerate living that close."

Did she like his dreams, or did they make her nervous? "Tomorrow you'll have a different brainstorm." Sid had talked about starting half a dozen different businesses. About moving to where there were jobs. Even about going to Africa to kill a water buffalo. No elephant or lion, just a buffalo. "Shoot a cow instead," she'd teased.

"Cows don't stick with making you dead like a water buffalo does," he'd explained. "With eight inches of horn over a buffalo's brain, once they get the idea of killing you in it, they got to use it up or die trying. It can't get out no other way."

Sid pushed her away and opened the creaky door of his car and withdrew a ratty plastic folder from beneath the seat. Inside were penciled graph papers, long lists of materials and prices. "I been thinking about this for a long time." He spread the papers on the hood. "Here's a living room, and a kitchen and a mudroom, a bathroom and one bedroom. That's all we'd have need of for a while." His face reddened. "Till we had kids."

Janet fingered the lines, trying to kickstart her imagination. "Hows come there's two outside walls?"

"That's the way you indicate stone veneer. I'll rock the whole house, once the top's put on. This is a big picture window. I know where the glass is, cheap. I can build the frame."

Janet turned her attention to Sid, trying to get a look at the new stranger. "Why didn't you tell me you were working on this? Maybe you planned it with some other girl." Sid's teeth still caught Janet by surprise, so white and straight that she ran her tongue over bottom teeth that were bunching in front.

"You know better." He kissed her sweet, not hot and sweaty. "I been fixing to ask you. This just made me pull the trigger quicker."

"How much would it cost?"

Sid pointed with a finger black-lined with grease. "$2,817.31."

The number was staggering both for its magnitude and for its possibility.

"I've saved near eleven hundred. And you could get a job, just till we had kids. It would beat squandering money on rent."

Janet's head was too full. She covered her eyes, then combed hair with fingers.

"Please don't say no."

"I'm not saying anything."

"I asked you too quick. Daggone it, I should a took you for a hamburger first. Or over to Morgantown to a movie." Sid put the papers back under the driver's seat. "Don't answer right now. Take however long it takes to say yes."

"Daddy won't let me."

"Will you say yes if he does?"

Daddy. It didn't matter what she said. "All right. I'll marry you, if Daddy says it's okay."

"Hot diggety damn." Sid danced a jig that showered gravel against her bare legs.

10

George slouched against white oak stall boards abraded shapeless by decades of cows' crowdings. His tongue fidgeted where teeth should have been. "I'm standing in cow manure, and you're asking for my daughter's hand." His coveralls were tattered, and his boots sported red-rimmed hot patches that Sid had thought were extinct. The kind of patches you clamped on, then set afire. Winter's chill lingered in the barn's basement; the heifers' breath clouded in the gloom.

"I never intended it that way. Here's just where you was when I found you."

"I can't imagine you having a thing to offer my girl. Maybe skunk spray."

Sid felt more akin to the heifers than to the man before him. "That wasn't my dog."

"You got that much going for you."

"I got a decent job. It's steady, and I go hard at it. Work don't scare me." Sid squared his shoulders, careful not to sprawl like George.

"You can lay right down beside work and go to sleep, huh?"

"I work."

George unzipped his coveralls part way and scratched under an arm. "We got a buyer looking at the farm."

"That's why I'm asking now."

"All the years we busted our hump here, we never made a penny." He gazed out a window, though it was so dusty and spiderwebbed you couldn't have seen a house afire through it. "Now the money we're getting for the place seems like more than we could ever spend."

A heifer humped her back and loosed a torrent that sounded like a waterfall. It was as good a comment as Sid could have made about George's money. "I'm glad for you."

"Just when it looks like your row's too hard to hoe, something turns up. But life works both ways. It can turn into a manure pile before you can blink."

"Janet wants your blessing. If you won't part with it, I'll have to wait. But I'll marry her anyhow."

"If I don't ever pull another cow tit, it will be too soon."

Sid kicked at the litter on the cracked concrete floor. An old three-tined pitchfork leaned against the wall, and he had a notion to give George a ram in the ass with it, get him on point.

Backlit by the window, George's ears looked big as rear-view mirrors. "Where would yous live?"

That George might consider his request momentarily stole Sid's words. "I've drawed plans for a basement, and got half the money laid back. I just need a place to build on."

George adjusted his cap and walked away, obliging Sid to tag along. Sid clutched George's sleeve before he could squeeze between the sliding door and the battered doorjamb. "Give me a answer. We got that much coming."

Close up, George's features had a severity that his vacant expression hid. "How would I stop you? Anyone who can beat on a rock like you done, there's no use telling him what to do. I could beat you in the head with a two-by-four, but you'd just be encouraged. I should have hammered your head the first time I seen you, but it's too late now."

He weasled free of Sid's grasp and walked away.

"Now hang on," Sid said, his voice hard. George's ears slid up against his cap, and he stopped without looking back. "Either give your blessing or say no. I want an answer."

"People in hell wants ice water," George said, and walked toward the house.

§

It was hot for June, the church windows propped open. In the parking lot, Tinker and Joybelle Dunham discussed the generalities of their upcoming divorce. Tinker's voice was a bull that horned through the church and out the other side, but Joybelle's fluttered around the ceiling like a bat and refused to leave. Her language was more inventive, too.

The congregation glared at Sid like he was a ventriloquist with foul-mouth puppets. "I only know them people from pumping their gas," he muttered to nobody. He'd had to invite someone. Shorty was working Sid's shift at the filling station, and only Greasy and Huck had come from the old blocklaying crew. Sid stretched at the clip on his bow tie. If Janet didn't come in that door right immediate, he was going out it.

The door creaked and Freda Ball gave a rip on the organ and everyone started to stand, but it was Joybelle, looking too sweet to utter the cusswords that still echoed. "If that music's for me, run it backwards, see if you can undo my wedding," she said. Someone tittered. Joybelle was drunk, and mouthy. "Your woman's right behind me, Sid. Run now, if you're going to." She laughed the way people should, though Sid couldn't manage it himself.

The door groaned again, and Freda leaned on the organ with enthusiasm. Janet peeked in the door at Sid and pulled back and shut it again. "Make up your daggoned mind," Freda said and crash-landed into a bad chord.

Sid's plaid suit stretched in all the wrong places and constricted everywhere else. Then the door flapped open and Janet marched down the aisle on George's arm. George tried to hurry her, but she would have no part of it. Freda ran out of song, and rather than turn back the pages, she just quit. Sid had never seen Janet in makeup, long black lashes and high-colored cheeks; he wilted when she smiled. She pulled up just short, all sweet smells and fine textures.

"Who giveth this hand in marriage?" Preacher Dunn barked.

George nudged Janet forward and mumbled, "Her mother and I do," then skulked back to his place. But he didn't say, "It got stold," like he had at rehearsal.

Dunn read from his little book, but Sid couldn't draw a bead on the words. He was bursting with Janet's scent, with her damp arm stuck to his, with the tickle of her veil.

Janet did her "I do" strong, and Sid got it croaked out too.

"What token of this union do you bring?"

Sid took the thin gold band from Roddy's shaking fingers. He'd been embarrassed at its plainness, but just then he held it proud and said, "This ring." Janet had agreed that he didn't need a ring. They were expensive, and dangerous. Ask Roger Kelso, who jumped off a delivery truck and left his ring and finger on the buckboard.

Then he kissed her, and someone hollered, "Save some for later," and the organ bellered and everyone shook hands with Sid and kissed Janet, except for Joybelle Dunham who did the opposite and left lipstick and whiskey in Sid's mouth. Sid's head was abuzz and it was all confusion like his mother's funeral. In the Sunday school rooms they ate cake and punch, and opened the toasters and towels and wall ornaments and some plastic doodad with a electric cord and from Roddy, a 6mm Remington bolt-action rifle with a 3-9x Bushnell scope.

"Now there's a practical wedding gift," Joybelle crowed, waving a glass of punch that had had turned a different color than the others'. "She might fall out of love, but she'll still be in range."

"It'll keep the family safe and put meat in the crock pot," Roddy said, red-faced.

"You never know when a skunk's gonna batter the door down," Harland Roomer said, deflecting laughter back Sid's way. Harland had kept a chew in his jaw so many years that it looked full even when it wasn't. "I never had skunk, but I've ate worse, 'specially them first couple of months we was married." He looked around for Dez, but his wife was chatting by the punchbowl. "Skunk done right would have been a treat." The other men laughed and glanced at their wives, wished they had the nerve to talk like Harland.

Then halfhearted rice throwing, Janet handing off her bouquet to Hattie who hollered *fank ooo, fank ooo* and mashed the petals against her chest.

The new motor home nosed in behind Sid's old Chevelle. George and Nettie had lived there the ten days since they'd closed on the farm; already it looked worn and dated. The stuff Nettie refused to part with rode in the second-hand trailer behind. George proposed to travel, but Sid figured a week after he parked it the first time, it would be underpinned. And have a porch, a crooked one like farmers built.

If a schoolbus waited too long at a stop there, somebody nailed underpinning to it.

Sid had put out the word that nobody had better mess up his car, but was disappointed to discover they'd heeded. No shaving cream on the windshield. Not even a tin can to drag so everyone would notice he'd just married the prettiest girl in the world.

Janet sat on the console and waved until they were out of sight, then she kissed Sid's neck and slid into her seat. "We done it." She loosened the hook at the back of her neck.

Sid had shed his bow tie and jacket and unbuttoned the top three buttons of his shirt and got a smoke going. "Was there ever any doubt?"

Janet worked her pantyhose off under her dress, looking in the rear view mirror. "Not in my mind." She humped back onto the console and stuck her tongue in Sid's ear. She considered the wadded stockings. "I hate these things." She tossed them out the window. Sid wasn't sure the car was going to be big enough to hold him. "Them too." Janet sent the flat black dressy shoes behind the pantyhose and Sid threw back his head and howled.

§

The motel room smelled of cigars and closets and of the love they'd made atop the fuzzy yellow bedspread. The redheaded woman who'd unlocked the door smirked at Janet's bare feet and Sid's unbuttoned shirt. "You come ready." She'd dragged the drapes closed and shouldered the door shut behind her.

Janet's towel did not quite contain her, nor did it catch all the water that dripped from the wet ropes of her hair. Sid watched indistinct figures tussle in a snowstorm on the old black-and-white TV. He'd turned it on five minutes ago, and hadn't yet determined what he was watching.

Janet sat at the desk opening cards, placing money to the side and writing the amount inside. "Ten from Elmira and Willie. That's over $200 we got now."

"From who?"

"The older, heavy couple that sat halfway back on my side. Her hair's going gray, and he don't have much left."

"That don't narrow it down." The afternoon was as fuzzed as the time Sid found the bottle of sloe gin in Roddy's toolbox.

Janet tapped the last envelope—the biggest—against the scarred table. "Here we go." She slit the fold with Sid's pocketknife. Neither had discussed the envelope George handed Sid at the last moment; there'd been no other gift. "You want to guess? It's thick."

Sid snorted. "A arrest warrant, probably. Or a bill for the wedding."

"Aw, Sid. Daddy's not as bad as you think. I bet it's a thousand dollars."

"If he'd a give it to you, maybe. But he handed it to me. If there's a surprise, it'll be like a fart with a lump in it. That kind of one."

Janet withdrew a card and a packet of blue papers. As she read, her hand rose to cover her mouth. She dropped the card in her lap and looked at the wall and picked it up and read it again.

"Well, what?" Hope wiggled its ugly snout.

Janet opened the folded blue papers. "It's a deed."

"Hot damn. You mean your old man parted with a little corner of all that property?"

"No," she said in a small voice. "Not off the farm. He wouldn't bust that up."

"Let me see." Janet left wet prints on the paper. Sid followed the words with a finger so as not to jump ahead. Other than that only Janet's name was on the deed—Janet Hollar's, not Janet Lore's—and that she was getting .27 of an acre more or less, the legalese made no sense until Sid came to *being the same property conveyed to Emerick Justin Taylor from Ronald Goodhope and Rebecca Starr Dumire in a deed dated September 14, 1958 and recorded in the land records of Union County.* "It's Ermie Taylor's place." It took a moment to remember that Ermie had started a worm farm last month when his liver gave out.

"I know."

"That's not big enough to build on. And we'd have to move that old trailer first."

Janet passed the card to Sid. Nettie had written in her flowery hand best wishes for a long and happy marriage. On the left panel, George had printed in block letters: MY LITTLE GIRLS NOT GOING TO LIVE IN A BASE-MENT HOUSE LIKE A GROUNDHOG. Something toxic worked in Sid's throat: Gasoline. Rat bait. Bleu cheese dressing.

Janet refused to make eye contact, but instead read the deed over and over. "Sid," she said after the air in the room had gotten as constricting as a bull band.

"Don't Sid me."

"Daddy's trying to help out."

"Hell he is. He's trying to shame us. I won't stay in that trailer. It's so old, it has round corners like a Studebaker. I'd rather live in a holler stump." It occurred to Sid that they hadn't been married an entire afternoon, and already they were fighting.

"Well, Sid Lore, locate a holler stump big enough for the both of us." She came and sat on his lap, naked against Sid's thighs, and kissed him on the mouth.

But Sid had the flavor of Ermie Taylor's trailer on his tongue, and he evicted her from his lap and stood up. Her towel fell away, and he deliberately didn't look. "I can't believe he done that to us." He went outside and slammed the door, but had to turn and drag it up over the sill. The motel consisted of steep-roofed cabins laid up from pine logs and river rock; the entire structure shuddered up to allow the door to close. Not that there was anyone else in the cracked parking lot to see anything if it didn't.

§

She found him down by the river. The South Branch of the Potomac was low, clear enough to show every poptop and shard of broken glass. Janet's hair had dried fluffy, blossomed like a milkweed. She'd changed into shorts and a white pullover top so thin the darkness of her bellybutton showed through. Sid scootched over on his rock to make room. The smell of suntan lotion was exotic as elephant dung.

"See him?" He pointed where a rock broke the surface.

"What is it? A goldfish?" She squinted the way she did when she could see fine, but couldn't nail down what she saw.

"It's a golden trout."

"It's pretty."

"It's a insult to nature. Stands out like a mouse turd in the mayonnaise. Ospreys snatch them out as quick as they're put in."

"They must do all right, or they wouldn't survive."

"They don't. The first one was a freak. Some biologist down at the Smoke Hole hatchery kept working at it until he got a whole new strain of trout. But they have to raise them in a tank, then put them in the river."

"How do you know so much?"

Sid shared the shiny brochure he'd picked up in the motel office.

"They're awful pretty, anyhow."

"I bet they're dumb as a box of prunes, like things are that people's fooled with. Like cows. And chickens. Turkeys. Even a Republican's not as dumb as a turkey. I bet you could hook them golden trout on baloney. On a booger, if you didn't have baloney."

Her arm slid around him and she pulled herself close. "You won't run out of baloney. Boogers either, with your schnozz."

Sid grinned. "Those mongoloid trout go against the natural order of things. They ought to be let to die out."

Her fingernail cut little doodads in his back, made him shiver inside his sweaty shirt. "They're like us."

Sid tried to lean down and kiss her, but it was too awkward. "You're awful pretty, but I don't know any other way we're like them generical-altered misfits."

"I mean as long as we stay in the hatchery, we're okay. But get us outside that, and look at us." She giggled. "We got lost not fifty miles from home."

His ears felt warm again, and he looked up at the mountains, wished he was up there. Where it was cooler, where people didn't talk funny. Where it didn't smell like mud and chickenhouses. "It's hard trying to drive, someone trying to half rape you."

She either nuzzled him or wiped the end of her nose. "You ain't hard to half rape, if that's what you figger it was."

"No, it was the whole deal." They watched the trout drift and rise and dimple the surface, then ease back behind his rock.

"Tomorrow we'll go to the Smokehole Caverns." Sid had two more days off from work for the honeymoon; what they'd do with the other day eluded him.

"I can't wait. Will it be spooky, do you think?"

"Naw. It'll be cool. And I'll find a moonshiner's jug, go on a toot."

They were quiet, imagining being married. The rock bit into Sid's skinny flanks, but he didn't want to rupture the mood. Finally he just had to, or he was going to be crippled.

Janet stirred like he'd waked her. "Why'd you get so worked up about Daddy giving us a place? It's a start, anyhow."

Sid envisioned the future with a clarity the present seldom offered. "It's an end, not a beginning." The death of his dream of building a home. He'd mend the rotted plumbing and patch the leaky roof and pay real estate taxes and electric bills and to pump the septic tank every time the ground staggered with water, and they'd never budge from it. They'd be stuck like caddis fly larvae in their grubby little tube houses, only they'd never float to the surface and take wing. Like Bud said when Sid talked about building a house: *you'll work on it till Jesus comes.*

On the other hand, they did have a place to live. Him and Janet in their own place. A stirring was underway in his undershorts, and he shifted again to make room. "It'll be all right, I reckon, if Jesus don't tarry."

Janet shook her head. "Sometimes you don't make no more sense than a June bug." But she'd discerned his problem, and led him by the hand back to the little rock room. Sid forgot about Jesus coming again long before they got there.

II

Tear Down the Mountain

Who knows if the spirit of man rises upward

and the spirit of an animal goes down into the earth?

Ecclesiastes 3:21

11

"Got a postcard from Mom," Janet said, more to attack the silence than to convey information.

"Where they at now?" Sid poked for lead shot before he put squirrel meat in his mouth.

"Same place they been for years. Still at that trailer lot in New Mexico." On the front of the card was a falling-down red clay sunbaked ruin. "She went with some friends to the Quari Indian mission. You ever hear of them?"

"They was probably extincted before my time."

"You think someday people will take pictures of where we used to live?"

"They better do it quick. We should take pictures ourselves, so we could recollect it the way it was before it rotted down. If we had a camera. Maybe I could daub pictures on a rock."

Stung by his sarcastic tone, Janet forced herself to rinse her plate rather than smash it over his grouchy head. All she'd done to make the trailer livable—the doodads and doilies and rag rugs—was wasted on him. But if the rug was in the wash, he stood at the door like someone had pooped in his lunchbox. That day it all felt cheap and tawdry. Outside, the flowerbeds looked like what they were: treadless tires stuffed with black-eyed Susies and chicory she'd transplanted from along the road. Even the wooden duck that flapped when the wind blew looked like something pasted together at vacation Bible school.

In fact, she had made it at Bible school. But as a helper, not a kid. Hers had lines penned between the feathers, and little nose holes in the beak. But it was still a homemade duck, and it flapped crooked when the trailer shivered in a gust of cold air. She examined the duck through the bird-watching binoculars she kept on the counter. "You shot my duck," she said when she saw the freckling of holes and splinters of wood. "You shotgunned my dag-gone duck."

He pushed his plate away. "It isn't hurt none."

"Why'd you ruin my duck?"

Sid looked childish, trepidatious. "I just seen it there and popped one at it. There wasn't any call for it. I didn't think."

His tone surprised her. Apologetic. A little bit scared.

"I was hoping you wouldn't notice."

"Aw, Sid, why do you got to shoot everything?" She lammed the binoculars down harder than she'd intended. When she looked through them again, twin offset images made her feel crosseyed. "You blew the flag off the mailbox. You shot a hole in the birdbath."

"We don't get mail anyhow. And it would have froze and busted, come winter."

"You splintered up the croquet balls. You shot holes in the hubcap I found and set up where the rightful owner could find it." Running out of steam, she looked through the out-of-line lenses. "You shot my mountain ash tree off. Why don't you just shoot me?"

"Good geeminy, Janet. I'm not crazy."

Bad as she wanted to stay mad, she had to laugh.

He slid down in his chair, either relaxing or taking cover.

"What's wrong, Sid? Why do you shoot stuff?"

"Don't know. Time I think about it, I done yanked the trigger."

"Then don't carry a gun all the time."

Sid looked as though she'd suggested he wear a dress. "I can't shoot nothing without a gun."

"That's the point."

"I don't mean the duck and the dog dish and stuff." He coughed, glanced her way.

Janet leaned over the sink and looked hard to the left. Sure enough, the dog dish was ragged with shot. Sidemore lay beside it as though he'd taken a load as well.

"Stuff like this squirrel. A deer now and then. I didn't hear you complaining when you had a turkey to eat."

The bird was stringy, but she'd been respectful of his pride in bagging it. Venison, that was another matter. Saliva blossomed beneath her tongue.

She felt his forehead with the back of her hand, then hugged him and pulled his face into her stomach. "Sid, Sid. What am I going to do with you." She turned his head up to look in his eyes. "What's wrong with my man?"

Like he'd done every time she tried to get inside, he pulled back. In memorial to her splintered duck, she locked his ears in a death grip. "You're not acting normal. Tell me why. If you got troubles, fork over half of them. We promised we'd share."

"That don't mean tribulations."

"Yes it does. Especially them." She'd have bet she could tear his ears off, but they slid through her fingers when he pushed her away in favor of his work-boots. "Is it your job?"

He straightened in the chair and allowed the strings to dangle. "It's just the opposite."

"Your play?"

He shook his head. "Unemployment. That's the opposite of job."

Janet straddled the warm chair he'd just vacated. "But you got a good job. Especially since Shorty's sold out, and they're building the new station."

Sid worked his lips and opened the door and spit across the stoop. Sidemore barked when the door screeched. "You looked close at that building?"

"It's twicet as big as Shorty's."

"There's no service bays. It's a big store, or a restaurant. Nothing to do with cars."

"Well, look at all those pumps. You'd never keep up, not and do service work too."

"What if they're self-service?"

"Shorty wouldn't do self-service. How'd he keep up on the gossip?"

"Shorty don't own it now. Philip Fitch and his buddies do, just like everything else. The marina. The ski slope. The Trading Post. The Pizza Den. Look what they've done there."

A tenuous unease built inside Janet, like a fart or a belch that could go either way. "They're busier than ever, now that they're spruced up nice."

"Look who works in them. College kids. Town folks. Slick Willies. You don't see hillbillies nowhere. Not mowing grass on the golf course, or making snow. They'd as soon have someone that looked right than someone that knowed what they were doing."

"You'll see. You'll have a job. If not the one you have now, a better one." Even to her own ears, her optimism sounded punky.

Sid selected a gun from the teepee of blued barrels in the corner—their first big investments after Sid got a decent job—and went outside. Within five minutes, a shotgun's flat bark interrupted her thoughts. "Don't worry, Sid," she said aloud. But she didn't get up to see what he'd shot.

§

Sid groaned when she wiggled in beside him on the couch. His unbuttoned shirt revealed a brick red vee against a pale chest.

"You going to make it?"

"Do I got a choice?"

She stroked his arm, trying to knead strength and confidence through his skin. "Sure you do. If this job is too hard, get another one."

"It's the lifting. Levering sheets of plywood onto the roof, hoisting beams. If it wasn't for that, I could do carpentry good."

"It ain't no sense to cripple yourself."

It must have stunk between the back and the cushion, because he only kept his head buried there for a moment. "I won't flip burgers or scrub floors. I'd ruther break my back clear in two."

"Then just quit." Janet took a deep breath, plunged in. "I'll get a job."

Sid chewed that cud for a while. "All right."

"Till you find something better. At least till then."

When Sid went to bed, he didn't kiss her or meet her eyes. He lay apart, awake until late into the night.

When Janet woke just after six, bacon smoke singed her nose. The kitchen was rank with grease and coffee. Eggs hopped like frog legs in the skillet. Sid tended them at arm's length, away from the spatter.

"Go set down, Sid. I'll finish."

"Maybe she's too hot."

"Go set."

Grease scorched his hand and he jerked away and yielded his space. "Just this one time."

When he'd sat at the swaybacked table, Janet scraped all into the dog can.

"That grub cost good money. Don't squander it on the dog." His teeth were stippled with coffee grounds; the filter collapsed if you didn't load it right.

"I doubt the dog will touch it. If he does, I ain't buying no more dog food. I'll torch a brush pile, feed him ashes." She scooted fresh slices of bacon loose before they could stick to the skillet, spooned hot grease over the eggs to firm up the chicken snot.

"I'll recall how. I used to cook some. Tomorrow it will be perfect." The same cocky tone he'd used the night he'd crawled in the door and climbed the frame to where he could halfway focus on her, and said, "I'm not drunk."

"What you laughing at?" Sid loved for her to do it, but not at him.

"I've been thinking. There won't be no tomorrow."

"If I knowed you was in command of the future, I'd a treated you nicer. Hell, I never even suspected."

"You won't be cooking tomorrow, because I'm not going to work."

"Now hold on here . . ."

"You can't have my job."

"The Bible says you're to be my helpmeat. You vowed to honor and obey and love me. Not break promises before they've even dried good."

Just as the toast popped up, she slipped four eggs and six slices of bacon onto Sid's plate. "I'll cook your meals and clean your house." She'd almost said "trailer," but caught herself in time. "Because I love and respect you enough not to shame you."

Sid interlaced knife and fork and sliced eggs like they were leather. "That's just a womany way to declare that when the bills come due, I'm on my own"

"I *will* get a job, but not till you do. Then I'll help make money and do housework too."

With his toast, Sid wiped egg yelk from contaminating his bacon. He ate one thing at a time, the same way he lived. "That wouldn't be fair to you."

Did she comprehend her own words? Did she mean them? Thoughts so tidy in the night spun away like dishwater down the drain in the light of day. "I'll help just till you don't need me to."

"If there's work in this county that my back can handle, I don't know of it."

Janet forked her single egg onto a slice of unbuttered toast and joined Sid at the table. "It's not your back that concerns me."

"That's because you're not the one has to shower because they can't get up from the tub. Who can't wipe their hind end without hollering out."

"It's your cojones that won't take the strain if I work and you keep house."

Sid's eyes skittered away like lard in a pan, his man-version of a blush, and Janet loved her little prude anew. "Just cause my back give out don't make me less of a man."

She stretched to refill their cups, awkward as she tried to keep her gown from falling open. "A man don't blow the feathers off a Bible-school duck to get over what he sees in the mirror."

"That don't have nothing . . ."

"You listen for a change. If I work out while you do woman stuff at home, you won't be fit to live with. Go find a job you can do, one your back can stand. It don't matter what, or how much it pays. We'll get by."

Sid brooded into his coffee while Janet poured grease into a soup can and stacked dirty dishes. "What's that for?" he said when she wiped out his lunch bucket and began to spread mayonnaise onto eight slices of bread. "I've already quit that job. I told Troy I won't be back."

"I know." Janet layered pickle loaf and Velveeta cheese and green pepper onto the bread. "But what if you find another job before noon? You'll have to eat." She deliberately didn't look his way.

Not until she'd filled his thermos and nestled in the Ho-Hos and dill pickles did he speak. "I told you there wasn't no service bays in that new station. Didn't I say Philip Fitch wouldn't have a job for me?"

"You were right, honey." Janet kissed him and offered the lunch bucket and a hug and a silent prayer that he'd find a job. Quick. Before what had been so clear in the night got any muddier. Already the idea of escaping the trailer, of creating something more than rag rugs and doilies and Bible-school ducks, gnawed away at her common sense. Just like a caterpillar, with ravenous little teeth you couldn't even see. When the old Dodge ground into life, she turned to her blackened pans.

Maybe if they'd had kids. Maybe it was something simple a doctor could fix easy. But she was afraid to ask, to find out that the problem might be with Sid. They both were.

For sure, she'd have to get some new clothes when she went to work.

12

Sɪᴅ ʜᴀᴅɴ'ᴛ ʙᴇᴇɴ ɪɴ ᴀ ғɪɢʜᴛ for at least two months—not one that required stitches. Stitches in Sid, anyway. Sid felt that one coming from the moment Horse opened his mouth, from the way he hunched on his barstool like a toad with the piles.

"Look at this French fry." Horse examined it in the light from the Iron City Beer sign. "Long as my whanger." He fantasized that's why they called him Horse. "How'd you come by such magnacious taters, Larry?"

Larry muted the sound from the CBS evening news. When Pike Baggart said, "Turn it up," Larry glared until Pike shrugged and looked into his long-neck bottle of Bud like there might be alternate programming inside. The lake woman at the end of the bar glanced back and forth between Dan Blather and the butthole who'd killed the sound.

Larry tipped the trashcan from under the bar and shot snuff juice into it. "I growed em. Where you think potatoes come from?" From atop Larry's septic system, such as it was.

Sid pocketed his change and drank his Keystone down to the last swallow; too many beers went to waste when a fight started.

"How'd your garden do, Sid?" Ashes dribbled on Gilpen's apron when she talked, into the food when she cooked. A spare cigarette was stuck under her hair net. "You grow any whopper potatoes?"

If Gilpen was a guy, Sid would bust her. She knew damn well what happened to Sid's potatoes. "Mine didn't turn out."

Pike didn't sense a thing coming, because he lit right into the conversation. Pike never fought, but got the worst of every one. Like the time he'd hid in the bathroom and the rubber machine fell off and broke his glasses when someone slammed against the other side of the wall. "My taters was a flop, too." He licked his lips with a tongue like a run-over snake. "I dug a quart of em the size of peas, then a whole bunch of little ones." He stole a fry from Horse's plate and stuck it in the side of his mouth that had the most teeth. "Umm. How much you take for ten pounds of them taters, Larry?"

"I ain't cutting a tater for nobody. You'll have to buy a whole one."

"Now I remember, Sid." Gilpen wouldn't let it rest. "Your dog tore out your garden."

"It wasn't much to start with." Sid found it hard to believe that he'd gotten drunk enough to tell Gilpen anything at all.

"Sid's dog's chain rusted loose from the trailer," Gilpen said, "and then hung up again on the rotor tiller Sid left in the garden. His dog made a crop circle with no crops around it."

Horse stuck a half-dozen fries into his red mouth, like he was feeding bundled firewood into a furnace. "What is it with you and dogs?" He chewed with his mouth open. Way open. "If it ain't the welfare board, you got a predicament with some dog."

Jukebox lights flashed in Gilpen's eyes. "Dogs feel threatened by Sid."

Sid finished his beer. "I never hurt a dog in my life."

"They aren't scared you'll hurt them." Gilpen couldn't hold her laugh. "They're afraid you'll take their place, and they'll have to move up. Get a job and stuff."

Larry was digging in the cooler, getting Sid another Keystone, and Sid couldn't walk away. He rolled his head, loosening up.

"They wouldn't need a job to take Sid's place," Horse said. "But a dog couldn't tolerate lazing around like Sid does. They have to scratch now and again, or take a poop." He didn't look up from his paper plate, but his eyes slanted Sid's way.

"I work." Pain sliced through Sid's back. "I don't draw a paycheck, but I work hard."

Horse lifted his feet to show how deep the manure was getting. Sid would have busted him right then, but the lake woman was coming down to talk, like tourons always did when they came out slumming. Make hillbilly friends to laugh about when they went home. "Hello, fellows." Close up, her face was fifteen years older. Bad skin underneath high-dollar makeup. A smile that indicated absolutely nothing. "I'm Debbie." She shook Pike's hand.

"Pike. That's my name."

"They call me Horse." He turned toward her, but not so far as to lose track of Sid.

Fresh beer icicled down Sid's throat.

"Why do they call you that?" She elevated one eyebrow in a manner that suggested she already knew.

"Because he's dumb enough to eat hay, and he shits himself a-walking." Sid dodged the first punch that whistled his way before the words were even out, and slipped his fist through to clatter off Horse's head. The cut-off cue stick rattled as Larry fumbled for it beneath the bar, but Sid stayed fixed on Horse's crooked nose. The cue stick was coming, he could feel it, but he hit Horse twice more, hard enough to slide the nose almost back where it belonged. Pike fell over a stool getting out of the way, but the lake woman held her ground, still smiling. Sid wished he could take a poke at her, too.

His last thought before the lights switched off was that Horse was stupid enough to think they were fighting about potatoes. The explosion of pain and light was almost welcome.

§

"I am not a damn doctor," Larry said. He oozed sweat and tobacco.

Sid's crossed eyes followed the trembling thread upward. "No, but you're right smart of a seamstress." He grinned at Horse, on a stool by the deep fryer with a bag of ice sheltering his nose. They were friends again since blood had been spilt. "It's your rule: you break it, you fix it."

"That ain't applicable to heads."

"Just hush up and sew." Sid grimaced but didn't flinch when the thread dragged through meat like a strand of rusty barbed wire.

"At least let me shave off some hair so I don't sew it into your head." Larry wasn't hesitant to use his cue stick, but he was squeamish when it brought blood.

"No, I can't tolerate baldness. That hair's going where it come from, just like plowing under a cover crop." He shook his empty beer can. "Nurse," he bellowed. "I need a IV here."

"Hold it down," Gilpen said from the far side of the curtain, tending bar while Larry played surgeon. "You already chased off half the customers."

Nobody had left but Pike, limping because of shins banged on a stool. Gilpen ducked through with another beer, and stopped to check Larry's stitching.

Sid felt of his ribs. "You kicked me while I was down, Horse."

"I never either."

Gilpen laughed. "He fell on you. He's so slow, he can be the first one down and still fall on top of the pile."

Scissors snicked, and the needle bit again. "Horse," Larry said, "you step out front. I need to talk to Sid."

"I never started it," Sid said. Being barred from Rooster's had a tendency to become permanent. "Horse swung on me."

"We got to discuss your bar tab," Larry said after the curtain closed behind Horse.

"Our deal works for me. But if you don't want to haul me to the store anymore, I can walk." It would be a hard walk, with bags of ketchup. Mayonnaise. Pickled eggs. Maybe he could catch a ride with someone else. "Make your list, and I'll go fetch it."

"The state's cracking down all over. I can't let you use food stamps to pay me anymore. And it bothers me that you got a wife needs to eat."

"She eats good. You think store-boughten cheeseburgers are better than venison steaks?" Before Sid sold the rifle there had been venison, at least. "Maybe we ought to give up fresh-killed trout, *purchase* some breaded fish sticks." He still owned a fish pole, but the line was rotten.

"It's going to be cash, here on out."

"Then I'll just take my business where it's appreciated."

"Do what you got to. Don't let the door hit you in the ass."

"How many more of them stitches you got?"

"Three. Maybe four. It's got to be sewed real fine to keep your brain from falling out."

"Well, get it done. I got to go. And don't worry about your door, nor my ass either. The two shall not come into contact." The kitchen was quiet, save for the exhaust fan and the freezer compressor and the grease-encrusted radio that played Merle Haggard and Buck Owens night and day and the rasp of thread and the snick of scissors. And Larry's whistling, like he was having one fine day.

§

Janet tossed bobbed brown hair like a schoolgirl, but she wasn't too schoolgirlish around the eyes. "What did the other guy look like? Or did you just beat him in the fist with your head?"

"You ever consider maybe it was a girl this time?"

Janet's eyes slid out of focus while she worried at what he'd said. She'd been in the depression pills again. "You wouldn't smack any girl but me."

"Well, you're wrong. I made a pass at this Debbie, a lake woman. Legs up to her collar, big blinkers. She did foo-young or something on me. Before I even seen her move, I was on the floor. First thing I knowed, I didn't know nothing, and half of that was knocked out of me. Never got in a single lick."

Janet's laugh was time-delayed. "Your knuckles are barked. And you're scared of girls."

Disgusted was the look Sid tried for, but he felt heat in his face. Women were worse than dogs; there was no way to fight back with them. "You go on thinking that. It'll make it easier to get away with it when I pick up a little strange."

She laughed dreamy, empty-headed. "You ain't keeping up with the woman you got."

Sid went to the bathroom to examine the fresh damage among the old. While he tried to figure out how to break the news that they were leaving that godforsaken place, he ran his tongue along the gumline to loosen threads of blood collected there. It was time to go. Go where there were jobs that didn't hurt your back, that paid more than it cost to live. Where dogs and women didn't run loose, snatching and yapping at everything that moved. Where it didn't snow in May, then mold clear over in June. Where you could find better friends than Horse and Larry and Pike. Where everybody didn't know you, and didn't care to. Where you didn't have to plant no damn taters for the dogs to rip out. Buy them at the supermarket, with that big check from a good job.

Sid cleared his throat and examined his teeth one last time. "Janet," he said. "I got something to say, and I don't want to hear no argument."

13

JANET LAMMED SID IN THE MOUTH with a flowerpot, and then she bawled hard little tears that sprinkled her bare feet like it was raining BBs. It was her last flowerpot, and she'd never know what had finally humped the soil and threatened to break free and grow, and the ivory pieces scattered among the terra cotta meant that the money they might have used to get wheels again would go to the dentist instead. Or the doctor. She'd got him good.

She'd dislodged more than teeth; Sid's determination drained away when the crockery landed in his pie hole. Or maybe he sensed the difference in these tears and those that fell at Janet's time of the month or when her lotto ticket struck out, and felt sorry for her. Whatever the reason, he comforted her, though he blotted his lips in her hair while he massaged her spine, but she couldn't really hold that against him. His long fingers touched each vertebra as though he were tuning her, high notes to low, except for where the missing finger should have hit. As reckless with a chopsaw as he was with words.

When he ran out of keys he picked her up by the cheeks and snugged her into him and carried her to the bedroom. Her heel hit the dryer's doorhandle as he wedged her back the narrow hall, and it thunked onto the swelled particleboard floor like someone had dropped a tangerine, and she wished she had a tangerine. The dryer was broke too, along with her last flowerpot and Sid's straight pretty teeth, and she'd have to go to the laundromat. She didn't have a thing fit to carry clothes in, and she wasn't going to walk along the road carrying Sid's undershorts.

Then they made love. Sweet love, where she nibbled the ruptured lips and felt the broken tooth stubs with her tongue and sampled his blood as if he were a honeysuckle and she a bee, and fun love, where the trailer rocked until she heard Sidemore's chain rattle out from underneath the bedroom. He'd sit outside slumped and dejected until they settled down, then he'd rattle back in.

Sid sat on the edge of the bed and cried too, though he didn't shed tears or let on. "You can't get away with that." He didn't sound like Sid with his mouth rearranged.

"Will you look at the dryer before you leave? Something fell off."

"Set up," he said. "You can't be beating on me. It's got to halt." She obeyed, and he hit her in the side of the head, careful as always that his fist landed above the hairline where it wouldn't screw up the week with paperwork if some busybody happened to notice. Her cheeks flapped and a harl of snot strung from her nose, unraveling from inside her head, and then it slipped loose and was gone, and she wondered if she'd made loops and fancy twirls like the bulls on *Professional Bull Riding* did, and knew that she'd forgot to try.

That's what fascinated her, that snot, back when they had a TV. Not whether the bullrider was laying on the spurs with his outside leg, or if his free hand touched, or if the eight-second clock run out before he plowed into the manure and got to throw a fifty-dollar hat away if the bull hadn't stepped on it until it wouldn't fly, and after you seen his bare head maybe the hat would fit better if the bull did step on it. Janet watched those shiny ropes of snot that curlicued from the bull, and she imagined the bull watching them too, crosseyed and artistic, moving his head loose and casual but just so, and the man on his back was there to encourage him and give him cause to do his best. Bodacious had been her favorite. He'd jump higher than a man's head standing up, and then write longhand in snot all the way down. Like Chinese, top to bottom instead of left to right. But Bodacious was hard on the help, and they laid him off.

Except Janet wasn't sure the good stuff—the tangerine and the honeybee and the waiting dog—had happened. Maybe Sid had just smacked her and she'd hit the dryer door on the way down. Since she'd started taking one pill for depression and then another when she got too un-depressed, things were hard to pin down right, like butterflies she'd tried to put in her collection that weren't clear dead, and earlier that day she'd been way too un-depressed. She settled on the other way, the first one.

She was in the bed, after all, and naked. She was positive she'd got up that morning, and put clothes on. The pills didn't make her that far gone.

While Sid worked on the dryer door, Janet screwed the bulb into the bedside light and read in the *Readers' Digest* book section about a woman who lived with gorillas until they became her folks. Janet shivered without meaning to, then tried to and couldn't. She closed one eye to single her vision. The big black stud gorilla, arm around the woman like he'd won her at a turkey shoot, didn't take long to look at. Gorillas were all the same.

But the woman wasn't. Skinny, not enough tit for a cat, half-starved looking. She probly couldn't find a man that would hug her. Gorillas must be like lawyers: do anything for a nanner.

Sid's rattling at the dryer door ceased. By the soft crunches, like when you step on a bird that's knocked itself out against the glass, Janet could tell the door had rusted to where it wouldn't hold a screw.

"The duct tape's under the sink, behind the dog can."

Sid's footsteps firmed where the floor did, and when he returned she knew she'd remembered right. Lately her memory had been wormy. But if she didn't hide the tape in a new place each time, it would be gone when she needed it.

Tape peeled from the roll just like a deer hide coming loose from the meat. Janet swallowed twice, and still had a mouthful of saliva. Sid didn't whittle a hide off an inch at a time; instead he put a rock in the hide and tied a rope around the knot and yanked the skin off with his pickup. How she loved that tenderloin. Not the backstrap, but the sweet little strips up inside that her and Sid ate raw while he cut up the meat. Would summer grass have the laurel worked out of the deer yet, so they'd be fit to eat? Would a riding mower jerk off a hide, did they have one? They had a push mower, but it was missing a wheel. Or something. Sid sold the deer rifle, too, to the same man that took the TV. And without teeth he wouldn't be able to chew meat, so he wouldn't be in any hurry to get another gun. A tear landed on the gorilla's nose.

The gorilla woman's straight gray hair appeared to have been cut with a steak knife. A face like a splitting maul without looking as mean as one. Gray eyes, gray all over, even her red-looking blouse felt gray. Not sink-drain gray, but kingsnake gray.

And depending on which eye Janet used so the woman wouldn't have four, the woman's eyes looked different. Protean. Janet flipped to the "It Pays to Increase Your Word Power" page to make sure she'd thought it with the right enunciation. Had knowing that word predisposed Janet to apprehend the woman's eyes in a particular manner—had she extrapolated some unassailable meaning from an ephemeral implication? She checked again to make sure she'd got them all right.

Sid spoke from the kitchen, but the ear he'd beat on was still ringing. She thought he'd left after he taped the handle back on. At least some of the pill's confusion had slopped out when he whacked her. "Yeah, Babe." She went naked to sit with him at the table. He didn't look bad, considering, and she couldn't help but love him.

Sid couldn't get words going. No wonder, since she'd rammed him with a flowerpot the last time he'd attempted it. He didn't have to say it. She knew what he wanted again: to tear down the mountain.

He surprised her. "You know how old I am, Janet?"

She raised her eyebrows, waited.

"I'm asking. I'm not sure anymore."

Janet realized she'd forgot his birthday, and felt terrible because maybe that's all he'd been going to say when she'd busted the pot. "Twenty-nine?" Sid didn't look twenty-nine, not his face and hands or the missing finger or empty mouth that looked a hundred and twenty-nine, or his body that looked nineteen, long hard ropes of muscle stretched tight across a big-boned frame. 'Cept for his little potbelly.

Sid nodded. "I was thinking along them lines."

He said nothing more, but sat solemn and puckered till Janet squirmed on her chair and made that duct-tape sound, and she hoped she hadn't pulled any finish loose. Hers or the chair's.

"About what I figgered. We been here a long time," Sid said, and left.

He would return stinking of beer, which Janet could drink with squirrel gravy but not with shortcake, but she tried to believe that he didn't really drink. She'd snuck down to Rooster's Bar one night and looked in the window, and he wasn't there. When she went inside and asked, folks looked sheepish, and she knew he hadn't been there at all. Then at midweek prayer meeting, kneeling in the pew not really praying but just getting un-depressed with her head on the rough brown cushions that they'd added to the oak seats when folks complained about the long sermons, she'd caught Sid's unique smell. She'd know it any-where, cause she smelled it in their own bed, and on the couch, and anywhere he sat for long.

She'd pieced it all together then, how Sid laid on the church pews in the dark, dreaming about tearing down the mountain. The first time he'd said it, she thought he'd meant dip the top off the mountain and dump it in the holler, like the coal companies did. "If flat ground's that momentous to you," she said, "it'd be simpler to just move down off here." The word didn't fit quite right, like jeans the proper size but the wrong brand, but if you didn't put them into use, there wasn't no reason to learn them.

"That's exactly what I just suggested we do."

Then Janet understood he'd meant tear down *off* of the mountain, not tear the mountain down, and it saddened her that Sid didn't have a better grasp on language. Sad too that he wanted to leave just because there were no jobs or even a hope of one there, and because they'd lost the truck, and because the dryer had rusted up and was falling through the floor.

Sid believed the things he didn't have would make him euphoric. But he failed to consider that moving would cost them their friends: Horse and Larry, and Pike, and Pike's woman, what was her name? Sally, or something just as dumb.

She shouldn't have laughed at something Sid took so serious.

Serious or not, there'd be no tearing down the mountain while she had any say in it. She was born there, not like Sid, and to do what he wanted, to hurry the hell down off of there, would knock the top off *her* mountain and bury her in the valley.

Sid was a hypocrite in reverse, pretending to drink but really laying on the quiet, peaceful church pews conceptualizing that he wasn't on the mountain no more, then gargling with Keystone Light before he come home—the beer he thought Janet didn't know about, hid in a holler stump just beyond the yard—so Janet would think he was having nice clean alcohol fun, wouldn't suspect him of anything sinister like thinking about moving away. Sid always tried to act worse than he was, but he got confused about what worse was.

Her heart went out to poor old Sid.

Poor old Sid had made one hell of a mess before he left, she realized when she rediscovered the dirt and broken pottery in the living room. Too dumb to duck. That's what women were for, to clean up after men's mistakes.

Janet located the Super Glue in the peanut butter jar and licked it clean, and realized she'd have to find a new hiding place since Sid didn't have teeth to get gummed up. She sat on the dog food bag they used for a beanbag chair, but the

paper stuck to her bare butt, so she slid onto the green shag carpet and worked
at restoring her only flowerpot. She sat aside tooth pieces in case Sid would want
to fasten them back in. He was a genius with the Bondo.

Sometime during the reconstruction the pot became attached to her left
hand, and she delighted in the possibility of pretending to hurl it at Sid again, but
it would stay in her hand instead of knocking out his gums. She'd bet a dollar he
still wouldn't duck.

Janet raked the dirt into a pile between her legs, sifting it for missing shards,
and among the pottery and teeth she discovered a seed, larger than she'd imagined,
the size of a hominy, with a long white sprout that wrapped around it, like a
slinking dog's tail, before it set off in search of water and food. She stared open-
mouthed for a while, unable to shake the notion that it had fallen from inside
her. There on top of the dirt pile, the sprout filled her with a longing so quick
and intense that she bawled, a long mournful howl that Sidemore answered,
and like their baying had called Sid to come, she heard him scraping his feet on
the stoop. So he hadn't gone to church at all, and she was aggravated at his
attempt to fool her.

The last piece of the pot fell into place just as the door opened. Sid sat on the
dog food, funny looking with his puffed-out purpled mouth, and she didn't have
the heart to scare him with the flowerpot. "Look." She shook her hand palm down
to show that the flowerpot wasn't going anywhere, and had the sudden irrational
fear that she'd never be rid of it.

Sid looked as though he'd say something, but he couldn't get it going for a
spell. "You got it all back together." Not sounding too happy, maybe because of
the teeth. Strange how something laying on the floor could affect the way you
talked.

"If you're wanting to insinuate the notion of tearing the mountain down
into the progression of our discourse, now would be the time," she said, and
shook the pot again to show him just how safe it was for him to feel safe.

Sid shook his head, and she knew she'd got it wrong. "Tear down *off* the
mountain," she said, feeling as stupid as she ever had. There wasn't any right
way to remember it but his way, but she wasn't going to. Not then. Not never.

14

When Janet confronted him with the sneaking-off-to-lay-in-the-church thing, not five minutes after he'd returned from the dentist, Sid looked more poleaxed than when she'd lammed him with the flowerpot. "You got to get off them pills. They're making you goofy. I wouldn't go in that church if they was passing out free hams, and homemade bread with cow butter. I'd set outside and eat acorns." He pronounced it A-kerns the way he'd learned it as a kid among Logan County hillbillies. And he wouldn't change. Wouldn't learn.

"Don't lie to me. I smelled you there. And I checked at Rooster's, and you weren't there. It's nothing to be embarrassed of." Her eyes had wet theirselves, made him look old and blurry. His cheeks, dead from the dentist's numbing, collapsed into his crowded toothless face.

His hand against her forehead was callused, though he hadn't worked for six weeks or more, since he sprung his back again. "You aren't running a temperature. You been grazing on jimson?" Blooded gums showed in his grin when she slapped his hand away, but he backed his chair away where she couldn't reach him.

"Is that what you think I am, a old cow?"

"A pretty one, if you are." His soft voice sucked the fire out of her. She hated when he did that.

"I smelled you in the pew cushions. Smelled your essence."

Sid's workboot patted the linoleum, and he watched it with curiosity, like he was wondering what tune it heard that he couldn't. "You know what you need, Janet?" Before she could say a car or a new dryer or a venison roast, he answered for her. "You need to look elsewhere for good things. You won't find any in me."

"You were there. In that church."

"When you came to Rooster's, I'd went with Larry to cash food stamps to pay my bar tab. And you smelt essence of shit in the cushions, not essence of Sid."

As clear as spring water, Janet knew that she'd wanted him to be there so bad that she'd clamped onto whatever could make it be true. She'd known she was smelling everyday farts. Ubiquitous farts. Homogeneous farts. "Well, maybe those essences are the same thing."

"That's exactly what I just said."

Putting him down made her feel worse than when she'd busted his teeth out. Sid was a good man; he just didn't know it yet. That and a couple million other things. "I didn't mean you was bad. I just wish you'd go with me once in a while."

"I haven't set foot in that church since we got married, and I won't start now." Any softness was gone, his voice like new barbed wire strung on peeled locust posts.

"They're good people. They never did you any harm."

"They're probably the finest folks in the world. But I'm not one of them. They're like Puritans; if you're not a chose one, you're not good for nothing." His mouth drooped, sadness hung to dry on a clothesline. "And I haven't been chose."

Janet was sorry she'd brought the subject up; how did you get it down again? "You don't have any perception of Puritan life." Her finger twisted at brown hair that had lost its shine from being inside all the time. She made it quit.

Instead of turning the conversation, she'd stirred his dander. "Just because you took to learning big words, it don't make me any more ignorant. I say what I need with the words I got. You don't need nine words for every little cat's ass of a thing."

"How many synonyms you have for poop? Or booze, or nooky?"

"I know why you go to that church, even when you can't teach Sunday school or be on a committee because you don't talk in tongues. You go because they make you feel lower than frog droppings, and then you figger you've made payment on your sins."

Janet wasn't going to think that, even if it was true. "Then let's go to another church, since you hate ours."

"Those other churches don't have the religion of a coal hod. I see Piscopalians at Rooster's all the time. Baptists come one one night and one another so they don't catch each other."

"Alternate nights."

"Hellfire and damnation." His jaws flapped like a deflated inner tube when he shook his head.

"Pentecostals are too good for us, and the other churches ain't fit."

"That's what I just said." He acted like she was the one that didn't know anything. "Roddy said one time that church was people, not a place. And I asked what did they do, carve God up and take him home so that He was only there when they all come together?"

"That's just plain ridiculous."

"I come to realize we was both right. When they chopped Him up, they give me the bunghole. Long as I stay away, they got the God they talk about: the One with the little lambs and the still waters and whatnot. But when I show up, He's got a touch of nasty to him. Like when He fried up all them Israelites cause one of them didn't bury their poop and He tromped in it early of a morning. Those folks like God a lot better when I'm not around."

"That's blasphemy. Sacrilege."

"It's not meant to be. It's just how I honest feel. And I don't figure I'd do better to lie about it. That don't get you a front seat by the throne neither."

§

"I been thinking." Sid's finger worked down the thin newspaper's half-column of employment ads.

"I'm glad you been doing *something* for the last month." Sid's mad faded quick, but Janet's frothed for a while. She jammed her fingers under her arms where they wouldn't pester at her hair. They found the soft knots in her armpits. Lymph nodes. "I was thinking to check your pulse."

Sid scratched a scar on the back of his hand. "What you need is a job."

Here they went again. "What I need is . . ." She didn't know where to start.

"A good job. Not waitressing or cleaning like you tried. Listen." He read in single syllables, without inflection: sound-beads on a string. "The Union County Health Department Home Health Agency is currently accepting positions for a Human Services Aide. Must possess Geriatric Aid Training, a Certified Nursing Assistant License, a valid driver's license, and provide own transportation."

"One for four ain't bad."

He looked puzzled for a moment. "Aw. You still got a driver's license."

"I'd have to steal a car to get it revoked."

"Or this one. Help Wanted—Customer-oriented office manager. Must be familiar with office machines and procedures. Must have . . ."

"Sid." He flinched. "I don't have those things. I don't know that stuff."

"You're smart, Janet. You can learn it."

"Don't read off jobs for me. Find one you can handle." But the spores of nursing or bossing had blown in her ear and taken root.

"Carpenters." The paper tore when he stabbed it too hard. "Loggers. Delivery men. That's the only kind of work there is for me."

Until the refrigerator rattled to a halt, Janet hadn't noticed its whine. Sid stared too, and Janet knew he was asking the same question: Had it ever quit running before? Janet determined that she wouldn't be the one to check if it was getting warm inside.

Sid rested his forehead in his palms and plowed long fingers through thinning blond hair. "My back's no better. Unless we move where there's jobs I can do, it's up to you. Or we can set here and starve." His eyelids hung red and watershot like an old hound's. "You could go to college, learn that stuff."

"I can't afford college. Not even our little pee-ant community one."

"You could get a scholarship, I bet. You got a diploma, and your grades was good."

Janet's fingers were busy again, squiggling on the tabletop. "I can't go to school and pay the bills and keep house too. I won't do it."

A crooked-looking tongue wet Sid's lips. Had it always been like that, or had she bent it with the flowerpot? "If you can learn college, I can learn to cook. I done it when I lived with Roddy. And I could run the sweeper."

"We don't have a sweeper."

"Whatever it is that women does. Up to a point. I'll get odd jobs when I'm able. Keep a little cash flowing."

"You'll drink it up."

The desk she pictured was always too small—a child's desk, part of a little chair—but not uncomfortable; it made her feel super growed up. The professor was old and grouchy with dead-possum breath, and kept her after class to chastise her for struggling so. She couldn't put a face to the other students.

"Didn't I quit smoking when cigarettes got too high? You chuck them pills down the terlet, I'll lay off the booze, except for parties and whatnot. Special occasions."

She saw thick books with tiny writing sprawled across the kitchen table, watched herself glance at the clock. It always said 2AM. She sighed, returned to her text.

"If we're going to live here," Sid was saying, "we got to find a way to get it done."

"I'll think about it."

"Will you?" Life stirred in dormant eyes. "For sure?"

"I said I would." After a while she went into the bathroom and rattled pills in one of the brown containers and let several splash into the commode and then flushed it. While it was gurgling she emptied the two vials into the folds of a towel. When she tossed the empties to Sid, he let them bounce off his chest and roll across the cracked linoleum.

He looked too old and hopeful and innocent for his own good. "This here's the first day of the rest of our life. You ever hear anybody say that before?"

"No." Not precisely like that.

"I made it up, I think." He came and hugged her, and she momentarily felt lightened of the past and happy with the future, and hugged him in return. "Don't never look back," he said. "Something might be about to grab you."

She touched his bruised lips hard enough to make him flinch. "All right, Sid Lore, let's go lam-on into tomorrow. We'll leave the past where it is. It'll be like getting saved. We'll get born again again."

He frowned at the comparison, but nodded. "That's what I just said."

That night, though, just before the last little slide into sleep, the void that had brought them together hove up into her thoughts and crowded sleep away. Sid's unshuttered eyes glittered in the moonlight, and she knew he was giving the past a good harrowing, too. Maybe that was the way to get shed of it. Cultivate it, like weeds.

15

"You sleep?" Janet's eyes puffed like Sid had whacked her on both sides. Other than that, she looked tempting, but Sid knew not to fool with her in the morning unless she hinted she was in the mood. She hadn't.

"There's something you ourta learn about sleeping."

"You got to hold still to do it. You told me that before."

"Well," he said.

"What was you thinking about all night?"

She rolled toward him, and he eased back so she wouldn't bump his piss boner and think he was wanting her bad. Then he'd never get none. "Just stuff."

"If I was to go to college, what would I study?" Janet's breath smelled full of canned peaches. "Where would I sign up? Who do you talk to? Could I still get in for fall classes?"

Sid crabbed to the bathroom with his back to her. "Go to the school and ask," he said when the pressure subsided. He rested his hand in the worn place on the wall. "Go find someone. Janitor or the president, it don't matter. They'll tell you where to go." He brushed his gums, careful of the tender spots where the dentist had rooted out the broken stumps.

Janet's eyes were closed when he returned. He sat on the edge of the bed and pulled on his socks, squigging his toes to get the seam crostways where it wouldn't worry a blister. Her hand was cold on his back, and he jumped. "What did you really think about all night?" she said.

The morning felt heavier than Sid could hold up. He knew better than to say, but the questions had been pent up all night, and one jumped out before he could pinch it off. "How do you clean a carpet if you don't have a sweeper?"

Janet laughed and pulled him down against her, breath rasping in his ear.

Sid tried, but he couldn't keep from thinking about having to wash the sheets afterward. Janet was plumb wild, like she thought she was a daggone cheerleader. Or a linebacker. But he got the job done, like always. And she never did tell him how to clean the carpet. Ol' Sid would have to get that job done on his own.

§

"Ummm," she said without looking up from her schoolbooks when Sid asked how she liked supper. When she tried to cut it, her sausage broke in two. "What did you do to it?"

"Broiled it. S'posed to be better for you." He spoke around a chunk he'd been testing with tender gums.

"Maybe cut the cook time back a smidgen." Black specs in her teeth when she grinned. Like she'd been eating coal. "Maybe a hour or two. But the beans is good." Since she'd flushed the pills, her eyes twinkled again.

Sid glanced toward the kitchen counter, but the can was turned so he couldn't read it all. "Big Northern beans. Like soup beans, but fatter."

She'd returned to her books, turning the pages too fast for reading, but there weren't any pictures. "What's that book?"

"Comp 101."

"What's that?"

"It's to teach you how to write good. This one book by itself cost $37, used. I'm glad we don't got to pay for them."

"Why are you reading, if you're wanting to learn to write?"

"That's the way you do it. This book is Psych 101—that's psychology—and here's Math 95. Our Phys Ed book ain't come yet, and Art don't take one."

Sid tried to read some of the words upside down, but the print was small and split down the middle like a Bible.

"I done good on my placement tests, 'specially English. My vocabulary was exceptional. I got to do a catch-up in math, though, since I never took geometry or trig."

"I don't even know what them things is for sure. Why aren't you taking nurse classes, or computer ones? Phys Ed and Art won't get you no job."

"Education is a comprehensive undertaking." Janet stared into space as though at an audience. "Learning incorporates not only mental stimulus, but also emotional and physical well-being."

"Hell's bells." Sid could conjure nothing to follow. Her whistling while he did the dishes worked at him like a skinning knife. When he scraped the skillet, he left gouges.

§

The leftover sausage patties were so hard Sidemore couldn't gulp them down without gnawing them to swallowing size first. His tail, too long and skinny for the rest of him, warped against the frozen ground, and Sid wondered if it hurt. Sid arrested the end of the tail, but the base labored on like it was run by a windshield wiper motor. "You going to get smart, too? Get so I can't talk to you?"

The dog moved to the end of his chain and resumed his chewing. When his tail wagged, his little anus looked like it was blowing kisses.

Sid's back lurched as he fished the last can of beer from the hollow stump. He groaned and massaged his spine. All afternoon he'd stacked brush away from Hube Smouse's fenceline, and he was just about done in. The beer was flat from being frosted at night and sun-stroked all day. They needed drunk faster, but then he wouldn't have any. He listened hard toward Rooster's for a trace of the jukebox or an old pickup starting, but all he could hear was Sidemore tormenting the sausage. What had Janet called it? Defecated? Desecrated? Desiccated, maybe. Sid drained the beer and flattened the can and sailed it into the woods. After one last look toward Rooster's, he went inside.

Janet was asleep with her head in her books, not yet eight o'clock.

Sid sat across the table and watched her, as if through close attention he could grasp what she was learning. Plumb wore out, she was, from walking down to the highway to catch the People Movers bus. From gnawing her pencil while she agonized over big words in bigger books. Sid held the pencil to his nose, and the hot tacky smell tore loose a remembrance of school: stiff jeans, mucilage fingers, confusion. Standing at the blackboard not knowing what to expect, what was expected. Not even knowing what he'd missed, off with the hives.

He opened her smallest book—*Harbrace College Handbook*—and read a few sentences, his lips shaping the words:

Sometimes, a semicolon (instead of the usual comma) precedes a coordinating conjunction when the writer wishes to make a sharp division between the two main clauses.

The female bees feed these lazy drones for a while; but they let them starve to death after the mating of the queen bee.

"I can't believe she's learning that kind of crap." He leafed forward and read again.

Use the semicolon between two main clauses not linked by a coordinating conjunction.

Small mammals tick fast, burn rapidly, and live for a short time; large mammals live long at a stately pace.
—STEPHEN JAY GOULD

He shut the book harder than he intended, then froze until Janet settled and breathed steadily again. She seemed no bigger than a squirrel when he gathered her in his arms and eased her onto the couch. A slow pulse burrowed in her pale neck, and he touched it lightly with his finger, felt the blood creeping just under the skin. When she was covered and tucked, he unscrewed the bulb and went to bed. He lay awake for a long time, too tired, too sore for sleep. A barred owl eight-hooted in the hollow below the trailer, and a faraway hound answered with a single condensed echo. Sidemore's chain rattled beneath the bedroom. Sid wedged Janet's pillow under his throbbing back and rolled over to face the wall like he'd done as a kid, when staring out into the universe got him to feeling so little he couldn't stand it.

16

When Sid got his head gathered up he heard the snowplow, and he knew what had woke him. The big blade's steel grumbled against uneven macadam, and for a moment it was January again and his sap was jelled and frozen, and he sorely missed his teeth. Then he shifted in the bed, where he and Janet rooched back-to-back in the hollowed mattress, and the strength of April's sunshine reached through the hand-knotted quilt.

Sid especially missed his teeth in the mornings, even more than his job or his truck. More than the deer rifle he'd sold to pay the electric bill. Five months after they'd been cracked out, he still expected them to be there. Overnight, his hide relaxed until he had enough to cover three jawbones. When he yawned, his puckered mouth barely opened, a reluctant anus.

He stood to look out, shivered one hard tremelation near the leaky jalousie panes. Sid's movement hadn't escaped Sidemore; the dog oozed from under the trailer and looked over his shoulder, nonchalant but hopeful. Like somebody checking a lottery ticket. His chain undercut and rearranged his tracks in four inches of wet snow.

Maybe winter finally had that out of its system.

"What's it doing out?" Janet's voice was full of dirty dreams and night matter.

"The snow's quit." The voice not his own from his baldheaded pie hole. He turned from the window with the feeling that if he watched, the snow wouldn't melt. It would lay there till Memorial Day getting filthier and sadder, unless he looked away.

Janet was easy to look at in the morning, soft and guileless, armor not yet up, guns unprimered, eyes like a feather pillow. She patted the space beside her. Sid pretended not to notice, but slid into cold jeans and socks as baggy and inelastic as his face. Her hand warmed and softened his back.

Had the weather been nice like it should be in April, or had he been twenty years old instead of thirty, he'd take her up on it. But when she said he was like a turkey gobbler, horny only two weeks in the spring, she didn't miss the mark by far. He wondered how quick and high and often her sap would rise had it happened the other way, had he knocked her teeth out.

Women could denut a man quicker than a vet could a bullcalf, then pine for the swole-necked stud they thought they'd married. And if the women took a day off from castrating, life in general would fill in.

Maybe he'd jump her bones the next morning, if nothing went haywire that day. Just in case the deal fell through, he hadn't told Janet he'd been dickering on a truck. The snow meant Sid wouldn't be getting paid for raking the lake-house yard he'd been laboring at for two days—a job he would have finished that morning, but for the snow. Even Knobby wouldn't hold up the deal for one day. Sid's word was the same as cash, more than Knobby Jerden could say.

Sid brushed his gums hard, like maybe teeth would sprout anew if he raked them good. While Janet took her turn in the bathroom, he spooned Sam's Choice coffee into a plastic glass, then filled it with warm tap water, stirred it with a fork, and swallowed it down in one long pull.

As he went out the door, Janet hollered out the stuff that needed done while she was at school. He never let on that he heard; the thought of doing the laundry gave him the hives, and since she didn't have to wash them, Janet shed dirty clothes like dandruff.

Out of sight of the trailer, he paused to lace long leather shoestrings and button his flannel shirt, then he set off for Knobby's place just down the road. The tang of a waterlogged septic system flavored the air, one more promise of spring. A warm spell before the snow had popped the sarvis blossoms. A mayflower thrust unfolded from a snowed-under mound like a little green man was sleeping there, and had woke with a hard-on. Steam curled where the plow had skinned the blacktop.

Sid loosened the top button of his shirt before he reached Knobby Jerden's junk-bright cancerous house. The mother tumor was scabbed with Insulbrick, and each new growth followed the landscape and the progress of the home-building industry: tarpaper, corrugated steel, aluminum siding. If Sid hated anything worse than a trailer, it was Knobby Jerden's house. Trailers tried to be livable; that place didn't even attempt it.

Junk continued where the house left off. There was a blaze of teal in the white, further over red or rust, hard to tell with colors uncoupled from shapes by the snow. Sid yelled a howdy, then waited for Knobby to call off the dog. While he waited, he rebuttoned his collar.

Slobber looped like jewelry from the dog's wrinkled face. The beast was some unholy mix of Doberman and bulldog, with devil thrown in. Sid wondered if it would still look as mean if it lost its teeth, and decided it would. It moved closer, stiff-legged and front-heavy, and Sid caught a smell like an old-folks' home afire. The dog tremored but didn't bark, silence more threatening than bared teeth.

One section of the house moved a few seconds before a plywood-paneled storm door flapped open. "Lucy," Knobby snarled, "git back unner the house." Lucy stilted backwards a few steps, then squirted bloody-looking drops at a rusted bed frame before retreating to one of the house's dozen corners where he sat and licked his balls.

"Hows come you call him Lucy?"

Knobby was as squat and mongrel and mean as the dog, but soft. "Cause that's his fucking name. You want the truck?"

Sid considered the vomit-colored lump of decrepitude that had once been a pickup. The FARM USE painted on the side was faded except where the paint had run. "Like to look at it again, anyhow. Will it start?" He imaged it fixed up, himself at the wheel. As the vehicles he could afford slid down the scale, they became more alluring.

"You think I'd sell something that wouldn't start?" With a snow ski from which the bottom surface was peeling away like a bad toenail, Knobby swiped snow from the hood.

Inside was the stink of mouse and burned grease and gray foam swelling from the ruptured seat. Where the speedometer should have been, a black hole fell beyond the vehicle's dimensions, hard to look away from. The bench seat, he found when he shifted to adjust the mirror, latched only on the passenger side. The way the mirror had cracked, you could see anywhere you wanted. "This is a Ford, right?"

"The parts that count is." Knobby's laugh was as breathless and startled as if he'd inhaled dandelion fluff while blowing up an air mattress.

Sid examined the starting mechanism—a dangling house light switch and a chrome pushbutton epoxied to the dash.

"Pump her a time or two," Knobby said, then sidearmed the snow ski toward the house and stepped further back than seemed necessary. Sid pulled the door into an approximation of shut. The side window spasmed down, dropping six inches every second turn of the knobless crank; he didn't try it the other way.

Leaves rattled from the defroster slits when Sid flipped the dangling switch. He pumped the gas pedal, thumbed the chrome button. The truck's skeleton shuddered and the engine turned rowWWWww rowWWWww and it hiccupped greasily and was running, choking on its own smoke, smelling its own farts, breathing easier and relaxing the clatter of push rods as age-blackened oil explored the engine's dark hidden warren. Some small animal flitted from under the dash and momentarily shuttered a hole in the floorboards, hawked up by the engine.

Sid felt for the moment when stiff grease would allow gears to mesh without raking. Almost. "I'm going to run down the road," he said. Knobby grimaced like it was his daughter leaving, or maybe coming back.

The truck lurched out of half-moon holes, stumbled on flat-faced tires. The rear wheels didn't track the front, but the steering didn't pull like a truck with a wrecked front end would; likely a broken king bolt. How could you not like a truck that made four tracks in the snow? The brakes squalled but held when he U-turned through Rooster's parking lot. The wheel trembled, but a good quivering like the ripples on that first drink.

Maybe he'd put a plow on it. Make money when it snowed, like the ski resorts did. A power-angle blade with auxiliary headlights that stuck up like a wingnut, high enough to shine down into a tourist's big Suburban.

Knobby was as Sid had left him, a misshapen stump. Sid wallowed alongside, but didn't shut down the engine. "Thirty-five."

"Forty."

A jolt of satisfaction, then concern at the too-easy ten-dollar reduction. What had he missed? He pursed and spat, still not used to having more lips than mouth; he wiped his chin on his sleeve. "I'll pay when the snow melts, when I finish this job I'm on."

Knobby's arm—an elephant's trunk, fat and boneless and smelling of exotic waste—shot in and turned off the light switch. The engine dieseled one great whirr and died. "I ain't running no damn finance company." He never looked back or acknowledged the names Sid suggested.

When the door clattered shut behind Knobby, the dog stiff-legged toward the truck, teeth bared and hair enough for two dogs. Sid had to shuffle backwards all the way to a wreck-battered white ash at the corner of the dog's territory. Out of sight of the house, Sid scuffed in the snow for rocks. The dog retreated far enough that Sid couldn't hit it, watching cold-eyed, licking slobber from its teeth. "You sunsabitch." Sid wondered if the dog was deaf.

Sid glanced up the hill toward his waiting laundry, then toward the raking job he'd intended to finish that day. Anger set his pace, and his back was sweated till he got to the lakehouse. He scraped snow to find where he'd left off, then lit into raking the whole mess: snow, leaves, twigs, and the soft red-dog gravel the snow plows threw into the yards. He saw not his work, but the Ford pickup. Not the way it was just then, but the way it would be after Sid fixed it up.

The wheelbarrow was cheap, with a wheel that slid side-to-side on the axle. Sid staggered with heaping, shifting loads to the woods' edge and threw the handles up with a grunt. Just after four o-clock—noon, had it not snowed—he stowed his tools in the cedar shed and knocked on the house's mahogany door. Shadows flickered behind the etched glass, and a golden brown manicured feminine hand slid out a check.

"Thanks," Sid said to a closed door. The check was made out to cash; they hadn't asked his name. Three days work for what they made scratching their nose, and they couldn't even ask his dad-blamed name. He read their name with the notion of knocking again to give them a sermon on respect, but couldn't pronounce it. *Foreign* flatlanders. At driveway's end, he rolled down his cuffs and threw the gravel trapped there into the yard for next year.

Rooster's was not the place to go with a pocketful of money, but the only place nearby that would cash a check. The bar frothed with the after-work crowd—pickup-and-stepladder carpenters, realtors' maintenance men, the chronically unemployed—but Sid found a solitary stool near the jukebox. Larry looked hard at both sides of the check, then brought back a fifty, a twenty, and a five. "Bust that fifty for me," Sid said.

"Be glad I busted it at all." Larry grabbed the five before Sid could pocket the small bills and force him to change the fifty.

Halfway through his beer, Pike Baggart sidled down the bar. "Hey."

Pike followed life as though in a funeral procession, pleasant and mindful of his own affairs, but life always stopped and backed over him. Sid liked him, but Pike was the only person Sid could treat like dirt and not feel bad about it. If Sid didn't, somebody else would.

Pike tried again. "Hard to get used to the way you look without teeth."

"It's no worse than your broke nose."

"My nose ain't . . . oh." Pike slid back where he belonged.

Sid's tongue felt dilitary when he left, a sure sign he'd drunk too much. Darkness had fallen without warning. Figuring to come back in the morning, he almost snuck past Knobby's without rousing the dog, but his foot scuffed gravel and instantly a blacker form firmed in the night. Six feet away a star reflected from an eye, or a tooth. The stench of maleness, panting breath like peeling Velcro. The dog came no closer, waiting for Sid to move, and it didn't take an Einstein to cipher what a bad idea that was.

Sid started to yell for Knobby, but his rage came unstoppered in a growl. Gravel shifted under the dog's feet. "C'mon," Sid whispered. "I'll kill you, or die one."

The dog was closer, but not near enough to get a steel-toed boot into. Waiting for Sid to turn. "I'm not stupid." Sid backed away, weight on the balls of his feet so he could lean into an attack. Back, back, he shuffled, dog following, until the big white ash slid past Sid's shoulder. The dog stopped and raised his leg to the tree, but really pissing on Sid.

"When I get my truck, first thing I do is run over you. If I got to wreck it to get you." Sid turned and walked away, not looking back. He stopped short of his own yard, brimming with adrenaline and beer. While his stream frothed in the gravel, he looked back toward Knobby's, then at his own trailer. Janet waited there for the details of his day, every daggone minute of it.

How did the laundry go.

Did the stains come out of her one white blouse.

Or did he wash it with the socks again.

Then he'd hear hers. How she outsmarted the professor again. How the boys give her the eye. How she believed she'd get a tattoo. Did Sid think that would be nice. Did he like blue or red. What did he think it ought to say.

Sid wearied of pissing before he was through and headed back the way he'd come because there was no place else to go. He hated to spend all his money at Rooster's, but wasn't up to the alternative.

But there was that hell dog to get past. Sid sat on the bank, halfway between the dog's territory and Janet's. If he had a flashlight, he could slip through the woods, but he wasn't about to try it in the dark.

He'd be quiet.

Sid smelled the dog before he saw it. Waiting. Like it knew Sid would be back before Sid did.

Sid stumbled back in a mudslide of startlement and fear and disgust for his cowardice. As before, the dog stopped at the tree and raised his leg.

Too much beer drunk too fast was cooking in Sid, that recipe for a restless reckless edge that skinned his knuckles and busted his head. "You mark all of Union County as yours if you want to, but this spot right here belongs to Sid Lore." Cold air washed his crotch like an alcohol swab. He staggered as he turned, made oblong the dark circle he drew on the pale road.

The size of his claim was not even adequate to lie down in. He enlarged it, squibbing flatfooted so as not to wet his jeans. The dog growled. Sid pushed the boundary further. "Now you know how it feels. Everybody squeezing from one side or another. Push you clear out if you let them."

The dog scratched gravel like a bull, its breath an obscene whisper, a dirty joke told behind a hand. That it would work itself into such a lather over a slab of potholed blacktop, just because it could, angered Sid. Suddenly piss was not enough. He wanted blood. His or the dog's, he didn't care.

Sid felt for his old Boker Tree Brand knife, thumbed open a blade much diminished by sharpening. He lunged at the dog. It waited, unafraid and patient. Sid stepped closer to the tree, found himself as dry as a popcorn fart. The dog panted, laughing. "Don't watch me." Sid's voice strained with the effort of mustering a few final drops.

As though sensing those drops' formation, the dog gathered into a tighter ball. Sid's eyes bugged as he finally powered a tiny squirt toward the white ash. Before it splashed against bark, the black shadow launched, struck Sid's chest like an anvil, heavier and harder than could be possible. Before he realized he was no longer upright the ground slammed his back and his air went out pulling guts hand-over-hand behind, and when he was empty the tearing continued, dragging forth sounds he'd never made before, or known that he could.

Sid struck with a knife that scissored shut on his fingers, steel grating on knucklebones, then skittered away into the ditch. He was inside the dog's mouth, old meat simmering in insecticide, and Sid bit at the invading tongue but his gums failed purchase and the dog's teeth slipped from Sid's loose cheeks, snarled toward his neck, and Sid jammed a forearm between them and felt shirt fibers penetrate his arm. Light flickered amid tree trunks, Knobby's voice Lucy, Lucy, and they froze, dog and man, rasping in each other's ears, shifting and gathering but neither making noise beyond that of living, waiting, waiting. Sid felt for and found the knife but it was instead a finger-sized stick he clasped and waited, waited, and the storm door rattled and the light died and he drove it into the dog and it snapped and folded against the tough hide, and teeth clamped his arm and shook and Sid's pain escaped in a long moan that inspired the dog to a flurry of biting and scratching.

The dog strove for his neck and a great hairy leg invaded Sid's mouth foul and gritty and he bit till blood spilled, his own, and he shook his head till bones rose beneath his gums and found flesh and new hot bright-penny blood filled his mouth and the smell and taste like Epsom salts, and he gagged and swallowed and bit again. The dog's teeth loosened as it whined, then tore again at Sid's arm. Fingers found not a knife but a back leg driving, driving, a stump of tail, then a soft hairy change purse holding two small potatoes that he squeezed, and he ground his gums deeper. The dog fell away howling and one of the potatoes lost its consistency under his grip, the dog's wail a pencil of pain in his ear and it tore away and moaned down the road a fleeting ghoul.

Sid staggered to his feet and ran after the dog, running from and to the sounds that poured forth from his own mouth. The porch light flared, the dog a slippery shadow that shot across the yellow-bright patch to cower in the same corner from which it had bared its teeth that morning. As Sid approached, it slid away, corner after corner.

The door opened a few inches and Knobby was there, hanging back where Sid could just make out his shape. Sid pulled up ten feet away and waited. Knobby said nothing. Sid looked around, looked at his torn and bloody shirt, pulled the shirt from his wounds. He wiped his good sleeve across his mouth and examined the black hair and blacker blood that came away.

"I come for the truck," he said and fished in his pocket for the fifty, all that remained of three days of work. Knobby's misshapen hand sneaked out the door the same way the manicured one had delivered the check earlier, took the bill and slithered in again and the door closed. Knobby didn't move.

"You said $40. I got change coming," Sid said.

The lock snicked, a soft little roach of a sound, and Knobby said, "That was before the dog. You don't get none now."

Sid looked at the pickup slouching in the light's edge, at the black form of dog beyond. "That's no ten-dollar dog."s

"No, he ain't now. But he was." The rough voice squibbed away at the end. "He sure as hell was."

A great laugh built in Sid like a gas bubble, hard and malignant, and it came out that way, battled the dark beyond the light, battled the dog, battled Knobby and the manicured hand that had proffered the check and those who laughed at the holes where his teeth had been and where his heart and his balls had been. It battled all that, and all that waited, then it dried up, and Sid felt no less humorous for its going, or more. "No, as you hillbillies say it, he ain't now. He sure as hell ain't now." Then the starting button was under Sid's thumb, and he drove his pickup home.

Janet glanced at his wounds, at the blood and mud, at the torn clothing. But mostly she looked into his eyes. "You got us a truck," she said when he returned from the bathroom.

Sid nodded.

"Was it hard?"

"It wasn't nothing I couldn't handle." His eyes moved over her contours the same way his little sander was going to glide over his new truck, soon as the weather warmed. Some things could get started before that. There wasn't no use to wait.

17

JANET WAS THE ONLY ONE WORKING since Sid's back clear gave out, so they agreed not to shoot the moon on anniversary gifts. Ten dollars, no more. Sid found at the Southern States Farm Cooperative something Janet might like, a *Comprehensive Guide to Appalachian Wildflowers*, stacked with a half-dozen other books of various titles in a bin of gloves and hose nozzles. Each was less than perfect: a broken back or a torn cover. The flower book had some shit-muckle-dun-colored goop on the bottom edge, but the book wasn't hurt.

Sid intended to buy flower bulbs, maybe tulips, but the book was better. Though the Southern States had never stocked books before, or blue plastic dishes, both were on sale. The book's flowers were prettier than any Janet would ever grow. Sidemore couldn't dig up a book, and a late frost wouldn't kill it.

He almost bought a bowl he liked, but lost his nerve. Groceries he could buy without turning clear red, but wasn't yet ready to purchase women's things.

The clothbound book cost four dollars, but it had $16.95 printed on the cover, and the sale sticker peeled off clean. Janet would love it, especially since it cost more than they'd agreed. She read a lot since she'd took college classes, and she was partial to any old kind of flower, from Johnny jump-ups to sneezeweed.

He figured right.

"Aw, man," Janet said at breakfast past a mouthful of popcorn with milk and sugar, after she'd untaped the bag. The brown of her eyes sparkled, set off by the whites from a thin face sunburned just as dark. "I couldn't have done better if I'd bought it myself." Her dangling spoon rattled against her teeth like the toilet's trip lever. Sid didn't care for it. The goop stink was stronger after being cooped up.

"Look at this," Janet said. "Viper's bugloss. Ugly ol' name on such a pretty flower." Sid didn't like the sound of the pages peeling apart, either. "Lesser broomrape." Janet giggled and repeated the last word, making it two, and looked at Sid like he should bust out laughing.

The popcorn had been another one of her money-saving ideas. Actually it wasn't bad, though it soggied up faster than cereal and the hulls stuck under Sid's new false teeth. But he wouldn't eat it in front of her. Not after he'd made fun. "I'm tickled you like what I bought."

Janet looked at her watch, a nice black one, though the Velcro band was frowzy. "I got to git. Open yours before I go."

Janet was flagging for a paving crew, daylight to dark. She'd quit the Not Quite Right when Fat's sweaty hand had snuck where it oughtn't one too many times. She'd shucked a coat hanger from a factory-second sweatshirt and hooked it in his nose and towed him out back to the dumpster with the other trash. While he was hunkered to work the hanger from his snothole, she'd laid her foot into his lardy butt.

"You're fired," Fats hollered after he wormed the hanger loose, but Janet said it was too late, she'd quit two minutes ago. Then he'd screwed her out of her final paycheck. "Make an issue of it. I dare you." The tape and gauze on his nose made him sound like a hillbilly.

She'd been hard to live with for a few days, till her period was over. Till she got that flagging job. Word of what she'd done to Fats got around, and the men on the paving crew made her into a goddess they could fear and brag about. They gave her a nickname, even stenciled it on her hardhat. When someone arrived at work surly or hung over, the foreman threatened to have Ripper give him a nose job. She wore a tank top that showed off the knot of muscle in her skinny little arm.

Sid knew they did it for a joke, but she took it serious after waitressing and cleaning cottages and being called honey and babycakes.

Sid ripped the red Santa Clausy paper off his package like he couldn't wait. Janet would like that. He'd guessed a camouflage undershirt, so the coarse red material surprised him. For a moment he thought he'd gotten a hunting jacket, but long tie strings fell forth. He felt suckerpunched. Then he laughed at Janet's sense of humor.

She was too sunburned to change colors, but she looked into her popcorn as though she were blushing. "I was scared you wouldn't like it."

"It's a apron." Sid looked around and realized there wasn't another gift. He held it up, tried to make sense of it. It smelled like new female clothes do, like a woman had already been in it. His name was on an embroidered patch that he recognized from his old Sunoco uniform. The patch was where his belly would go. When he examined the back, he saw that his name was covering a hole. Janet had bought it at the Not Quite Right before she'd quit.

"Now cooking won't make your shirt greasy."

Sid had clear opinions about putting a dress on a man just because his back was out of whack and he had to do woman stuff, but was cloudy on how to offer them without the conversation circling to bite him in the ass, as in Janet paying the bills. He was still turning the apron this way and that, searching for the right words, when Janet kissed him. She left behind sugar grits and a popcorn shell casing. "If the next nine years are anything like the first nine, I can't hardly wait." She ricocheted out the door like a hickory nut falling through limbs. "Happy anniversary, Sid," she threw back over her shoulder.

The pickup ground and roared, and she was gone. Sid laid the apron on his lap and looked out the window until the oil smoke cleared. When he tried the apron on, the name patch rode on his little potgut like there was a baby in there, and they'd named and labeled it. Sid wadded the apron and threw it into the corner with his nuts.

§

Sid redded up the living room and made the bed, then sliced Spam into a hot skillet and broke brown eggs over top. When the mess would hold together, he divided it and slid each half between bread. He ran a thumb around his waistband; he'd lean up when he went back to work.

He chewed as though splitting firewood, steadily and harder than necessary. The new teeth chafed and chattered, but they were better than gums, and his mouth didn't pucker like a bunghole. He looked thirty again, not eighty.

While he ate, he prized open pages of Janet's flower book. Some he knew—Dame's rocket and Joe-pye and bindweed—and some by a different name—rattleweed instead of blue cohosh, and jimson, not purple thorn-apple. He was surprised and put off to see ginseng. A root. To call it a flower defied the natural order of things.

Several flowers Sid had never seen, and he'd walked over every inch of Appalachia around. Some cityslicker made them up, he figured, to impress other cityslickers who didn't know better. The names were haywhack, made to sound countrified, or like someone thought countrified *ought* to sound: stitchwort and puttyroot and lopseed and sleepy catchfly.

The pages peeled apart okay, but they didn't go back together right, and the book got fatter on one end like a white oak in low ground. He opened to boneset, and tasted the boneset tea Grand Annie had make him drink whether he was sick or not—he was always sick, afterwards—and Sid pushed his half-eaten sandwich away and closed the book. It lay fat-ended for a moment, then rolled onto its spine and fell open like a five-dollar whore, and Sid closed it and hit it with his fist. He hit it harder and harder until his fist started getting the worst end of the deal. He rinsed his teeth and fitted them to his gums and fetched the dog can from beneath the sink.

He partially filled the can from the hundred-pound bag of Generic Pride dog food they also used as a beanbag chair, then scraped his leftover sandwich on top and went outside.

Not yet eight o'clock, the air was thick, and the pools of transmission fluid where the pickup was parked smelled like town. Another 70-degree, 100-percent-humidity day where if you moved you sweated, but shivered if you didn't. The lousy mountain weather they'd have through June, till it sharpened up in late summer. Over the hill toward the lake, a backhoe bulled in stumps and rocks, sounding mad, scraping a hole where another vacation home would pop up like a toadstool. Where some other fool could ruin his back rassling timbers for a rich man's playpen. Sid spat in that direction.

The Worker's Compensation man said he'd never known a West Virginia back injury that didn't heal up come deer season. That's five months from now, Sid said. Trout season, either, the man said, and returned the papers to Sid's folder.

Sidemore sat with front legs spraddled and belly hanging down like he'd swallowed a rock. His nose came up when he smelled the Spam. Sid threw the sandwich in the dog's bowl and dumped dry food on top.

The dog stared into the bowl, head tilted sideways, then rummaged among the hard tan lumps with a foot until the bowl caught a root and flipped over. The way the dog wolfed the sandwich, finding pleasure in what Sid had discarded, pissed Sid off. A foot jumped into Sidemore's ribs.

The dog humped up, but slashed at the Spam like it still had life enough to escape, and in two gulps it was gone. The black-and-brown-and-tan-and-dirty-white mongrel sidled to the end of his chain and arched his back and extruded a hard red turd among a boneyard of rust-colored ones, rolled-back eyes showing muddy whites and red rims.

"You dirty little mutt." Sid picked up the water hose and turned it on the dog instead of into the bowl. Sidemore yelped and ripped back under the trailer. "Come out of there. You need a bath." Sid knelt and tried to squirt over a sagging plastic sewer pipe, but the hose was knotted up. When he yanked on it, the water petered out to nothing, then squirted up at the bib where he'd ruptured the cheap plastic. The spray made a rainbow in the morning sun.

Sid's back lurched out of place when he scrambled up; he said uhhh and the dog answered. Water saturated his shirt before he got the spigot shut off, and damp as it was, it would still be wet come dinnertime.

Sid saw how his day was going to be, and nothing he could do about it, and he laughed and looked under the trailer again, and said, "Come here, dummy," in a whole different voice than he'd used when he'd invited him to bathe, but Sidemore wasn't ready to make up. "I didn't mean to kick the shit out of you." The dog yawned.

On the way back around the trailer, Sid examined the windows he'd promised to wash. The only thing visible through the dirty panes was the red of the apron, afire in a beam of sunlight.

From the kitchen faucet Sid ran hot water into a bucket said hell and poured it out. He changed his shirt and wet his head so the hat hair wouldn't be so bad. After he'd tamped a pinch of Skoal into his lip and checked his nose for night stuff, he walked down the hill to Rooster's.

§

The bar didn't open till one o'clock, four hours yet, but Larry's scabby-topped Oldsmobile was parked out back, lolling like a sunburned walrus. Sid squinted between cupped hands through the glass, and thought Larry was dancing with someone, until he realized Larry's partner was a mop. Sid rapped on the glass, and a few minutes later the kitchen door lock rattled and Larry's beardy face emerged.

"We're closed." A mop handle clunked against the doorjamb, and Larry turned and kicked at it.

"I figured you might use some help cleaning."

"I ain't hiring."

Sid nibbled a few grains of snuff. "Wasn't asking for a job." He looked toward the trailer and combed his hair with his fingers. "I decided to take a day off. If you'll let me shoot pool afterwards, I'll swamp the place out for you."

Larry kicked again and the mop rattled away. "A day off from *what?*" he said from back in the dark.

"Just cause I don't punch a clock don't mean I lollygag all day. I work as hard as anybody you know, and some you don't."

From further in a bucket clunked and Larry cursed. "You got to pay for the pool. Fifty cents a game, like always."

"I didn't ask for free pool. Just the chanst to practice without having to wait half a hour between pokes."

"All right, come on. Lock the door before some other asshole sneaks in."

With the beer sign lights extinguished, the bar's smoked surfaces devoured the ceiling lights like they weren't on. Daylight raking low across the wood floor made it look like a plowed field, but not as clean. Without people, the smell was different, lonesome and sickly. Larry had mopped around the pool table without sweeping first, transformed dirt into mud.

"You got a broom?"

Larry's face didn't spring back when he worried the corners of his moustache, just got longer and skinnier. "I can't find it this morning."

"Take a break, I'll find it." Sid wanted to get the hung-over old fart out of the way, get the job done, get on the pool table.

The storeroom was a boar's nest of pasteboard boxes and stacked beer and fire extinguishers charged and empty. And a broom, fallen between the walk-in cooler and a refrigerator that limped bad. Reaching for the broom, Sid discovered a stickum trap with a dead mouse in it. He wiped his fingers on a case of beer, but the more he rubbed the bigger the sticky patch grew. It spread to his other hand too, and felt like it was even in his shorts till he'd scoured it off with Ajax in a cracked concrete utility tub.

"You was back there long enough." Larry sat on the customer side of the bar, drinking coffee and glaring like Sid had guzzled half a bottle of Crown while looking for the broom.

Sid swept the main space, working into the corners where dead millers were getting deep. What would it be like to work there every day? "You got a mouse in one of them glue traps."

"Good. Little bastards."

"He's been in it a while."

"Shows the rest of them what happens when they fuck with me." Larry slid off the stool and flipped up the drunkstop at the end of the bar and went into the kitchen and slammed around in the pans.

Sid used a *Vacation Guide* off the bar for a dustpan. Flies boiled out of the trashcan. He shook out the guide and replaced it on the pile and hoped the tourists would catch something off of it that would cause them to shit themselves to death. Over a week or so.

§

Sid chalked his cue and studied the table. His eye was sharp, like it got sometimes after a beer or two, but his back ached from rassling the mop.

"You done good on that floor. How much you have to have, was I to put you on?" Worms of fried onion escaped from Larry's sandwich into his beard, and the food in his mouth didn't look ready to eat yet. He shoveled food in constantly, but got skinner all the time. Larry's food was like firewood for a stove that dried him out like beef jerky.

Sid sighted and stood and leaned and sighted again, like the nine-ballers on the TV did. The six popped in crisp and the cue ball drew back for a dead bank on the two. "I wouldn't need much, with the tips and all." Sid saw the line and snapped it in without chalking or hardly aiming.

"Hows come you don't shoot like that when there's money on the table?"

Sid ran the five hard down the rail but got some perverted English on it that made it hook the side pocket's tit and fly back to jam the eight ball into the corner pocket. Sid barely got his hand out of the way.

Larry laughed. "Spoke too soon."

Sid emptied the can of Keystone that had gotten warm and pissy, wiped his mouth on his sleeve. "I done that a-purpose. A trick shot." He glanced at Larry and drank again, as if the can was half full. "I'm not playing eight ball. This is my own game, different rules."

Larry turned back to his sandwich, and the way his neck and shoulders worked, just like Sidemore wolfing Spam, filled Sid with the urge to give him a ram in the ribs, too. He pocketed the rest of the balls without missing, not taking real hard shots but not picking ducks, either. A drop of beer had collected in the can, so he turned it up and nursed it out. He didn't realize Larry was watching him in the mirror behind the bar until he spoke.

"You want another one, or you going to suck that one inside out?"

Sid felt the short stack of quarters in his pocket, all that remained of the change from Janet's book. "I'm hair near broke. Just enough for a couple of games after you open."

Larry wiped his mouth on a handful of napkins and belched and smelled his fingers and wiped them on his pants. "Grab a few on the house. For the floor." He nodded at the stainless cooler behind the bar.

From behind, the bar was all crooked sinks and tangled pipes and wires, junky but attractive as a homemade spaceship. Sid pictured himself being fast with a joke or a comeback, pouring liquor from two bottles at once without having to look in a book for the ingredients of a Grasshopper or a Slippery Nipple. Maybe he'd wear a little red vest.

"Don't move in. Get your beer and get out."

Sid nodded and sidled past the drunkstop and fed two quarters into the pool table and ran a rack of balls, shooting hard and quick.

§

"Where you going, slick?" said the guy in sandals and baggy shorts. "Give me a chance to get even." The reflective sunglasses worn on top of his tight-curled hair squirmed with neon lights.

The beer was a cold core in Sid, and a hot skin. He fingered his single quarter. That guy—Charles, gym-trimmed and boat-tanned, crooked little nose and politician's teeth—Sid could beat all day, any day. It was only bad luck that Sid had lost the last game. He'd been hooked on every shot until he got flusterated and tried a cut on the eight he wasn't comfortable with, and scratched. "Got to go. Chores to do."

"One more game. I'll rack, play you for ten bucks." Charles' ring twinkled when he dug though a fat money clip and winged a bill onto the green felt.

"Play him, Sid." Larry leaned on elbows at the end of the bar. "I'll front you ten."

Sid hung his stick in the rack, wiped talc from his hands onto his pants legs. "Was you serious about giving me a job?"

"You can start this evening. Work tonight and see how you do, and then we'll talk money."

Sid's guts went a-judder with an instant case of fantods. He wasn't sure how to draw a draft beer, much less mix a drink.

"You going to play or not?" Charles said.

"Shoot him," Larry said. "I'll bet on Sid, if he won't, Charlie."

"Charles. Not Charlie."

"Same damn difference."

"I ought to be going," Sid said. But Larry's confidence was like a shot of bourbon. He reclaimed his stick from the rack.

"All *right*." Charles threw his ten atop Larry's and shook down the balls and slapped them in the rack. Two strangers further down swiveled to watch.

Sid made a solid and a stripe on the break, then stood a long time ciphering the table.

Charles clapped a sandal between his heel and the floor and whistled through his teeth. "Think long, think wrong."

"Whenever it gets quiet, maybe I'll shoot."

Charles shook his head and muttered something Sid couldn't hear, but he settled down while Sid sunk four big ones and allowed one of the remaining two to trickle down tight on the eight where he couldn't budge it without losing. "Dammit." Sid jammed the butt of his cue into the floor. Larry retreated to a chair behind the bar, just his head sticking up.

Charles moved like he was on roller skates, hardly taking time to aim, pop, pop, pop, but his last ball caught a piece of the eight and skinned it off the rail where Sid's ball could see daylight.

Just when Sid was lining up, Charles said, "Five more he can't run them off," and Larry's head nodded slow. Sid reconsidered, found it still just as easy. He goosed the nine down the rail and sucked the cue back just perfect, then greased the seven past the eight and the cue ball followed around off two cushions and left him a dandy shot, longer than he liked but easy.

Charles was still and quiet. "This is my last game." Sid chalked his cue. "I'll start tomorrow. I need to study up first." Janet had tended bar, had a little book. Sid sighted, pictured the shot.

Larry laughed. "Study what? How to flip a hamburger? I heard you could cook."

Sid froze. "I thought you wanted me to tend bar."

"You think I'm going to cook while you stand out here and flirt with the women?"

Larry already had a cook who came in at four. "What about Gilpen?"

"She's got plenty mouthy lately. Lazy, too."

Sid stroked the ball but the eight rattled in the cup and died on the edge of the hole. Charles whammed it into the pocket while Sid was hanging up his stick, and Larry said to Sid, "You owe me $15, you damn choker."

"I got no bet here. You ram your $15 and your cooking job up your scrawny ass."

"Here, get us all a drink." Charles set his empty glass on the fanned bills.

Sid shut the door softly behind him, afraid he'd tear it off the hinges if he turned his anger loose. Halfway up the hill, he looked back at the black Bronco parked at the corner of the lot where it wouldn't get dented by parts flying off the locals' vehicles. He sailed a gravel the size of a lug nut toward it, but was drunker on free beer than he'd realized, and hit the bar instead. His fire and strength and balance ran out and he sat down in the road and watched the rock ricochet up the roof's slope and make a u-turn, dinging holes in the tarpaper everywhere it hit. Sid put his head between his knees and wished a coal truck would smoosh him. But it would probably just break an arm so he couldn't shoot pool. Or bust his new teeth.

He sat surrounded by no money, no respect, no beer. All he possessed was love, and she was working thirteen hours on their anniversary because Sid couldn't cut the mustard anymore.

He thought about the windows needing washing, and how he'd felt when Larry said "I'll bet on Sid," and about the red apron. How it would be to have a paycheck, with a dollar left over. And about his back—he'd wrenched it again when he threw the gravel. Sid got up and brushed himself off and returned to the bar.

Larry was talking with Charles, best of friends. After a while he said "Yeah" in a louder voice without looking up.

"Sorry about blowing off steam. I could use that job."

Larry looked at Charles, but spoke to Sid. "I been thinking about that. There ain't no doubt you'd work harder than Gilpen, and a blind retard could out-cook her." Food showed in his grin. "But she's got the *cutest* little butt." He looked at Sid. "And you ain't."

"I just don't want it said around that I turned down work."

"Turned it down? That ain't exactly the way I recollect it."

§

Getting the apron on Sidemore was like shoving noodles up a wildcat's ass. Instead of poking his legs through the slits Sid had cut, the dog would pull them in and turn clear around inside his hide and pop them out somewhere else. He never snarled or bit, but just kept squirming, his eyes rolled back at Sid.

Sid was determined. When Janet saw the dog decked out in Sid's anniversary present, she'd know how Sid felt—what he didn't have words to say.

Five minutes later, Sid was covered with as much dirt as the dog was with apron, but Sidemore was dressed in red. Sid released him to see what he'd do.

The dog looked over both shoulders to see if he had a good side, and then started walking every place his chain would reach, just walking, walking, like he could outlast the apron if he couldn't whip it. The apron slipped back over his bony flanks so that he hopped with hind feet together like someone trying to take their pants off standing up.

Sid straddled him and worked the apron forward again. That time, though, he stretched the neck loop over Sidemore's nose and under his neck. The dog had quit struggling, like he knew he could outsmart Sid. Or maybe he'd started to like it. Sid pictured the dog pushing the loop over his head with his forepaws. He unclipped the chain from the collar, intending to rehook it on the other side of the loop.

When the snap came loose, Sidemore wiggled backwards through Sid's legs. Sid grabbed, but with the apron wrapped around the dog, there was nothing to latch on to. Sidemore lunged and Sid took a bellyflopper at the trailing strings, but missed.

Sid chased him down the fill bank, bramble slashing his arms. He yelled once, then held his wind and tried to keep the dog in sight. The dog looped toward Rooster's, where he usually went when he got loose. Where Gilpen would give him a burger. He put on a burst of speed at the thought of a row of faces looking out the window at a dog wearing an apron with "Sid" embroidered on it.

The trailing strings were like a wind-blown paper, always just out of reach. Then Sid tripped and rattled between a stump and a pignut hickory just like the eight ball had rattled in the corner pocket. Sidemore faded to a red flash once in a while.

Sid felt tremendously drunk and especially dumb, and he wondered whether he should get up at all, or just lay there for good. After a while he sat up and dug leaf mold from his lower lip and spat twice and wiped his mouth on his sleeve, examined what he'd wiped off and spat again and wiped with the other sleeve.

Sidemore barked, not toward Rooster's but down in the bottom toward Crupp's Creek—one panicky sound more yelp than yap. Sid whistled and called, but the dog didn't answer.

It was wet down there, tangled with jack oaks and ninebark, and before he'd gone far his jeans were slicked with frog spit and his face was sutured with spiderweb. He said "hey" not too loud, and a whine came from ahead. Sid glimpsed red in a tall flurry of skunk cabbage, and fought his way toward it.

Sidemore's apron strings were caught over an alder stob. If the stupid mutt would have backed up or changed directions, he'd have been loose. But he just leaned into the apron and waited for someone to free him up again.

"You dumb little buttlicker," Sid said after his breath caught up. Sidemore wagged his tail and looked off in the woods where he wanted to go. "I ought to just cut your throat and let you here." But after a while he gathered dog and apron and headed toward the trailer. Sidemore lay back in Sid's arms with his eyes shut and issued a contented little sound that Sid wished he could make, or have cause to, just once.

§

Sid's back was afire when he woke on the couch. It felt late. The air was heavy with the smell of popcorn; Janet was home. Just after midnight. The apron he'd been sewing when he dozed off was on the coffee table, folded nice. Sid knew without looking Janet had finished the job Sid had started, mending the slits he'd cut for Sidemore's legs.

Sid didn't think he'd been dreaming, but his half-awake thoughts were fresh with how Sidemore had looked at him while he squeezed out the turd Sid had kicked loose; how he'd hunkered when Sid turned the hose on him; how he'd waited for Sid to tote him home when he got hung up in the skunk cabbage.

After Sid had carried Sidemore home, he'd repaired the hose. He stripped right there in the dog lot and turned the hose on himself. Sid hollered at the spring-cold water, but he kept at it till he was clean. "You're next," he told Sidemore, but the dog crunched away at his Generic Pride and paid him no mind, even when Sid shot a little foosh of water his way, so Sid petted him and scratched behind his ears instead. After a while the dog tired of that, and yawned and went back under the trailer for a nap.

Janet had sneaked in and sewed his new apron and made popcorn for the next morning's breakfast and gone to bed, while Sid lay there with a bad back and a beer headache. She'd picked wildflowers from the roadside while she worked; blue and purple and pink blossoms hung from the pages of her fat little book.

Sid smelled the flowers, but got instead traces of feed store chemicals and sweet soft women and of piney floor cleaner and cigarette butts and stale beer and money and skunk cabbage and hot dirty dogs. Even after he pushed the book away the smells persisted: transmission fluid and dead mice, talcum and dog food.

Sid browned a frozen venison roast like a man does, flames licking the sides of the skillet. He put the darkened lump in the crockpot with a slop of water and looked at the clock and hoped it would get done in time to slice off a nice sandwich for Janet's lunch. Then he lay on the couch and listened to the sounds that he couldn't quite hear: the crockpot; the country at one o'clock in the morning; Janet asleep.

He slipped into the bedroom and lowered himself onto the bed, careful not to wake her. She was turned toward him, snoring softly. He eased close until he could feel the glow from the gentle furnace inside. He breathed her milky breath, taking it in as she cast it away. Stars were soft through the dirty glass of the uncurtained window beyond her, candles at a table.

Sid opened his eyes one last time to stare at the woman he couldn't see. He breathed her in, released her, breathed her in, released her, breathed her in, released her.

In his dreams, he was a hero. Not so strong as patient. Brave with hope that fists couldn't bruise. Formidable in kindness. In his dreams, that was enough. In his dreams, that would do.

He touched her chapped lips with a fingertip grown soft as the stars faded away into morning. She grasped his wide hand in both of her smaller ones and kissed it, and he realized she'd been awake, listening as he slept. In dawn's first light, it was enough. In dawn's first light, it would do.

18

Horse Wilson pictured himself an oversized load on the highway of life, slipping along without escort or lights or permit, dodging the scales and beating the system. He'd said so. Sid figured he was a runaway garbage truck with a drunk teenager at the wheel.

It was late, and something deep inside wanted to be home, even if Sid couldn't translate that desire into a thought. Either that or the pickled egg had give him gas.

"Tell you what I think." Which meant Horse would repeat what he'd heard someone say, though it wouldn't be recognizable after it had composted inside Horse's head. He wiped a beer moustache onto the back of his hand and pointed a finger remarkably like a parsnip at the television over the bar. The finger was fat but pointy, pale and strewn with hairs that looked more like roots.

Sid glanced at the same scene they showed every night on the news: cater-wauling women, angry bearded men pumping a fist into the air.

"The only way to get peace in the Middle East is to pave it." Horse looked both ways to make sure everyone had at least smelled the bait, even if they hadn't taken it yet.

"It is paved." Larry lifted Horse's glass and wiped the bar underneath. "Israel ain't Stumptown. Look at it."

"I mean the whole continent, or whatever it's called over there."

"The Good Book says there won't be peace till the Lord returns to set up his kingdom?" Pike Baggart ended sentences in a manner that left him room to dog paddle if the doodoo got too deep.

Fats Compton said, "He'll have to set her up without sandniggers, then. They learn to fight before they learn to use the terlet. They'd ruther show off their manhood than eat." He groped at his crotch, then augured in his ear like he couldn't decide whether to be a gangbanger or a half-deaf idjit. Fats had gotten rich before he'd figured out who he was, and then there was too much at risk to try to find out. Success had knocked all options in the head. Some said he was worth a quarter of a million if you took his property into account.

"That's my point," Horse said. "They had sand in their diapers, and now it's in their beards and in their bedsheets. You know how cranky you get after a day or two at the beach."

Sid's concept of beaches reshuffled with that new clue.

"If you paved the place over, you'd seal up all that sand. And there wouldn't be any rocks to throw." As though Horse had scripted the news, Palestinians flung stones at an Israeli armored carrier.

"Don't cast the first stone." Pike again, inserting the Bible like a suppository.

"Give me a rock and someone to hit, and I'll heave the first one." Sid was feeling good about himself. Maybe in comparison to his company. Or maybe it was the beer.

"Both sides got a point, so there won't be no peace?" Pike said.

"Bullcrap," Sid said. Not at or to any one particular thing or idea or one. Just staking out a general position. He recalled Roddy's Jew girlfriend that he'd never even got to meet, and wished he could go back and undo what he'd said about her. Maybe if Roddy had married, he'd still be there.

Pike had worked up backbone enough to argue. "The Israelites got their land fair and square, paid for it, and never took land except when they was attackted, but the Palestinians don't have a home. You got to consider that." He peered into his bottle for the rest of the argument. "And don't you wonder where the Jews got the money to buy it with? Honest, you figure?"

"Home's where you go and they got to let you in. Someone said that." Larry read those evaporated books, thought he was smart.

"I wish he'd a said it to Janet," Sid said.

"Home is where the hard is." Larry again.

Horse had found something to get mad at. "Before they built the dam, my granddaddy owned the whole holler from Thunderstruck to Pinetop, the big-money end of the lake. Six hunderd and fifty acres he sold for ten bucks a acre.

There's lakefront lots—lots, by hell, little bits of land you couldn't grow a tater on—that sells for more'n a million bucks nowadays."

"In the land of the suckers, a carp could be king. Or the other way around." Larry shrugged.

"There wasn't no other way to raise a dollar but to sell out, not in the Depression. And Grampap was bad for drink."

"Look how much better you're doing," Sid said. "You can't drink up your wealth, because you don't have none."

"He was took advantage of. It wasn't right."

"I don't reckon he complained till the money was gone." Sid was already sick of the subject. "When Roddy quit the papermill and moved to Baltimore, I should have had the first crack at his place. But he put it up with a realtor and hauled out like he didn't know me. I didn't even get the money that was supposed to be mine from when we sold the home place down in Logan County. You hear me bellyaching and whining about it?"

"Ain't that precisely what you're doing?" Fats wasn't worth a response.

"Baltimore." Larry drove the word into the conversation like it was a hoe. "I was on this train to Baltimore back when I was a teenager."

"They have trains back then?" Fats said.

"The conductor was asleep in the back of the car, and this woman was changing a baby's diaper, and the conductor roused up and sniffed and hollered 'Baltimore!'"

They'd heard it before. The beer beat against the inside of Sid's head, and he wanted to be home where he could hear it. "And you think Janet got any of the farm when her folks sold out, or the money? Her folks ride around in a motorhome till the old man has a nanurism and she has a stroke, and the money gets gobbled up by some nursing home out in Phoenix. That's just the way it is. Git 'er done on your own, or it don't get done. The only home we got is that old round-shouldered single-wide. And when it rots down—I give it six more months if it don't rain, but it will—we won't have nothing. That's nobody's fault. It's just how it is."

Horse's face had acquired a purple tinge that was unrelated to his drinking. "That kind of thinking is why we get tramped down till the worms has to look through their legs to see where we went."

"So what you going to do?" Sid nodded toward the TV. "Set up your own country?"

"I'm going to do something."

Larry spat into the trashcan behind the bar, or at it. "You're always going to do something."

"Make fun, if it makes you feel good. But I'm going to set some things straight." Horse's mug marked the bar when he sat it down. He stopped at the front door and aimed his parsnip-finger their way. "Don't forget whose side you're on. Don't forget that."

"I'm a Mountaineers man myself," Fats said, but the door had already slammed behind Horse.

"He'll most likely whizz in the lake, think that will even up the score with the tourons?"

Sid had the munchies. "Give me a can of them sardines."

Larry blew dust off the tin and found a plastic fork beneath the bar and picked coins from Sid's change.

"They're eighty-five cents at the WalMart. Sardines is high this year," Sid said.

"I know that. Where you think I buy them?"

"Then hows come you sell them for seventy?"

"They was only fifty when I bought the last."

Sid peeled back the tin and stared at the four bodies, packed shoulder to tail. After a while he said, "Give me another one."

"You ain't touched that one yet."

Pike made a face. "Another one won't be no better."

Sid tapped the bar with a forefinger, and Larry said hell and brought him another. Sid opened it and sat it beside the first. "Now, show me the difference between one and the other."

"There ain't no difference. That's why they call them sardines."

"What if you went to the WalMart and got two more? Would they be different?"

"Why don't you go see. We'll manage without you."

"Let me get this straight," Sid said. "I buy two cans at seventy cents, and you go pay eighty-five for two more. You still got two identical cans of sardines on the shelf, just like before, and you just lost thirty cents."

"You obviously don't know nothing about business. I'll sell the next ones for"—Larry closed his eyes and made a snoot—"a buck and a quarter."

"And then you'll go buy two more for a dollar and a half apiece, and lose another fifty cents."

"Larry knows how stuff works," Pike said. "You don't."

"Why don't you just eat your little fishies and shut up," Larry said.

Sid examined them some more. "I believe I looked at them too close." He pushed them away and collected his change and made for the door.

"That Sid can come up with the stupidest ideas for a white man." Had it been anyone other than Fats, Sid may have taken offense.

§

Sidemore was wailing after a bear until the old sow turned on him, then the chase went the other way, toward Sid. The dog veered off, and it was all Sid, all bear. Sid clawed at what covers he hadn't kicked off, then woke enough to recognize a fire engine caterwauling toward the lake. He pressed a bicep over his ear and tried to go back to sleep.

Janet was at the window, her head lopsided with pillow hair. "Looks like the world's afire."

Sid grunted, rolled to face the wall.

"Let's drive out and watch."

"Come to bed."

"Ain't you even going to look out the window?"

"Daggone it, Janet, we got to get some sleep. It's most likely a brush fire."

Janet was feisty, like she was before she got awake enough to remember what life was like. "There's a pillar of fire and smoke just like in the Bible. And tomorrow's Saturday. We can sleep till dinnertime."

Sid sat up in bed, any remnant of peace gone. "We'll not lay up in the bed daytimes like white trash. We'll not start that." Beer lingered in the corners of his head and stale cigarette smoke filtered from his hair. He scraped a furry tongue on his upper teeth before he remembered that he didn't have any upper teeth, or lower.

Janet didn't miss it. She laughed and sat on the bed and thrust herself toward Sid when he fell into the hollow she made. "Don't you lick at me unless you mean it."

But Sid still smelled cigarette smoke, and his fuzzy head couldn't shake it loose from the red glow that flickered in the window. He rolled away from the saggy place and hung onto the mattress edge for dear life, sorry as it was.

159

Janet's voice was mad or hurt; Sid never could differentiate one from the other with any reliable results. "I'm going to look at the fire. There sure ain't none here anymore."

Sid didn't have the energy to argue.

§

Janet's eyes seemed to look under Sid's skin, down where it wasn't fit to look, the way they did when she had her contacts out and couldn't see the sun on a hot day. "It was that house you raked the yard at last spring. Where those foreigners live? I can't say their name. They don't live there anymore. What a fire." She said it "far," like all the hillbillies did.

Sid swished cold coffee in his mouth, savored his jubilation at the news.

"You don't have to look so *tickled*. That was somebody's home."

"No, that was somebody's *house*; their *home* is somewhere else. Arabia, most likely. And they'll take the insurance money and build one twice as big."

"I bet those big trees are done for. You could feel the heat clear up on the road."

Now that was sad.

"It was arson, someone said. The house and the guest cottage was both afire."

"Guest cottage." Sid had figured it for a fancy outbuilding. There was no good place to spit, and Janet was looking inside him again. "Put your contacts in. You'll fall down and black your eye, and them Social Service people will think I done it."

"My contacts ain't out."

The dirty window glass made the outside air looked tinged with smoke. Sid examined his grounds-speckled cup.

"I shouldn't a said what I did last night." She stroked his arm hairs.

"Don't say things you don't mean, you won't be obliged to apologize." He wasn't sure what she'd said, but he wasn't going to let it pass without comment.

"You sure are acting funny this morning." Apologies flitted through Sid's life like winter wrens, scarce and beautiful in their drab unremarkable way; if you grabbed at them, they were gone so fast you were never sure you'd even seen them.

"You going to be using the truck? Figgered I'd run down to Rooster's, see if Larry's about yet." If something big happened overnight, Larry would open early so he could get his opinions firmly established before they ran head-on into facts.

"Last night's booze ain't even out of you yet. And I got to get some groceries."

"I'm not going down to drink." He rubbed his headache. "Just to see if anyone knows anything. About the fire."

"I need the truck. We're out of dog food, and shortening."

"Don't get your tail in a knot. I'll walk down."

Sid had barely gotten out of sight of the trailer when the burble of a big engine running easy crept alongside. Sid glanced at the deputy's light bar, then jerked his eyes away like he'd encountered his grandma in a nightie.

"Sid Lore." Even if Tinker Dunham was telling a joke, what you heard in his voice was the click of handcuffs. "Where are you walking to this time of day?"

"Hey, Tinker."

"Hop in, I'll give you a ride." The car crept Sid's way to make room on the passenger side to open the door.

"I'm just going to the bottom of the hill. You go on."

The car stopped. "Get in."

"Right." Sid walked around the back so Tinker couldn't run over him without changing gears. The inside was all Naugahyde and cords and microphones and gadgets, black and menacing. The old Crown Vic had a sense of empty space and unlimited power the new slick carpeted ones never developed. Bill Anderson played on a cassette player that hung under the dash: *Still, after all this time, Still, you're still on my mind*.

"I haven't seen much of you lately." The same way Larry would have said it if Sid had abandoned Rooster's, had started hanging with the muckety-mucks over at the Silver Cove Inn. Tinker had run for sheriff in the last three elections, had never figured out that law-abiding citizen voters were just as juberous of him as your everyday homegrown criminal. Tinker radiated suspicion like a Burnside stove broadcast heat, and if you stood too close you found yourself with an urge to make a run for it. "You behaving, Sid?"

Not that Sid voted, but if Tinker kept up like that, he'd start. "Hell yes, I been being have, like you wisht everyone was." Tree-shattered sunlight flitted strobe-like across the windshield and jumbled Sid's thoughts. "Let me out right down here. Like I said." Larry's Oldsmobile was parked out back of Rooster's, and Pike's Chevette and a pickup Sid didn't recognize nosed the wall like nursing shoats.

"Sure thing," Tinker said, and burbled onto the highway without slowing. The floorboards throbbed as they accelerated toward the high-dollar end of the lake, just a few miles away. Tinker ejected Bill Andersen and adjusted his rear-view mirror, then let his arm drop across the bench seat with his hand on Sid's shoulder. "There was a fire out here last night. But I suppose you know that."

"It would be hard not to. I'm not deaf, nor blind. Janet went out to look at it." Sid's fingers worried at the seam in his jeans.

Tinker's fingers drummed on Sid's shoulder. "I noticed. And you didn't go."

"I was tired. And I'd had a couple. Just beers." Though he didn't take strong drink or left-handed tobacco, sitting in the car with Tinker, Sid felt like he did. He felt himself becoming more criminal with each click of the odometer.

The doublewides and ranch houses and weed-scabbed yards had dropped away into a no-man's land—a strap of land around the lake too expensive for the locals, too far away from the water for the tourists—then the road curved back to follow the lake's contours. Where the first blue water flickered through the trees, stone-and-cedar mansions sprouted like cheese mold. The stench of burnt plastics hung heavy where Tinker turned into a paved driveway broken-edged from the fire trucks' weight.

Where a manicured hand had slipped an anonymous check past an etched-glass door, a sullied stone fireplace stood alone in a smoking ruin like a fat, abusive sun-baked heathen god who had got drunk and tore up its king-dom. Leaves hung shriveled on blackened branches, and tree trunks oozed sap through steaming fissures. A white official-looking car was parked further down, and two men in coveralls and hardhats probed around the edges of the ash pit with some sort of electronic gadget.

"What do you think?"

Sid stared at the lake, where a big ski boat bobbed at an aluminum dock. "That's some shit. But it happens."

"This particular defecation had some assistance." He nodded at the cover-alled men. "They're from the fire marshal's office in Charleston."

"Good for them."

"They were here before daylight. And I've already talked to the neighbors." Sid looked at his watch.

"The people up the road saw what they took to be a pickup go tearing out of here just before the fire sprung up."

"There you go. You got you a clue, anyhow."

"The lights set up high, and the exhaust was loud, they said. Not like this"—the Crown Vic torqued sideways as Tinker revved the engine—"but like it didn't have an exhaust pipe."

"You already narrowed it to half the vehicles in Union County."

"Where were you last night around a quarter of two? Say between one and two?"

Sid didn't normally remember dreams, but the bear nearly gnawing his hindquarter off lingered in his mind. "I was rassling a bear."

"What time did you get home from Rooster's? I saw your truck there."

"I don't recall exactly." Eleven forty one. Three aces and a four, the best alarm-clock poker hand he'd had all week.

"Take a guess."

"I don't recall."

Tinker hauled the shifter into reverse and backed out of the driveway without checking for traffic. "You suppose Janet would recall if I asked her?"

"You'll have to try her and see. I don't speculate when it comes to women."

"You rednecks beat on your women all weekend, then they testify in court for you on Monday morning. I never could figure that out."

"Maybe Joybelle could explain it to you." Tinker's ex-wife. "My woman don't get beat, and I've never been to court in my life. Not on my own account."

"You been lucky. I'll grant you that." Tinker hitched sideways in his seat like someone who spent a lot of time under the wheel. "Who else was at Rooster's last evening?"

"I don't recall. Who else's truck was there?"

Tinker idled along no faster than a man could walk as they approached Potlicker Road and Rooster's. "You recall driving home?"

"I remember that good, but there wasn't nothing notable about it."

"Maybe I should follow you a night or two, see just how unremarkable your driving is." Tinker idled into Rooster's lot, but didn't offer Sid permission to get out.

Sid wondered how it would feel to bury his fist Tinker's nose. He'd most likely break his hand, and Tinker wouldn't even blink. "Look," he said, then started again without the whine. "I never once caused you any problem. I don't do drugs . . ."

"You can't afford them."

"... and I don't steal or ..."

"Too lazy."

"... get in fights that needs help to get it ended. Hell, I don't even speed."

"Probably not an option, considering what you drive."

"I'm a pure-as-the-driven-snow law-abiding citizen. What do you want out of me?"

"I want to know who set that fire last night. The department ought to solve that, not some bigshot from Charleston."

"It wasn't me."

"From what I hear, I'm not so certain." Tinker removed a little notebook from his shirt pocket, held it unopened like he was offering it into evidence. "Did there ever come a time when you might have publicly showered verbal abuse onto the selfsame people whose house was consumed by fire? Did an occasion ever arise for you to knowingly and with malice aforethought insert a living opossum into those selfsame people's mailbox?" He leaned toward Sid and whispered, "That's a federal offence, fucking with a mailbox."

Sid tried to identify the dark face behind Rooster's smoky glass. "You're making that stuff up." Both instances had been the other buttholes from Pittsburgh that lived way down past the burned ones; the ones who'd stopped at the house and asked Sid if he'd pick up trash along their road, did they pay him good. "Nobody would tell you stuff like that, even if it was the truth. Which it isn't."

"Then I wonder where that information came from?"

"We don't talk around behind each other's back."

"Some do, obviously. And you're talking to me right now, aren't you? What do you suppose those people inside think we're discussing?"

Sid expected the latch to be inoperative, but the big door lurched downhill and dragged Sid out like the car had gagged him up. "I'll be seeing you, Tinker."

"Yes, you will."

Sid blinked inside the doorway till he could make out the ball-capped figures hunched over beers at the far end of the bar. Pike, Larry, and Horse.

Sid took a stool beside Horse, or the shed skin of someone by that name. Horse was pale and pukid, liquid-looking under skin that strained to hold last night's misery. Only his eyebrows, as wild and unruly as one of those dusting hickeys they sold on the TV, offered any evidence of ongoing life.

"How you feeling this morning, Horse?"

"Way better'n usual." Horse lowered his head into his hands.

"Where's your truck?"

Larry drew foamy draft into a pint Mason jar.

"Did I say I wanted one of them?" Sid said.

Larry plunked the jar down in front of Sid and added tomato juice from a can, and Sid overcame his gag reflex and drank half of it down. "Swallow, so I don't have to get up again," Larry said.

Sid obeyed, and felt better for it while Larry drew the second mug.

"It ain't your business where my truck is. I'm driving my sister's today."

"I didn't know you had a sister." Sid attempted without definite results to imagine the same couple spawning Horse and anything without chest hair.

"Then I guess you don't know much. Most flatlanders don't."

"Well, excuse me all to hell," Sid said. "What brought this on?" He made a show of looking at the bottom of his shoe. "Did I track something in?"

"I thought Dort was your stepsister?" Pike said. Maybe chest hair after all.

"Nothing you can't tramp back out when you leave," Horse said. "What you doing riding around with Dunham, anyhow?" The deputy's big engine still burbled outside.

"It's not me that tells tales out of class. And I've heard enough of this flatlander talk. I grew up in the hills, and I've lived in these ones since I was fourteen." Seventeen, but fourteen sounded better. "My woman was *born* here, and if we'd had kids, *they'd* a been born here."

"If your woman had any kids, their *pap* would have been borned here. Considering." Horse's eyes considered up and down Sid's frame.

Sid gripped his jar in a fastball grip, but Tinker Dunham sat just outside the door, waiting for exactly that to happen. "You sonofabitch," was the best he could do.

"Our cat had kittens in the oven," Larry said, "but we never figured them for biscuits."

Pike uttered a nervous bray that encouraged Larry. "Though our hound must have, the way he eat them up." He snorted and honked like a hog that had inhaled a bumblebee.

"I ast you a question," Horse said. "Why you riding with Dunham?"

The air went still and hard, like bar air did when trouble started.

Sid took in all the beer he could in one swallow, then pushed the mug away. "Yous go to hell, all of you."

Horse caught at his sleeve, and Sid stopped to keep from tearing his shirt. "What I said last night was just drunk talk." His breath hissed sour and rank, like an uncovered kraut crock. "I had nothing to do with that fire."

Sid peeled Horse's fingers away one by one, and gave the last a twist to show what would happen if they lit on him again. "I don't know what you're talking about. You think you got the patent on drunk or something?"

"What happens here stays here. Right damn here. But nothing happened. Don't you forget it, neither."

Sid brushed where Horse's fingers had gripped his shirt, knowing the stain would always be there whether you could see it or not. "No, nothing happened here. And I don't reckon it ever will."

Tinker let Sid walk far enough up the hill for him to think he'd gotten away before the engine rumbled Sid's way. "I've been thinking," Tinker said when he'd idled alongside. "It would probably be best if I didn't cause too much of a stir about a fire that nobody will care about come election time. I believe I'll just let the fire marshals handle it. Me being from downstate and all. After a while it'll all go away like nothing ever happened."

Sid had been determined never to speak to Tinker Dunham again, but the words crowded out like calves from the barn in the spring. "You're not from around here either?"

Tinker's lips grew long and straight and thin, like he'd attempted to take a bite from a piece of window glass. "You can't tell any difference between me and these hillbillies?"

The realization that Sid had come uncoupled from his destiny was like a breath of dry air: as long as he lived in such a place, these things were going to happen. And the longer he lived there, the less suited he was to live anywhere else. And he'd been there way too long. "Now that you mention it, you don't seem near as intelligent."

Tinker laughed. "I'm smart enough to let fires to the experts. I'm going to concentrate on drunk drivers. Domestic disturbances. Loitering, and vagrancy. Things the voters will appreciate. But if you hear anything about that fire, you know how to get hold of me."

"You betcha," Sid said, and turned from the road and scrambled up into a forest both intimate and alien.

"You know what I hate most about rednecks?" Tinker yelled after him. "They have no sense of humor. None at all." He laughed loud and raucous to show what one sounded like, then accelerated hard toward an election he still believed he could win, just like Pike still believed Jesus was coming back to take him home.

Halfway home, Sid sat against a tree and laughed himself.

19

"How's HE GET AWAY WITH THAT?" Sid said. "Why don't they fire him?"

Janet tried to aim her laughter at Jeff Foxworthy without slopping any onto Sid, but she could tell from the look on his face she'd failed. "Because he's funny."

Foxworthy strutted in grainy grandeur across their black-and-white TV. Sid leaned forward and whopped it on the lower left corner and the sound cleared up for a minute, like it did when you whopped it just there. "If anyone in your family ever died right after saying, 'Hey, y'all, watch this!' you just might be a redneck."

"You call that funny?"

Janet was cramped on the couch, kicking her feet like a groundhog that had been shot in the head but not properly. "No, it's hilarious," she said when she could breathe again.

"That's exactly what happened to Pike's little brother, and you can laugh at it? I mean, the boy's *dead*."

The lizard inside her that the church had never rooted out—the part that could laugh at a four-wheeler accident—rose up and took control of her breath. "I can't help it," she wheezed.

Foxworthy was still at it. "If your pickup has curtains but your house don't, you just might be a redneck."

Sid glanced out the window and said, "What's funny about that?"

Janet covered her eyes, but could still see the wrinkled aluminum camper top, the faded paisley curtains. She shook her head, the only response she could make.

"Well, we can't hardly go camping without curtains. People might look in and see us in our birthday suits. But not here. Sidemore would bark, and then I'd shoot them in the butt."

"If your grandmother ever said, 'Anybody want to see this before I flush it?' you just might be a redneck."

"That's just disgusting, that is." Sid felt in the cracks between the cushions. "Where's the tuner, anyhow?"

"Here," Janet said as the mirth ran out of her. She handed him the pliers, knowing his mood would turn even uglier if he didn't find them.

Sid clamped down onto the chewed brass shaft and switched to what was either a western or wide-hatted Eskimos riding horselike creatures in a blizzard. "We don't say nigger and raghead and faggot in this house, and we won't start with this redneck talk."

"Aw, listen to Reverend Sid. We don't say those things because we don't have anybody to say them about, or to. That's the only reason."

"Hell we don't." Sid stood in the open front door where he could look toward the lake. In silhouette he looked wide but thin, like a sail cat she'd seen leaned against a mailbox post after someone peeled it from the pavement. "What about those colored people from Wheeling, and the A-rabs that had their house burn down? And Billy Corst, you think his wires aren't crossed somewheres?" He waved the other way, toward town.

"But you don't even get around those people, and Billy's just a nice man. But different. There ain't none of them any part of our life."

"If I did get around them, I wouldn't call them what they was. I'd call them who they are."

Janet wanted to get mad, but it was hard to do around Sid. Something funny always ran out of his mouth. "Is there a difference?"

"If you don't know that much, you don't know nothing. Foxworthy's making light of what I am, and he don't know me, or *who* I am."

"He's making fun of himself. He knows that stuff from being a redneck."

"He's no redneck. He lives out there in Vegas, makes $50,000 a year making fun of his grandma's turds. Probably hadn't been out of town since he graduated from college."

The word "college" shot nostalgia Janet's way, hard enough to knock her back to that little bit of time when life still offered promises. She felt her voice changing, and her thoughts. "The reason they can joke about us is that we're comfortable with what we are. We can laugh at ourselves, so they can too. It's something to be proud of."

"I never even heard that word till lately," Sid said. "Now it's everywhere, like welfare cheese. I don't even know what a redneck is for sure."

"A redneck is anybody that doesn't know what one is. If you'd listen to Jeff Foxworthy, then you'd know and wouldn't be one."

Sid turned and leaned against the jamb. In the raking light his face was lined and old, his eyes like the worn glass intermingled with rounded stones on a river-bottom. She'd not noticed how his hair had thinned, and her heart went out to look for the missing strands.

"I reckon negroes laughs at theirselves when nobody else is around, but the rest of us damn well better not."

"But they didn't choose to be what they are. You can't make fun of what people can't help."

Sid's voice was as dry and wrinkled as his face. "You reckon I chose this here? That I looked through God's big mail-order catalogue and said, yeah, right here, I want this redneck life, in this pretty little rotted-down trailer on the bottom side of the road where the trash washes out of the ditches and into the yard, with this bad back and no job and no education and no money. Yeah, Lord, I'll take that'n, cause it's funny and it'll make people laugh and feel better, and then I'll feel good for making them do it."

The way he talked in a monotone, and as though to someone standing just out of her sight, made Janet uneasy. "You could have left out of here at any time. Nothing holds you back."

"Yeah, just like a possum in a pack of dogs. He's got the option to whip all them dogs and go about his business, but he don't ever exercise it. He lays down and plays dead while they chomp up his ribs and gnaw holes in his gall bladder, and after they're finished he feels real good that he give them such a good time. That's why possums grin like they do."

Janet laughed, then thought better of it; it attracted his eyes, and she didn't want them on her right then.

"But let's say I did choose what I am. I reckon some garbage men does too. Artificial cow breeders. Butt doctors. Tree huggers, and Jews, and Piscopalians. Can you get on the TV and make light of them? Not if you want to keep your job, you don't. You treat them people with respect, unless they're a redneck. Life's got splashed down till we're all that's left in the terlet, and everbody that's clumb out turns and spits back in like they was never there."

Janet pushed past him into the kitchen and rattled around in the cabinets not for something to cook, but for something to derail Sid from working himself into a tizzy. "You always get this way when the days get shorter. You have that Seasonal Affective Disorder Syndrome I told you about. SADS. It comes from not enough daylight, and gets you all depressed."

"Maybe I'll go sunbathe, then." Sid flung his hand toward the sky. Clouds had set in Labor Day weekend, like always, but that year they hadn't departed. October's leaves fell in sullen solitude through mist and rain.

Janet shook a box of macaroni and cheese, ran a tongue over her teeth and set it back. "They got pills that do the same thing. You could take them, not be miserable till spring. You make everyone around you miserable, too."

"Yeah, I'll just take my insurance card and slip down to the family doctor and get me a bottle of them. What's a matter with that macaroni, anyhow?"

Janet reclaimed the box and closed the door and turned to face Sid. "Go to the emergency room. They have to treat you, whether you can pay or not."

"Well, let's just call the ambulance while we're at it. Tell em Sid's been struck down by cloud cover. Tell em to hurry, to bring some a them sunshine pills."

Janet leaned back over the sink, half worried at his tone of voice. "You got to lighten up, laugh a little bit. Life's getting way too serious around here."

"All right," Sid said, and laughed like he'd took her advice. "Try this." He took the pliers and turned back to Foxworthy's show, but the sound had faded away into a static buzz. After he'd studied the comedian for a moment, Sid started strutting around enough like his model to make Janet laugh out loud. "If you live up in the hills where your folks and grandfolks did, you just might be a redneck."

"But that's not funny. It ain't the same."

"And if you'd fight for what them old farts believed and thought, even though you haven't figgered out what's so special about it yet, you just might be a redneck."

"Aw, Sid."

"The fact that the rest of the world makes fun of it makes it good enough for me.

"If your house and car is paid for, even if they are rusted down to nothing, you just might be a redneck.

"If the only nose jobs you know of was done with a chunk of firewood or a cue stick, you just might be a redneck.

"And if you don't fix things that's not broke, or get a new one if it's not wore out, you might be a redneck."

Janet put a hand over her eyes.

"If you plant taters by the signs of the moon, but think the horoscope is of the devil, you just might be a redneck.

"If you don't call people niggers because there's not any here, and are pretty durn certain you wouldn't anyhow, you just might be a redneck.

"If you wear the same kind of clothes your daddy did, because they fit right and wear good, you just might be a redneck.

"If you hunt sang just because you can, and because you know what it looks like, and because it reminds you of Bud and because you like to do it and you sure got the time to, you might be a redneck."

Words beat like hailstones.

"If you bought your own clippers when going to the barbershop got to be about cutting hair instead of finding out what was going on around, you just might be a redneck.

"And if a paycheck still catches you by surprise, but the first frost don't, you just might be a redneck." Janet had forgot to pick up her pay in her rush to get home and cover her flowers, and Sid wasn't going to let it pass.

"If you try to make your yard look pretty with what you got, even if that's nothing but a old truck tire and a dumb wooden duck you made in Bible school, you just might be a redneck.

"If you can quote from the Bible, but can't recollect who wrote that *Moby-Dick* book they tried to make you read in college, you might be a redneck. So saith the Lord."

Janet felt tears begin to leak. Sid's voice softened. "If you keep your folks at home instead of burying them early in some pissy nursing home, you're most likely a redneck. Or would have if you'd had the chance, if they hadn't run off on you. I know you would have."

The box of macaroni dropped from her hand and the end popped open and the individual pieces crunched under Sid's boots. His arms went around her and squeezed the water out in earnest. His voice had gone low and soft. "And if you think all that's funny, you just might be a . . . hell, I don't know what that makes you. Some kind of a hog, or a ape maybe."

They stood swaying, dancing without moving their feet, and suddenly they were off balance, and the macaroni hurt Janet's feet too much to take her weight and they were falling and the floor was springing under her, not hard but resilient, and Sid was atop her but caught on his elbows and knees, and the jarring brought the TV sound up again. "If you see a billboard that says 'Just say no to crack,' and it reminds you to hitch up your pants, you just might be a redneck," it blared before it faded again.

Something began working deep inside Sid, like a baby kicking in the womb, or a mule, and then he laughed and she laughed and their laughter grew and consumed their anger and their pain and their misery. When she could, she reached up and tickled his butt where his jeans had slid down and they laughed some more and he kissed her and they rolled onto their sides amid the macaroni. She ran a finger down the ridge of his nose, testing its character as one might test a store-bought tomato for any trace of softness, and with the same results. "Let's move," she said.

"Just lay atop me," Sid said, and rolled onto his back. Like he would be softer than the floor. "I hate that couch."

"That ain't what I mean. Let's move to where we got a better chance. Maybe not right into a city, but close to one. Closer. Where you could get a good job that didn't hurt your back. Where we could be happy again."

Sid sat up quickly, like he'd heard a prowler, and stared hard out the open door. He bored in his ear. "I must have misheard you. It sounded like you said let's move."

She prized a piece of embedded macaroni from his cheek and sat up and kissed the mark it left. "I got nothing holding me here anymore. Mom and Dad are gone, and the farm. And this place is getting to be like a city anyhow." Lies rolled freely and without thought from her mouth, and as she lied she lusted for the things she'd always clamped down on before she could want them too bad. Money. Things. Places.

His eyes had livened, whether with liquid or hope she couldn't tell. "Don't you tease me. Don't say to leave and then won't."

Daring tremoloed her voice. "No, I'm ready. Let's just go."

"What about your friends? You gonna leave them behind?"

"I don't really have any. They tolerate me at church, but I'm not part of them. And the people on the road crew aren't my friends. All my real friends have already moved. We could go out to Canton where they all went, and it would be like going home instead of leaving."

"No. I'd not do that. I'd start clean over was I to go. I'd go to where I didn't even know who the sheriff was. Was I to go."

Janet laughed. "Now it sounds like you're dragging your feet. Don't you want to go? To tear down the mountain like you always said?"

"You'd change your mind before we got to the bottom of the hill."

"No. I'll stick with it." Would she?

"I'd go to school maybe."

"Sid, now you're talking simple. You hate school."

"Not a regular school. One of them trade schools, where you learn to do something valuable. Not in the daytime, when I was supposed to be working, but at night. We'd have money enough for two cars, so you could still have one when I was gone."

"I'd get a job too, and not because I had to. We'll be rich as Fats."

Sid looked at the TV, where a commercial for some kind of a credit card was playing, and a shadow fell across his face. "You reckon they'll make sport of us? We don't know nothing about living around people."

The full weight of how dumb and backward and poor they'd allowed themselves to become—all because of her silly refusal to leave the security of a place that had eroded around them until even the people she'd known were washed away—crashed down like the trailer roof had fallen in. Janet wanted to go, go right then, because by the next morning she'd lose her nerve, and her excitement had begun to fade under Sid's scrutiny. "They're making fun of us now. For staying here. So what difference if they make fun of us for leaving?"

"Well, let's think about it anyhow. The idea has some appeal."

"No. Let's just go. Let's go tonight. We won't tell nobody. Let's put what's worth saving in the truck and just go. We can put rocks in the other side of the bed to balance it up."

Sid grinned, but uneasily. "What about the electric and stuff?"

"It'll get turned off after while. After nobody pays."

"Where would we go? We've not picked out a place or nothing."

"It don't matter. Cities are probly like mountains, one just like another. Let's just go till we find one."

Sid's face was flushed, and his breath coming harder than sitting on the floor warranted. "We won't come running back if we go. I want you to know that clear."

"I'll not ask you to. But if you decide to, we'll just come. We won't make a big deal about leaving, won't tell anyone, so if we come back we'll just come."

"You're serious. You'd really leave this place."

Janet nodded and hoped her tears wouldn't spring out just then. "If we like it there, we'll call back and sell the place. Or rent it."

Sid looked around the inside of their little trailer. "You know anything about sardines?"

Janet shook her head. "More than I want to. What's that got to do with renting?"

"No, we'll just let it set. Let it rot down, like it wants to do." Sid crunched his way outside and stood on the stoop, looking all around. "Sidemore," he yelled after a while. "I hope you like them flatland dogs. Cause you're gonna be one.

§

Where Route 50 topped Allegany Front Sid pulled to the side of the road and killed the engine. "What's wrong?" Janet said.

"You want to give the mountains one last look before we fall off?"

"No man, having put his hand to the plow, and looking back, is fit for the kingdom of God. The Bible says that."

Sid laughed with more ease than she'd heard since she'd suggested moving. "I didn't figure it come from the *TV Guide*. I'm not fit for God's kingdom anyhow. I'm going to take one more look. That's all."

Sid's last look took a long time, but even when Janet's eyes were open, she never took them off the valley ahead. Not then, and not ever.

III

Bell's Hill Lane

And I saw a new heaven and a new earth:
for the first heaven and the first earth were passed away.

Revelation 21:1

20

Janet chimed a fork against her plate till Sid was ready to bust. Like there wasn't noise enough here, cars going by like blackbirds. She finally got around to what was chafing her. "The light in the fruit cellar doesn't work."

Sid created a haystack of beans and carrots, then scattered them across his plate. When the dinging started again he said, "You call the landlord?"

"Name one thing he's ever fixed."

"You didn't have a fruit cellar back home, and that didn't bother you none."

"Sid, we've been here fourteen years. This *is* our home. Please fix the light. Is that too much to ask?"

Sid wadded his napkin and added it to the vegetables.

"Finish your dinner first."

"I ate dinner six hours ago."

"Supper, whatever. Look, I fixed this specially for you."

"Yeah." Sid slid down to let his head loll against the back of the chair, eyes closed. A muscle ticked in his neck, and the evening sun warmed the hard ridges of his face. He felt like the little end of a broken stick, whittled down to nothing. He had so little hair left his fingers couldn't detect it when he scratched his head; his hat ring went clear to the skin. He looked square on at Janet for the first time that evening. "Jerry was inside all afternoon. It was busy, too. I couldn't unload trucks for fetching stuff for the customers."

Janet belabored her meat with a steak knife without hurting it much. He'd told her a thousand times you can't just throw beef in a skillet like you could venison, not if you wanted to chew it.

"His job is out in the yard, with me."

"Is that your problem tonight? You didn't have anybody to hold your hand?" Bitter words that dragged behind him like a tin can tied to his tail.

"I'll look at the light."

The fruit cellar's air was fluid with onions and old potatoes. A long cold damp room under the concrete porch. More a groundhog hole than a fruit cellar, no place for a light anyway. His groping fingers found a cobweb, then the light string. A broken switch, he could tell as soon as he pulled it. Not just corrosion, like the last time.

In comparison to the fruit cellar, the furnace room was dry and bright. He dumped a box of pipe fittings and phone connectors, rusty nails and broken receptacles on the floor—nothing that would fix a light. He picked most of it up, kicked the rest behind the water heater.

Dry restless leaves fouled the garage floor, crunched under his feet when he retrieved a flashlight from his pickup. Sid stood the flashlight outside the fruit cellar door, then sat on the basement steps and mulled over the day's developments.

When he went upstairs, Janet was on the couch, working on her toenails. "Is it fixed?" Firm chin on tanned knee, warm brown eyes that cut like a skinning knife.

"The switch is broke. I'll get one tomorrow. I set a flashlight there for you." His fingernails made scratching noises against his palm. Sid sat in his chair and rolled his frayed cuffs, removed his socks. Man, his feet stunk in that heat. The weather should have cooled by then. "There's no reason for Jerry to be inside, busy as we was."

"The slippery slope to solipsism."

"I don't know what that means."

"No, you sure don't." Janet tossed her nail file onto the coffee table and slid off to her bedroom. Later the back door clicked shut, then her car door. Headlights brightened the living room wall, and she was gone. Again.

And Jerry was inside, on a busy day.

§

Janet leaned against the cold empty range with arms crossed. Sid detoured around her and sat his lunch bucket on the counter and drew a glass of Chloroxy tap water. "I forgot the switch."

"Big surprise." Earrings flashed in a harsh shard of autumn sunlight that bared her beauty and her imperfections—glossy hair and faded roots, rosy cheeks with tiny pockmarks, a little wrinkle under a smooth chin, slim neck with the suggestion of bones within.

"I'll get it tomorrow."

"You can set a trap tonight, because now we got a mouse in there. I'm not going back in till it's gone."

Sid laughed. "Used to be you weren't scared of bats or copperheads or polecats, but now a mouse gives you the thimbleshits."

"Just get rid of it. There's mouse poop everywhere."

Sid blew his nose, refolded his handkerchief with care. "What's happened to you, Janet? You've changed."

Janet answered so quick that Sid knew she'd been waiting for the chance. "You haven't. That's the whole problem. You're the same redneck you always were."

"I never counted that something to be ashamed of. Like you did."

She wheeled away, and he knew he'd stung her, and was glad for it. "Get rid of the mouse." Somewhere back aways she'd started saying mouse so it started with moe, like the smart one of the Three Stooges, and house the same way, like a garden implement.

"There can't be a mouse in the fruit cellar. It's got block walls, and a concrete floor and ceiling."

"You tell that to the mouse," she said. "Talk him into not being there, then come up and talk yourself into dinner."

"Where you going?'

"Who said I was going anywhere?"

"Did you fluff up just for me? You got on earrings cause you're happy to see me, and you painted up so I'd feel thankful to have such a woman when I come home? We going to have a party? Fire up the grill, have Jerry and Darlene over?" Sid suddenly felt shamed by his nastiness. "I'm sorry. I don't mean to talk like that."

If she heard, she didn't acknowledge.

§

Sid discovered the hole behind the potato box. Somehow the mouse had found a chunk of loose mortar that would have been big as a bushel basket to a man, shook it with its little feet, thought a spell, then shook it again, dug around the corners, and finally rolled the stone away like Jesus Christ emerging from the tomb. Into a fruit cellar.

Sid shined his flashlight into the mouse hole: an alien landscape of cement and dust. The hole smelled of lime and potatoes and a fainter smell that belonged to something that breathed and defecated.

Sid had an out-of-body experience (that's what Janet would call it since she'd started fooling with stuff like that) where he saw himself on all fours, smelling a mouse hole. A primal growl built in the same place laughter was generated. "I'm coming to get you," he whispered into the hole, and tried to imagine what the mouse was doing. Was it trembling, or working on its toenails?

Janet's car was gone when he went upstairs to get a trap from under the kitchen sink, to bait it with peanut butter. The trap snapped shut on his finger, and again before the crossbar caught in the trigger; he carried it to the fruit cellar and set it just outside the mouse hole.

The peanut butter had made him hungry. A plastic package of crackers wouldn't open at first, then split end-to-end. He ate two with peanut butter, then scooped the mess into the pull-out trash bin.

§

Jerry waved him to a stop. Sid eased the pallet to the ground, then shut off the forklift's engine and removed his hard hat. Jerry propped a foot on the step-up and leaned on his clipboard.

"The Man wants to see you, pal."

Sid spat dust from his mouth. "What for?"

Jerry shrugged. "I'm just the messenger."

"Darlene ever fool around on you?"

"That's a hell of a thing to ask." Jerry flipped the clip on his board, again and again.

"What would you do if she did?" The forklift's seat creaked as Sid leaned back and scratched his sweaty stomach. "Would you shoot her, or him? Both of them?"

Air whistled from Jerry's puffed cheeks. "We don't act like that down here on the flat ground." He looked at his watch. "You need to see The Man."

"What would you do if you caught Darlene with someone else?"

"You think Janet's having an affair?"

"Maybe."

Jerry shook his head. "Nah. Darlene would know; they tell each other everything." He wagged a finger at Sid. "Thou shalt not discharge firearms. You might hit yourself."

"I considered doing that, too."

"Hey *hey* hey. This conversation's getting way too serious. Get inside. Mudpuppy's waiting."

"What are you doing inside all the time?"

"Whatever Mr. Moudopie tells me to." Jerry slapped Sid's leg with the clipboard. "Front and center."

Mudpuppy was on the phone when Sid peeked into his office, blatting about kids and college. He sat square and straight on his chair, like a child at the big cherry desk. "Sid," he said as he replaced the receiver. He waved to a chair covered in green burlap. "How's it going?"

"Good."

Mudpuppy said he wished he had time to get outside more, to experience "the grass-roots level of the operation." Sid sat like a stump. The boss fidgeted with a fancy pencil. "Sid, I guess you've noticed how much we're growing."

Sid waited.

"We're also improving our operation as we expand." He sat back in his chair. "We've been automating, streamlining our warehousing functions. Now we're in the process of changing our emphasis from product to service."

Sid stared at an ink smudge on Mudpuppy's white collar.

"Though we're growing exponentially, we actually have need for fewer personnel. People," he added, in case Sid couldn't differentiate a personnel from a forklift.

Sid inspected the crescents of grease under his fingernails. He not only operated the equipment, but he had to maintain it, too. How many people could do that?

Mudpuppy adjusted his tie. "Our restructuring won't commence until the first of the month, and the staffing decisions aren't finalized. But I feel it's only fair to keep you abreast of the situation." He looked away, thinking about kids and college, Sid figured.

"I been here five years. I done a good job, without complaining, without spending half my time in here begging for a raise. Now you're going to fire me."

Mudpuppy steeled up under Sid's stare. "Yes, you've probably been here longer than some who will retain their positions." He adjusted his pen parallel to a line on his desk pad. "We're going to be a lean, mean team. And you've not impressed me as the world's best team player. You're detached. A loner."

"Detached."

Mudpuppy looked at the wall clock. "Even more so, recently. Is there a problem I should know about?"

"I never seen any team helping me run the forklift. Load customers."

"Like I said, our emphasis is changing."

Sid leaned over the desk and misaligned the pen. "You want to know my problem? I got a rat hole in my basement wall, right through the concrete blocks." He stood and left, but turned before he'd even left the building.

Mudpuppy was on the phone again. "Excuse me," he said, and put his hand over the mouthpiece.

"You'll be sorry."

"Is that a threat?"

"No, I wouldn't bother to threaten you. If I wanted to do something nasty, I'd get it done, not warn you. I'm just saying you'll be sorry I don't work for you no more."

§

Janet was sweeping the garage, so Sid parked in the driveway. He watched her, how she wasn't as old as he felt. "I found out what Jerry was doing inside," he said when she stopped and looked at him with upraised eyebrows. "Getting promoted."

"You told me."

"I didn't even know it."

Janet turned away and poked into a corner with her broom. "You told me something like that. Did you get a light switch?"

"Jerry's going to take my job. I was there before he was."

"Nobody would want your job. Especially Jerry."

Sid walked past her and down the concrete steps to the basement. The mousetrap was untouched, but there were new turds around the hole.

The twelve-gauge pump shotgun he'd bought as soon as Janet's car was paid off was in the bedroom closet, behind the red plastic bag that kept dust off his suit. Shells were in his sock drawer; Sid selected two.

Janet met him in the kitchen, eyes wide at the sight of his gun. "What are you doing?" Her hand worked at her mouth like the flapper on a pinball machine, like the words were knocking her fingers out of the way.

"We got a rat needs shot." Sid found a pack of sliced Swiss cheese in the refrigerator, held it between his teeth as he navigated the doors to the fruit cellar. The flashlight cut a swath through dusty jars and slumped bags and boxes of recyclables. Sid shredded a slice of Swiss and scattered it around the hole. An old blue cooler felt familiar against his butt, brought back the camping trips they'd taken when they first moved there. When Janet still missed the country. He propped the flashlight on top of a gallon jar of pickles, its beam centered on the mouse hole. The gun's action was metallic and harsh within the close walls.

The door eased open. "You can't shoot in the house. The bullet will ricochet and kill you."

"Save you the job. It doesn't shoot bullets anyway. Just shot."

"Sid, you're crazy. Come out of there. Let's go out to dinner. Come on, honey."

"It isn't dinner that I want."

"Then what, Sid? What the hell *do* you want?"

"I don't know." Then he did know. "I want to go home."

Janet groaned. "All those years listening to how you wanted to get away, now you want to go home."

"I was wrong."

"Did you ever consider that it's not the place that makes you unhappy? That it's you?"

Sid eased her out the door. He selected a shelving board from a stack leaning against the wall and kicked it tight under the doorknob.

Not long after Janet gave up knocking, the mouse was there, all trembling whiskers and glistening eyes. "You're gonna die." The gun barrel's front bead edged over the mouse's body like a full moon rising till only the eyes showed. "The world don't tolerate rats."

"Sid! Who are you talking to? Open the damn door."

The mouse stopped chewing for only a moment. Sid tightened his finger against the trigger. "Goodbye, rat." The mouse raised his head and wiggled his nose. The finger pressure hung there, just an ounce short of firing. Knocking started again on the door. Sid swung the barrel to the side and fired the shotgun into a pile of newspapers stacked for recycling. The explosion was like a third presence in the small compartment, using all the space and air. The noise tore at Sid's intestines, ripped at his bowels. The pile of papers oozed sideways, then spilled across the floor with a thump. The fallen stack continued to settle, adjusting, getting comfortable again. A door slammed far away.

Sid laid the gun across his lap and waited for the mouse to return. It was there again in just a minute or two. Sid's talk flowed freely, once he got started. The mouse nibbled earnestly and listened attentively. Sid's words faded away as the flashlight dimmed. Gradually, then swiftly, the darkness absorbed them.

Sid was hungry again. Not just hungry, ravenous. An image of the mouse feeling its way through the block walls returned as he felt his way down the shelves. The jars of fruits and vegetables Janet had cold packed during the summer were cool and solid. The raised letters on the jars felt like the country. He traced *Mason* with work-hardened fingertips, knowing the letters before he touched them. He found a jar that felt just right. The flat top gave way under his thumbs with a pop, and a breath of sweetness washed his face. Smell, touch, taste, he identified the contents—sliced peaches.

Sid sat on his cooler and ate peaches and Swiss cheese with his fingers. He held a slice of peach above his face. Syrup tapped his nose, then his chin. He felt rain, fresh sweet spring rain untouched by smokestacks and exhaust pipes, cool rain that brought a green flush to the forest. The slice dropped in his mouth, dead center, and he smiled as he chewed. Nothing had ever tasted so good. "You there, pal?" He sensed the mouse, watching and listening and nibbling. They ate, and watched, and listened.

He heard voices as he drank the last of the juice. Thunder boomed and lightning flickered around door's edges with the first couple of crashes. With the third, the prop splintered and amber light from the bare basement bulb washed across him.

Jerry and Janet squinted into the cellar's gloom. Their sweat and perfume polluted the potato and onion and damp and sweet smells. They watched and listened, eyes bright and wide. The yellow backlight tinged the red around Janet's eyes purple. Mascara, leached into wrinkles, bound her in spiders' web. Thin lips puckered around a shock of chestnut teeth. Orange-nailed bony fingers clutched and quivered at Jerry's sleeve.

Jerry breathed as though he were preparing to venture underwater. "You're still here." He stood square-on, a cardboard man against the light, all eyeballs and open mouth. "We thought you shot yourself."

The laugh that rolled from Sid's belly was as rich and sweet as the peaches had been. One huge guffaw, then another, and then it came like a train. And then it quit.

"My God," Janet said.

The sound of the pump action drove Jerry and Janet a step back. Sid ejected both shells. The spent casing he dropped into the empty fruit jar, the charged one into his shirt pocket. He stopped to consider his friend and his wife, huddled like mice. "I'd offer you some peaches, Jerry, but they're all gone." Jerry involuntarily clutched the jar when Sid thrust it against his stomach.

Janet followed Sid up the stairs. "Sid, stop. Talk to me, honey." The shadow of her hand behind her back fluttered as she motioned for Jerry to stay back, but he followed them up the stairs. They were waiting in the hallway when Sid returned from the bedroom with the shotgun and an armload of jeans and t-shirts.

Sid sidled around Jerry, though he wanted to push him aside. His shirt ripped as Jerry clutched at his sleeve. Sid stopped. "There were these two rednecks, Jerry, that met on the road, and one of them had a bag over his shoulder. The other one said, 'Hey, man, whatcha got in the bag?' And he said, 'Chickens. If you can guess how many I got, I'll give you both of them.' And the other one said, 'Four?'"

Sid's shirt slid loose from Jerry's clutch. "I told you that joke."

"You didn't finish it. The first redneck give the other one the bag, and then he laughed all the way home. He was sick of packing them same two damn chickens up and down the road, day after day." Jerry recoiled as Sid reached their way, but Sid pulled Janet forward and kissed her cheek. "Check those eggs real regular." He patted Jerry on the shoulder, then walked out the door.

Janet caught him before he could back out of the driveway. "Where you going?"

Sid switched off the engine and looked off into the haze and streetlights toward where he knew the mountains eased up out of the flatlands. "Home, I reckon."

"This is our home."

"This here's a subdivision of hell we've paid rent on for fourteen years."

"But you hated it up in the mountains. We can't go back there."

"I never knowed what hate was up there. Not until we come down here did I get any grip on that word a-tall."

"That wasn't your home for long. You were born down in Logan County."

Home for long. Sid heard again the Bible verse his mother had said over and over, a tonic, a promise, a lament for a life of pain she was anxious to leave, yet afraid: *Also then they shall be afraid of that which is high, and fears shall be in the way, and the almond trees shall flourish, and the grasshopper shall be a burden, and desire shall fail, because man goeth to his long home, and the mourners go about the streets.* "This place sure isn't home. If that's not home up there, it will be. I'll make it so. Make it my long home."

"Don't leave me here. Not here."

Sid thought about that for a while. "You got a car, babe. Come when you're ready."

"What about your stuff?"

Sid nodded at the armload of clothing on the pickup's seat, the shotgun. "The rest is city stuff."

"Janet?" Jerry had finally got up enough nerve to poke his head out the garage door. "Is everything okay?"

Sid had a notion to run at Jerry, holler at him and scare him under the bed. But he started the engine, and Janet's hand fell away from his rear view mirror as he backed into the street. He wanted to look back to see if she was chasing him down the street, or if she was snuggled back in Jerry's arm, but he didn't. He looked ahead, a long way ahead, to where the mountains swelled cold and wet and empty and jobless and beautiful into the night.

21

As she topped Allegany Front, Janet worked the math, calculated the fourteen years since she and Sid had rolled across that same spot in a pickup with no tags, with FARM USE scrawled on the doors with green spray paint. How were they to know that wasn't legal outside of West Virginia?

Fourteen years of craziness. They'd let their values weather away untended. They'd replaced the trees and rivers of their minds with hardtop and litter.

Through the fog Janet glimpsed scattered pale hulks of dead white oaks amid seas of green forest. In '90, when gypsy moths had gnawed every green shred from the oaks, they'd thought it was the end of the world. But the moths were gone, and but for an isolated casualty, the trees remained.

They'd thought no jobs signaled the end of life.

They'd thought a change of scenery would mean a change of circumstance.

Jesus.

Janet rolled down her window to breathe the dank mountain air. Her glasses fogged immediately, and she tossed them onto the seat. Up there, what did it matter if you didn't see so good?

A silver SUV caromed from the mist, no headlights, straddling the double line that hadn't been there when she'd left. Janet swerved onto the berm, let the bigger vehicle slide past. She wondered if the driver had even seen her little Ford.

As abruptly as she'd entered the clouds, Janet burst into blinding sunlight, and again gravel rattled against the rocker panels as she lost her sense of direction on a road she could have once driven with closed eyes.

Leaves glistened with a million crystals of moisture in the clear air that welcomed her home. One of those rare upside-down days, where Union

County saw the sun while the rest of the world pined in the drizzle. An omen, maybe, made special for her homecoming.

Then the glare from all that glass slashed at her, and she braked without checking her mirror. A car she hadn't seen, a low red slinky thing, shot around with a wail of horns and the driver's upraised finger. For a moment she was adrift, and her equilibrium juddered as she regained her bearings. She pulled off the road and stepped out. Gravel bit at bare feet grown tender on deep carpet and soft lawns.

She shaded her eyes and tried to apprehend the glass-fronted homes that plastered the hills around the lake. Thousands of them, vacation row houses, the biggest ones shoulder-to-shoulder on the crests like raptors perched to swoop down and devour the rest. In the valley below, where there'd been only a bait shop and a dilapidated motel, a small city blinked and churned. A shopping center sprawled where Homer Markin's farm should be. Even from that distance Janet could almost read the marquee on the huge stone building that had to be a theatre. An eight-holer. Boats swarmed over the lake like maggots.

As though she were a maggot as well, Janet allowed herself to be drawn in.

A sense of the ridiculous swelled as she drove slowly through restaurants and banks and hotels and boat dealers. Familiar signs that she never expected to see there—Perkins and Comfort Inn and Burger King—instilled an air of the city she'd just left, but the remnants of the past scattered here and there—a red barn, a small cut-stone house nestled between a BP station and the Chamber of Commerce—made it all a mixed-up dream. She'd wake, and laugh at such a perverted fantasy world. She'd find herself in Akron, snuggled against Sid's back.

Even the road names had changed. Route 219 had become Union Highway, touted on overhead placards at every side street. She hesitated where the Dam Road turned off, confused by the Lake Vista Drive sign. But she recognized the lumpy red oak on the first hard curve, tumored from innumerable confrontations with late-night drunks.

McCumber's Inn Road. Who was McCumber, and what inn ever graced the Jawbreaker Road? More than the open fields and dark woods that had been buried under lawns and asphalt, Janet felt outrage for the missing names. Jawbreaker Road, where the Union County Commissioner and the State

Highway Superintendent fought with bare fists over whether it would even *be*. That special name had been reduced to McCumber's Inn Road.

Her own road, too. Bell's Hill Lane. "It's Potlikker Road. *Potlikker Road!*" she said, and turned up it. A Sheetz store sat where Rooster's once had.

Her confusion intensified as she drew near where her old trailer *had* to sit. There, but a house sat there, and the topography wasn't right. She pulled just past the driveway and stopped. The lot no longer fell hard away from the road, but eased gradually downward over terraced walks and flowerbeds. The house was crisp and modern, but stone and wood made it appear to have grown from the hillside. Rhododendron billowed around its walls, the grass meticulously edged around the clumps. Bird feeders everywhere.

It was not the right place.

Then she saw the old pitcher pump. It had been in a load of fill dirt that Sid had hauled in to level up a place for the dog box, and Sid had stuck it in the ground like there was a well there. Someone had painted it a soft teal green, with its own native-stone base, the handle extended toward the highway. On the end rested a cedar mailbox. Under it hung a carved sign. The Bells.

Bell's Hill Lane.

Janet backed into the paved drive and studied the house in her side mirrors. A high-gabled affair, the central section was glassed on both ends, offering a view of the inside. Janet could see it best in the right mirror, the one that made everything far away. She could see her old life in one take, like through the wrong end of binoculars, not magnified by coming home, but shrunk down to where she could see it end to end.

Janet started when someone said, "Can I help you?" in a soft, articulate voice. A woman stood in front of the car. She wore an earth-toned long-sleeved blouse and a wide-brimmed hat, the expensive kind that comes from L.L. Bean or Land's End. Under her waistband were tucked soft-looking leather gloves, and she held a pink-handled trowel in both hands, as one would a weapon.

Her skin was so pale and so fine she might never have been outside before.

"I was just turning around." Janet pulled the shifter into drive, but the woman didn't move. The engine idled too fast, and Janet had to ride the brake hard to keep the car from lunging at her.

"What business have you here?" She placed one hand on the hood.

"Please." Panic Janet couldn't explain quivered in her voice. "Move out of the way."

The woman eased along the car to stare in Janet's window. Janet looked straight ahead, but she could feel the eyes probing like the little trowel would seek out weeds in the flowerbed. Release the brake pedal, be gone. Release the brake. Release it.

"Who are you? What do you want?"

Janet turned to the blurry woman, until then unaware that her eyes had become wet. She wiped them with the heel of her hand.

"This was my home."

The gray eyes probed where Janet did not wish her to dig.

"There was an old house trailer here. Falling down. The floor was rotted away, and red squirrels had taken up residence in the roof."

Janet nodded. "That's it. That was my home."

"Are you sure you have the right place?" Her eyes flittered across Janet's yellow blouse, at the stylish purse on the front seat. "Another man was here last week. He said this was *his* home."

Janet imagined how Sid would curse and rage that another's home sat on land that had been his, that she knew he'd consider his no matter whose name was on the deed. "That's just papers," he'd said once when a block of bottom-land he'd hunted was sold to the Nature Conservancy. "It don't change the *land* any." Sid would threaten to sue these squatters, or to shoot them.

"My husband."

The eyes tightened. "No. A local type."

"My husband. Sid Lore."

The woman's eyes left her then, rested on the house, and Janet knew that she'd recognized the name. "I'm sorry. It sold at auction, for back taxes. That was before all this"—she made a sweeping gesture that encompassed all that had happened in Janet's absence.

"I have to go." Janet knew more with her gut than with her brain that that particular part of the past was gone, and that the quicker she pulled herself up out of the hole it had left, the better off she'd be. *Don't dwell on it.*

The woman touched Janet's arm, not in a predatory way. "Come inside first. I'll make fresh lemonade."

The change in attitude confused her, and Janet so wanted to walk where she and Sid had spent the best years of their lives, though they'd had no reference that would make them suspect it at the time.

She watched her own hand push the shift lever into park and switch off the ignition. As they walked down the stone walkway, the woman's hand supported her, urged her onward.

The door was heavy with beveled glass and polished oak. Inside, the air was cool and dry, not Union County air. "Come." She led the way to a kitchen all stainless steel and granite.

While the woman squeezed lemons beside the sink, her eyes seldom left Janet. Janet grew uncomfortable under her blatant inspection. "My husband stays at our home in Arlington during the week. That's near Washington."

"Does he work there?" Apparently some things hadn't changed.

"Carlton's an attorney. Not the criminal kind." She laughed. "An estate attorney."

"Estate."

The woman licked a finger, opened her mouth as if to speak, then rinsed her hands in a sink that seemed part of the countertop. Dark, and deep. "I think you could help us, Ms. Lore. This"—she made the circular all-encompassing motion again—"should be stopped." She poured juice into heavy glasses, slid one Janet's way.

Janet looked out the window while she sipped the tart and heady juice and imagined her trailer there, faded and dented. She again saw wildflowers, Johnny jump-ups and chicory and coltsfoot where cultivated beds of flowers waved in the afternoon's breeze.

"For a while, ours was the only home on this road. It was *lovely*. Now look at it."

"It's beautiful. I'd forgotten how beautiful."

"Not like it was." The woman shook her drink, clinking the cubes.

"What do you want from me?"

The woman came around the end of the countertop, and Janet thought she'd be touched again, but the woman stopped short and caressed with her voice instead. "Were you advised that your property was being sold?"

Janet thought of the reams of unopened junk mail she'd discarded over the years.

"You weren't. I know for a fact that you weren't."

Janet sensed where the conversation was headed. "We never gave anyone a forwarding address. We just left."

"I know. We tried to contact you before we bought it." She retreated to her pitcher. "When your husband came last week, Carlton had an idea. You could sue."

"Sue you? Why would you want me to do that?"

"We bought from a realty company. They bought it at auction. You could bring action against the company, and against the county." She leaned across and touched Janet's arm. "Carlton would represent you."

"I can't sue people I don't even know."

"You could get a settlement. Enough to buy another place." A large smile.

"You don't care about me. You just want to slow development. Now that you're here, you want the place to yourself."

The woman straightened, crossed her arms. "We're not new here. This road was named for us. Bell's Hill Lane."

"This road was named after a fucking dog."

"Oh, please." She made a face that matched her tone.

"Potlikker Road."

"Can you imagine that on your return address."

"Yeah. Yeah, I can." Janet set her glass on the granite top.

The circular motion again. "They're destroying this place."

"Somebody is." Then, because she was back in Union County, a different person again, "Thank you for the lemonade."

She didn't look back until just before the car dropped down the hill. The woman was standing at the road's edge, watching her out of sight. Janet's fingernails chattered lightly against the glass as she adjusted the rear-view mirror, but inside she felt as calm as she had for years. Country calm, like the bigtooth aspens along the road—leaves aquiver, but rooted deep in the rocky soil.

Janet was home. She switched off the air conditioner, cranked down the window.

§

Janet didn't find Sid, but she found out about him. Or as much as anyone might know. He'd stormed around the county for three days, breathing fire and sulfur smoke, then he'd driven away.

Janet found work, and a place to rent—a second-floor apartment over a Sunoco station. The slamming of car doors and the flicker of fluorescent pump lights made sleeping difficult, but she found it easy to nap just after dinner, when she was most tired.

Tentative footsteps on the outside stairs brought her eyes open.

"I saw your car," the woman said when Janet opened the door. She sported the same kind of understated, earth-toned clothing she'd worn for gardening, but a touch of makeup made her subtly elegant.

"Come in." The smell of trailing arbutus, an aroma Janet had thought perfume could never duplicate.

"I'm Katlin Bell." She extended her hand. "I behaved badly when you came to my home."

Janet took the hand, found it firm and strong. "It's okay."

"No, it's not. I've horribly misjudged you, I'm afraid, and I'd like to apologize."

Janet led the way to her Formica-topped kitchen table and offered Katlin a Diet Coke. She seemed not to notice the mismatched glasses. "An apology's not necessary, but I accept," Janet said.

"Your husband made quite a scene, threatening to sue everyone involved."

"Sid would."

"I wrongly assumed that you would share his sentiments. Carlton's notion to represent you was purely defensive, to turn your anger away from us, toward someone else."

"There won't be any litigation from my end. We didn't keep up the taxes."

Katlin pulled a tissue from her pocket and blotted her lips. "If you change your mind, or if your husband returns, please don't do anything rash. Speak to us first."

For one short moment Janet toyed with the idea of getting a chunk of money just because someone took advantage of their stupidness, then discarded it. "Sid'll be back, I figure. But if he's already blown his stack, he'll be simmered down. Staying mad's something he can't do. We'll just get on with it."

"If there's anything we can do to help you get re-established ... if a word here or there would help you find employment, please let us know." Making sure Janet knew she wasn't offering cash, just influence.

Janet tried to imagine a job she could do that the woman's recommendation would be of any account at all. *She can carry three plates at one time*, or, *She's hell on wheels with a vacuum sweeper*.

"I'm working two jobs, and taking real-estate classes at night. But thank you."

Katlin was openly evaluating her, as she'd done in her own house, in her own kitchen. "I admire your resiliency."

Janet shrugged. "You do what you have to."

"I'd like to invite you for dinner, and to meet Carlton. You'll like him. Maybe this Saturday evening?"

Janet stood. "Thanks, but I have to work. I hate to be rude, but I need to get cleaned up for class." She looked down at her tan slacks and white blouse, stained red and brown from a long day's serving.

"Another time, then? We'd like to get to know you. Carlton's really interested in the area's history."

"Sure. But some other time." She pictured how it would be, she ill at ease with every unfamiliar topic, which fork to use, what to say about the wine. Her face, stiff from forced smiling. Holding her water because she was embarrassed to use the bathroom again.

"Nothing fancy. Burgers on the grill. Cold beer. Bluegrass music."

Resentment, undeserved and childish, hove up against Janet's breast, and envy. Why should these people know so much about her, she nothing about them? "Sure." She glanced at the clock. "But not this weekend."

Janet eased onto the shoulder short of the house, then slipped behind the screen of witch hazel and sassafras that flourished in the sunlight along the road. She watched the house that sat where her trailer once had, seeing what had been more than what stood there.

A dog barked further down the road, and she saw bench-legged Sidemore waiting patiently to be fed, for his ears to be scratched, or to be even noticed. Then he'd yawn and crawl back under the trailer as though they were intrusions into his peace of mind.

When an oriole flitted past, she saw the orange-halves she'd fed them, stuck on a rusty nail, staining the porch and drawing bees. How Sid had growled about that.

She saw Sid himself, lean and hard and young, grubbing roots with a broken-handled mattock, peeling the hide from a deer, picking Janet off the ground as though she were a dandelion fluff. Older, squatted over an open fire beside the porch in his worn red apron, grilling tiny fresh-caught native brook trout just the way she liked them.

The beveled-glass door flashed in the late-evening sun, and a man stepped onto the cedar deck. Slim and painfully erect, chinos and a short-sleeved checked shirt. He lit a cigarette and leaned on the rail, staring down as if examining Katlin's flowerbed but not really seeing it. Janet had never heard his voice, but felt she knew it—deep and slow. Minutes later, Katlin joined him. They laughed about something, then looked concerned when she pointed to a crab-hole coned up six inches above the sleek grass.

Occasionally their eyes passed over the spot where Janet lurked across the road. All she'd have to do would be to step out, say hello. They'd ask no questions about why she was hiding there. *Never ask a direct question of these mountain people.* She'd overheard it a dozen times while waiting tables at the restaurant. *Let them work the conversation around to what you want to know.* Rural myths, like locals were black bears that must be treated with caution.

These people would comprehend her feelings, perhaps better than she did, or they'd pretend to. Then they'd share their concern without pointing it out like they'd done the crabhole. Not like country folk, chunking out hard bitter thoughts like they'd lopped them off with a dull hatchet.

Janet stood there until they went inside, then she worked her way back to the car in the gathering darkness. She accelerated up Bell's Hill Lane past her old home without looking or waving, though she felt them there.

"No," she said as the place snagged at her in passing. "Another time." A time she'd never find, a time and place that would again leave her behind.

22

BUT FOR A BLADDER that could no longer be ignored, Sid might have driven onward into the Pacific. But he didn't want to die full of piss. Anything but that.

Here was as pretty a place to end life as any. The ocean had caught him by surprise, soft breakers not fifty yards from the highway, afternoon sunlight glittering where they licked at a black rock the size of a doublewide stood on end. White sand, water that sharpened from pale gray near the shore to a shade of blue that made the horizon hard to locate against the sky.

Sid rolled the window up so he couldn't hear the water. There'll be a gas station or a restaurant soon, he'd told himself for the last fifteen minutes. The time for talking to himself was slipping away; time for action.

Sid accelerated around an old pickup—a dilapidated crate like his own or any other back in West Virginia except that the one he passed had a surfboard instead of a stepladder on top—then veered onto the shoulder at the first patch of forest. He jumped out of the cab and scrambled down the bank. The driver he'd just passed tooted the horn and grinned, and Sid waved.

As the pressure in his bladder drained away, the reality of his surroundings seeped in. Before him, like a table made for a god, lay a stump like no other Sid had ever seen, or even imagined. The downhill side stood a full eight feet from the ground, springboard notches still visible on the sides, but the upper end was an easy step from the ground. He paced across the stump, seven steps. The tree that once stood there was beyond the scale his imagination. He knelt and touched the annular rings, raised an inch proud of the summerwood by decades, even centuries of weathering. He tried to imagine the roots, how far they reached, how deep.

A blast of airhorns brought his thoughts to his pickup, barely off the road. Sid climbed the bank to his pickup, waited until Highway 101 was clear in both directions, then made a U-turn back toward the beach he'd passed.

Sid found a place off the road to park, then walked to the beach. Waves lapped at the soles of his tennis shoes, wet his feet. *And the rivers run into the sea; yet the sea is not full; unto the place from whence the rivers come, thither they return again.* In Wyoming, Sid had picked up a Bible in a motel room. It had fallen open to Ecclesiastes, a book the Pentecostal church he'd grown up in had pretended wasn't there, filled with verses he found unfamiliar and surprising. The words matched his thoughts. *Then I looked on all the works that my hands had wrought, and on the labour that I had laboured to do; and behold, all was vanity and vexation of spirit, and there was no profit under the sun.*

He'd tried Psalms, too, recalling it from his youth as an encouraging book: *And he shall be like a tree planted by the rivers of water.* He found it both whining and mindlessly optimistic: *Mine enemies would daily swallow me up; for they be many that fight against me, O thou most High.* Or, *I will both lay me down in peace, and sleep: for thou, Lord, only makest me dwell in safety.*

Sid's enemies didn't have to fight. They'd took over his land without knowing he even existed. And if he'd counted on the Lord for safety, south of Albuquerque where he'd slept overnight at a rest stop, he'd be under the sand, not squatting on top of it. Sid had slipped the 12-gauge Mossburg from inside his sleeping bag. "¡Cuidado!" the squat, strong-smelling man had said when Sid worked the pump. He'd climbed carefully back over the tailgate, then two pairs of feet had pounded off into the night.

Yea, I hated all my labour which I had taken under the sun: because I should leave it unto the man that shall be after me. Whoever Ecclesiastes was, he'd pretty well got life up on cinderblocks where he could get a good look at how it worked.

Sid dipped his hands in the sea that was never full, himself filled with the awareness that one ocean touched another, that oceans swallowed rivers, that rivers consumed streams, that springs bled from the land under his feet. His hands touched the same water that trickled from Union County's rocky soil; he squatted on the same land he'd left. There was no escape.

The next wave seemed to splash on through him like a great swell of despair. *That which is crooked cannot be made straight; and that which is wanting cannot be numbered.* He'd come to the end of his journey with no more hope than when he'd left. Somewhere, he'd figured, was a place that felt right to him. But everywhere he'd been a stranger, just as he'd been a stranger when he'd returned home after fourteen years away.

Sid spat into the water, watched the phlegm float in and out, in and out, relentlessly moving north without him. When it passed out of sight, he dug at an empty seashell that made a drift in the shifting sand. *For that which befalleth the sons of men befalleth beasts; even one thing befalleth them; as the one dieth, so dieth the other; yea, they have all one breath; so that a man hath no preeminence above a beast: for all is vanity.* "Shit," he said, and walked to his pickup without looking back. Again he headed north on Rt. 101, but since he'd come to the end of the land, he was drifting.

All the way west, Sid had avoided the tourist attractions. Tourists were the one thing Sid had had enough of. But just north of the beach he saw a sign for the Redwood National Park, and remembered the feel of the stump under his fingers. He swung into the narrow road that wound up a steep hill, ready to turn around if some guardian of nature wanted cash to see what God had wrought. But there was no entry kiosk, and almost immediately huge dark trees loomed in the forest, trees bigger than anything his eye could grab in one bunch. Not until he reached the parking lot at the Lady Byrd Johnson Grove did he get a clear look at them. Only four other cars were in the lot, and Sid parked beside a tree with a long diagonal slice across one side as if someone had tried to saw it down, but after a day or two had realized the futility of such an effort.

Standing outside his pickup with his head laid back against the cab to try and take in the immensity of the tree, he felt uneasy. As though he were trespassing. As though a deputy sheriff might show up to run him off, just like they'd run him off land that was rightfully his. He locked the truck, then set off across the arched wooden bridge into the grove.

It was damp there, and foggy. A whisper of surf came from the foot of the hill. Sid stopped to experience the bark, to test the span of his fingers across the crevices and crags. The path was interspersed with benches and placards explaining the forest, and though he'd vowed not to be a tourist, he allowed himself to be drawn along the route.

In the new scale of his surroundings, he felt nothing but an insect, and found comfort in the sensation. What could he matter to such a world?

What could such a world matter to him?

Where the path broke sharply from the ridge down through a switch-backed section of trail, he stopped at the largest he'd yet seen. Fire had hollowed its base and burned away the soil until the tree stood tiptoe, poised on its roots. A wooden bench was placed for comfortable viewing of the unusual growth.

Sid felt of the roots, three feet or more around, then stooped to glance at the room-sized void. Someone had discarded a Dr Pepper can inside. The can angered him, and he duck-walked through the largest hole to retrieve it.

Inside the tree, the sound of the surf was louder, as though he held a mammoth seashell against his ear. It was warmer there, too, with an earthy smell that made him nostalgic for something that he couldn't name, and missed more for its elusiveness. It was a longing for the earth, for the forest, for the hills, but not precisely. For another earth, maybe.

Just as he was ready to scrabble outside, voices approached. For no reason, Sid drew back, wiggled into a dark cranny between two roots.

The voices grew louder, the trembling rasp of an old man's voice, the softer, more persistent drone of a woman. They stopped just outside. "Look at that," the woman said.

"I'm too tired to look at anything." The man's voice rose and fell like the surf.

"It won't wear you out just to *look*, will it?"

Sid closed his eyes, leaned back into the roots, willed the couple onward. He allowed the dry duff to sift through his fingers, sent his mind up into the hollow above him, up through the fibers of the great trunk.

The surf whooshed softly as Sid allowed his trip to unreel behind him.

§

Just that morning, he'd descended beside the Trinity River for an hour or more. The river was fed with snowmelt, grew neither larger nor smaller as it tumbled toward the sea. A young boy pumped an old balloon-tired bike up the grade. To where, Sid couldn't imagine.

§

An angry-looking woman at the agricultural inspection station where he'd entered California. Sid passed over for inspection the two apples remaining in the bag he'd bought at a roadside stand.

"What if I had a whole truckload?"

The woman returned the apples to him and waved him forward.

"I was just curious."

"Move on." Already she was appraising the next vehicle in line.

§

The young man in a western shirt with sweat on his upper lip as he dodged from machine to machine at a backstreet casino in Reno. Two hands, or three, from each video poker machine, then he jumped to another, like a fly at a picnic. "This is fun, isn't it," Sid said, though the place felt dirty and desperate beneath the glitter. The man hadn't answered, or given an indication that he'd heard. Sid fed the last of his nickels into the machine and left. He'd planned to find a cheap room for the night, but slept in the back of the pickup again.

§

The modern art sculpture that stood in the middle of a salt flat west of Salt Lake City. A huge concrete affair like tennis balls on a tree, shed hulls beneath. Sid tried to imagine creating something like that, out where folks could see it. He'd been looking at the artwork, and nearly hit the multi-colored dog that limped along the edge of the interstate. One back leg shot crookedly to starboard, and the dog's long white terrible scar tore at Sid's own flesh. Sid pulled off, leaned across the seat and opened the passenger door and waited for the dog to limp alongside. "C'mon, boy," Sid said. Three donuts were left in the box from breakfast. Sid tossed one out. The dog snarled and turned, walked away across the white-crusted flat. Sid coaxed for it to come back, but it didn't even look his way.

§

The man who'd spilled a pallet of turf from his pickup in Salt Lake City's rush hour. His beaten posture under the curses of those he'd delayed, the way the police car's flashing lights played over his face. Sid wanted to stop and help him load the turf back onto the truck, disliked himself for following the trooper's signal to keep moving.

§

Wamsutter, Wyoming. Shit, Wamsutter. A frigid, stinking, windy glop of run-down buildings and a handful of half-alive businesses, a godforsaken filthy falling-down wreck of a motel. Too tired not to stop. Too cold to sleep in the truck.

Sid had gone to the office to complain that the television didn't work. He rang the bell and yelled into the gloomy room behind the desk. Waited. Sid was looking out the window, shivering in the air that leaked around it, when someone said, "What?" Sid turned not to the slight pert girl who'd exchanged a key for his money, but an older man who filled the doorway. His shirt pocket was torn, and his jeans were stiff with oil and sweat. Grease half-mooned his fingernails and coarsened the lines in his face. Weariness radiated from him like heat from the sun.

Asking for a new television was too much to load onto such a man. "You got a phone book?" Sid said instead, though he had no one to call.

"There's one in your room." His tone suggested that he'd just been informed of his mother's death.

"I didn't see none."

"Look again." The man disappeared from the doorway.

Sid discovered that there really was no phone book, and suddenly it seemed important that he have one. He looked under the bed, and found instead a Bible under a broken bed leg. Sid replaced it with a rock from just outside the door, and with nothing better to do, read it. It left with him at four o'clock the next morning, when the filth and cold became more than he could endure. Somebody owed him *something*. The irony of stealing a holy book was not lost on Sid, and he read it daily in payment for his sin.

§

The old woman in Ouray, Colorado, feeling with her cane and clutching at her too-thin jacket.

Southwest of Four Corners, the Navajo woman who would not meet his eyes when he'd asked the price of her roadside jewelry. He'd given her a twenty for a twelve-dollar hematite necklace, left before she could make change. "Asshole," she said.

Teal green McDonald's arches in Sedona, Arizona.

Abandoned cars along the interstate south of Albuquerque.

The low-slung understated class of Santa Fe's stuccoed buildings. The shambling gait of those who serviced those who could afford to live there.

The stink of Roswell, Dairy Capital of the Southwest.

The airborne manure in Lubbock, Texas. An ancient Ford Ranger pickup towing a new King Cab Chevy.

The wind. The absolutely unbelievable wind.

§

And there inside the redwood tree, someone was calling him awake.

"Sir?" A girl's thin face, topped with a Park Service ballcap, filled the hole through which Sid had crawled. Sid was confused, unsure of where he was, out of place—like a cowbird's egg in a wren's nest.

"It's nearly dusk. You have to leave."

Sid scrambled outside. She stepped away, kept her distance. He brushed debris from the seat of his pants and the backs of his arms. "Sorry." Sid showed her the discarded can. "I went in to get this."

"Move out."

Her tone made Sid feel like a convict. "I'm not a fruitcake or nothing. I didn't want to scare these two old people that come by, and I reckon I dozed off before they left." He shrugged. "I guess it's no use to be stupid if you don't show it."

A smile softened her face as they set off toward the parking lot. "You don't sound like you're from Ohio."

He looked at her sharply. "Aw, my truck plates. I worked there for a while, but I come from West Virginia."

"What's it like there?"

"Poor. And pretty."

"Most pretty places are poor. They're not good places for businesses. Not the kind that make good jobs. It's the same way right here."

"You got a good job."

She rolled her eyes, a gesture that reminded Sid of the difference in their ages. "Contract labor. No benefits. Seasonal."

Sid appraised with fresh perspective her neat uniform and the shiny white pickup that waited beside his rusted junker—bought brand new in Akron, Ohio, at the beginning of his new life. "Why don't you go somewhere else?"

They had reached the tree with the diagonal slice through the bark. She looked up at its looming silhouette. Her tanned throat was thin and vulnerable. "Leave this, for some apartment overlooking a shopping mall?"

As though payment for all the long days of driving had come due at once, Sid was suddenly exhausted. He said goodbye, but she didn't answer. She was still looking up into the trees when he left.

Sid idled down the curving road to the intersection with 101, hesitated there. How far it might be to a motel, he had no idea. On impulse, he turned left, back the way he'd come. At the beach area, he took his sleeping bag and a flashlight and walked north along the highway, searching for the tracks where he'd earlier pulled onto the shoulder. When he found them, he retraced his steps to the ancient redwood stump.

He unrolled his sleeping bag in the center of the stump and crawled inside without removing his shoes. Even through the bag's insulation, the stump's annular rings bit at his back. Almost instantly he could sense the roots below him, drawing him down, down into a dark as black as any Appalachian coal mine.

They weren't his roots, but they were roots, and he let himself go into them. A single star glittered in the treetops, then was gone.

§

In the Oklahoma panhandle, a solitary flagger had waved him to a stop, though the pilot truck was not yet out of sight, with nobody following. For more than an hour, the flagger had hung on Sid's side mirror as though physically restraining his passage, talking as though it were his first opportunity, or his last. He told of his wife leaving, of his dog having pups, of the reason new brake pads wore out so quickly. The pilot truck finally returned, alone, and the driver traded places with the flagger. After ten miles or so, the truck turned onto a side road, and the flagger waved Sid onward. If there was any road construction, Sid had missed it.

The wind.

Laverne, Oklahoma. A sign arched across the highway, "Home of Jane Jarowe, Miss America 1967." Nothing much was happening that day, either.

The Holyrood Baptist Church, the smallest pole-building Sid had ever seen, and the only bright blue one.

Concordia, Kansas, where Sid had walked in the narrow neighborhood between highway and wheat fields after dinner. Infant children played unattended in the dirt street. A dark-haired woman in a nightgown stumbled past them, past Sid, without showing any signs of noticing them.

Iowa. The ground itself dammed up with earthworks to keep it in the fields.

A station wagon with a back seat full of kids, none buckled in, one tapping the woman in the front passenger seat and pointing to the curtains in the back of Sid's pickup as the wagon slid past on the four-lane. She laughed. A sticker, crooked on the wagon's scraped bumper: MY CHILD IS AN HONOR STUDENT.

Crossing the Ohio at Wheeling, breaking loose once again of West Virginia's tentacles.

§

"Don't come here again," the deputy said. "Next time, your ass goes in the can."

"I come again," Sid said, "someone's ass is going in the ground."

"I could lock you up for those words."

Sid had pushed the fat little deputy as far as he was going to be pushed without pushing back. Sid took one last look at the land that had once been his, sold at a tax sale for next to nothing to a man who had next to everything. "I reckon you could." The last words Sid had spoken in West Virginia.

§

Coming home after fourteen years in Akron.

The taste of Knobby's dog.

The stunning impact of Janet's flowerpot. The feel of stubs, where teeth had been.

Janet's flowered dress, the first time he'd seen her.

His mother's funeral.

His father's lighter, snick snick in the night.

His dog. Goliath. Taller than Sid.

§

Sid's senses told him that midnight had passed when he woke on the redwood stump. He was hungry, and cold. The backs of his arms, when he sat up and hugged himself, were ridged from the stump's growth rings. He felt rested as he hadn't been for a long time.

Sid stretched and rolled his bag and walked back to his pickup. He ate sardines and bread on the tailgate, and when he tired of watching the ocean, he turned and watched the moon that rose over the redwoods. Over West Virginia. He laughed the way he did when he didn't really understand a joke, especially when it was on him, then wiped the tin clean with the last of his bread.

Sid stopped at an all-night gas station not far north of there, in Gold Beach, Oregon. Daylight found him far up the Columbia River gorge, the coast a hundred miles behind. Workers were already in the fields, planting from green boxes. One laborer straightened and rubbed his back.

Sid flipped down the visor and bored into the morning sun. During the night, while he ate sardines and watched the surf methodically stitch the present to the past, old friends floated by, drifting inexorably north with the tide.

Bud, risen from the grave clutching to his chest the five-prong sang they'd buried with him. *You had your brain out playing with it in the sand, and lost it.*

Greasy. Lestoil. Tom, and Huck. *Mud, boy, mud. We can't lay no block without mud.*

Janet's dad, George. *People in hell wants ice water.*

And Nettie. *Stay away from that man.*

Pike. *The Good Book says there won't be peace till the Lord returns to set up his kingdom?*

Roddy, arguing still in stubborn ignorance that church was about people, not place. Sid still couldn't let him pass without taunting. *They divvy God up and take Him home? So the only time He's there is when they come and put Him together?*

Janet, beside him on the console, her pantyhose and dress shoes cartwheeling down the road behind him. *I hate them things.*

Sid rolled down his window, and for the first time since he'd left Appalachia, a tune found his lips. The off-pitch whistled notes whipped around the cab and out the window, fluttered behind like trash strung from a ruptured garbage bag. Like pantyhose. The Ford's worn engine labored hard at that speed, one to which it was not accustomed. Sid tried the words that had been forming in his mind: "I'm home, Janet. I'm home. And I brought the bunghole."

THE END

Acknowledgments

Much gratitude to my mentors: Greg Jenkins, Ginger Broaddus, Brad Barkley, Barb Hurd, Mary Grimm, Bret Lott, and Larry Sutin. Thanks to the critics of my early work—Sue Biser, Sonya Craver, and Barb Custer—and to those special friends who carry me when I fail and kick me when I'm lazy: Kathie Smith, Gerry Snelson, David Snyder, and Layne Staral. I am grateful to the Jack Kent Cooke Foundation for giving substance to a dream; to Farley Chase and to Richard Nash for their tireless and patient work on my behalf; to Tennessee Jones for such sensible guidance; to Anne Horowitz and to Kari Rittenbach for putting it all together; and to Kristin Pulkkinen for making it go. Most of all I thank my family: my parents and sister, for their love and example; my sons and daughters-in-law, for inspiration and hope; my grandchildren, for being; and to Connie, always to Connie, who picks up all my slack and loves me still.

Photo by Asa Christiana

Appalachia has been Roger Alan Skipper's home since his birth there more than a half-century ago. There he writes, hunts wild ginseng, picks the banjo, and builds musical instruments.